The Name of an Angel

Clarissa stared boldly at the stranger who was looking at her, beyond caring about the salacious absurdity of it all. What was she doing here, allowing a strange man to look on while Nick, her student and young lover, kissed her so voluptuously between her thighs? Yet she wasn't embarrassed at all; indeed, she was coming to a new understanding of the full power of her unexplored sexuality. She invited his gaze; she welcomed it. She was utilising him in order to gain the maximum of sexual pleasure from the scene. The fact that he was as young as Nick only made it even more thrilling.

Other books by the author:

Haunted

The Name of an Angel
Laura Thornton

BLACK LACE

Black Lace books contain sexual fantasies.
In real life, always practise safe sex.

This edition published in 2003 by
Black Lace
Thames Wharf Studios
Rainville Road
London W6 9HA

Originally published 1997

Copyright © Laura Thornton, 1997

The right of Laura Thornton to be identified as the Author of
the Work has been asserted in accordance with the Copyright,
Designs and Patents Act 1988.

Printed and bound by Mackays of Chatham PLC

ISBN 0 352 33277 8

Chapter One

Clarissa Cornwall stood in front of the mirror anxiously inspecting her half-dressed image.

'*Dr* Cornwall!' she reminded herself crossly.

She was preparing for the first day of the new term at the university where she had recently begun teaching on a temporary but renewable contract. Clarissa's first lecture of the day was to introduce her course, 'Representations of the Erotic', which despite its name was actually a serious course of study of famous literary works. 'Nothing smutty,' she'd promised when proposing the course to her department. Instead, she planned to concentrate on the 'great' writers, poets and playwrights – H.D., James Joyce, Tennessee Williams and, of course, Sigmund Freud – and so in an academic context she would be discussing female sexuality, homoeroticism, masturbation and other sexual obsessions. Mindful of her audience – largely nineteen-year-olds in their first year at university – she was confident she'd have no trouble attracting their attention on the strength of the material alone, if not because of her jarringly American accent. Nevertheless, she was determined to look the part as well.

Clarissa considered herself a pretty woman but not a natural beauty, and only half-guessed at her reputation as the sexiest and most glamorous female lecturer on campus.

As she appraised herself in the mirror now, she concentrated on her hair, a source of both torment and constant pride. Clarissa's hair was a flaming mass of copper-coloured curls, a jumble of shoulder-length corkscrew tresses that framed her face in wispy tendrils and untameable wayward waves. In vain she attempted to pull it back, for it invariably escaped from its constricting plait or French twist, and feather-light curls would creep forward to tickle her throat, ears and forehead. Today, therefore, she'd abandoned her customary French braid and instead let her hair fly free, though as usual she was critical of its excess; instead of saying her hair had body, she considered it simply frizz, and she thought its tendency to cascade at will just made it unmanageable. However, today she simply slid a brush through her jumble of curls and moved her inspection on to the rest of herself as she carefully applied her make-up.

She stroked gel on to her thick, arched, reddish-brown brows in an effort to tame them, combed black mascara on to her lashes, and smoothed cocoa shadow over her hazel-green eyes. She dusted rosy blusher over her fair, freckled cheeks, wishing she had a more pronounced bone structure, and painted her luscious, ripe mouth a dusky shade of mauve. Her face complete, she stepped back to examine her body.

Clarissa often complained to herself that she was several inches under the tall, willowy stature of popular supermodels and sought-after film vixens, but she underrated the sensual appeal of her well-proportioned, voluptuous figure. It seemed to Clarissa that her legs were too short and her long waist cut her height in half, but now she admired the creaminess of her rounded shoulders, the curve of her full, though not large, pink-tipped breasts, the deep indentation of her tiny waist, and the circular arcs described by her firm buttocks. Years of aerobics classes and sessions at the gym had carved enticing hollows into the panels of her thighs, moulded firm muscles along her shoulders and arms, and grooved indentations along the sides of her slightly curved stomach. Clarissa worked hard at maintaining her appearance, and she was proud of her self-discipline and determination which resulted in a body which was strong, curvy and voluptuous; she had the shape of a woman, not a girl, but her youthful face and trim figure made her seem much younger than her actual 35 years.

Clarissa glanced at the clock and tugged frantically at her lace-topped hold-ups. She arranged her silk blouse over her front-fastening bra, rose-painted fingertips flying, and hastily checked to make sure that her nipples weren't immediately visible. She zipped up her clingy black wool jersey skirt, clasped the black patent leather belt round her slim waist, and fastened the silver buckles of her black suede shoes with the slightly stacked heels. She cast one last glance at herself in the mirror and clicked her way out of the room, leaving behind an expensive trail of designer perfume.

As she drove the short distance to campus, singing along loudly to the music on the radio, Clarissa tried to picture the faces of the students who would fill the classroom today to its maximum capacity. Her course looked like it was going to be quite popular, no doubt because of its sexy title, and her class register was completely full, with a few hopefuls pencilled in at the bottom in case any students dropped out and a space opened up. Although she recognised a few names from courses she'd taught last year, Clarissa was unfamiliar with most of the young women and men who had signed up for the class – hoping, no doubt, for an easy term of saucy reading and simple essay assignments on racy subjects. Ha! thought Clarissa, carefully manoeuvring her Honda Civic XL into one of the cramped parking spaces allotted to faculty members. This is going to be one tough course! she mentally promised her students while silently rehearsing her opening address to the class. As Clarissa pulled open the heavy glass door to her building she debated to herself the use of 'deconstructive' versus 'post-structuralist', and contemplated the various pronunciations of the names of the French theorists Felix Guattari and Luce Irigaray. She was so busy conducting an interior monologue that she hardly noticed where she was going and so blundered into a wandering student body which was suddenly in her way.

'Oh! Dr Cornwall! Sorry – didn't see you there for a minute!' blurted out a red-faced and evidently very embarrassed young man who was steadying himself by means of his hand upon her arm.

'It's OK – don't worry about it,' replied Clarissa, gingerly removing his hand while desperately trying to remember this particularly anonymous student's name. Daniel? David? Derek? Oh Lord, she hoped he wasn't one of those annoying ones who silently panted after her in class and obviously had a crush on her. Hell, though, she remembered cherishing a few of those crushes herself when she was in college.

Happily, this one seemed relatively immune to her charms because he was now rapidly backing away from her, but then he turned to call out after her, 'See you later – I'm in your nineteenth-century literature class this term!'

Great, Clarissa muttered grimly to herself, shaking out the keys to her office. I hope I remember your name by the time I take the register. Clarissa was hopeless at remembering students' names unless they possessed some outstanding characteristic which acted as a mnemonic guide: spectacularly good – or bad – writing, a speech impediment, a strong regional accent, or – especially in the case of her male students – remarkable good looks. Not that there are ever enough of those, Clarissa thought briefly to herself, then brushed the thought aside as she switched on her desk lamp and began her final preparation for the first of that day's lectures.

Ninety minutes later Clarissa stood at the front of her classroom preparing to recite John Donne's erotic poem 'The Flea'. As her manicured nails located the proper page, her eyes caught those of the tall, lanky lad leaning insolently back in his seat, staring openly at her. He was seated in the very last row in the left corner of the room, but his eyes raked over her body in a manner that was profoundly and immediately intimate. Even had he ignored her, how-

4

ever, one look at his face told Clarissa that his would be instantly memorable to her, though as usual it would take her weeks to memorise the faces of his classmates. Reddish-brown hair, though not nearly as brightly coloured as hers, flipped over a broad forehead overhanging arched, fringed brows, narrowed eyes, long, strong nose and wide, sensual and, Clarissa noted in self-amazement, eminently kissable mouth. He was wearing a black rollneck sweater and black leather jeans, and his black boots were set firmly on the floor pointing directly at her. His body was turned purposefully towards hers, and she had to avert her eyes from his brazen stare.

This is unbelievable, Clarissa said to herself. This boy is showing me that he wants me. He is barely nineteen years old and he's actually turning me on in front of my class! To her horror, she discovered that his eyes on her body and his evident desire for her were provoking a rush of warmth between her thighs and a tightening of her nipples beneath her blouse, which she devoutly hoped remained invisible to the class. To cover her confusion, she began to read the poem, her voice falling automatically into the cadenced rhythm.

As Clarissa read the poem aloud, lingering over the deliberately erotic inflection of Donne's repeated use of the word 'sucked', she listened out for the predictable sniggers of embarrassment from her class, but then the movement Clarissa caught out of the corner of her eye nearly caused her to skip a line. Knowing the poem by heart, she recited virtually from memory as she tried not to look in the direction of the strangely compelling youth, yet the barely discernible motion drew her eyes directly to him. He can't be! she thought in disbelief. This boy cannot be masturbating in my class! But he was. He was positioned in such a way that she was the only one who could see him, she knew, yet the unmistakable rhythmic movement of his arm was keeping time to the pace of her voice. She could feel the heat of his eyes as they caressed the shape of her breasts under her blouse and the curve of her backside as it was gripped by the tight jersey of her skirt. His hand was buried under the desk and he had hunched forward over his lower body, but there was no misunderstanding that gesture. Indeed, no doubt sensing her eyes on him, he looked her boldly in the face as he continued what he was doing, daring her to guess at the nature of his actions. She could almost feel the motion herself, could nearly clasp her own hand around what she was sure to be a heavy, thick shaft that pulsated and throbbed, and she could nearly smell his maleness as his muscular arm pumped up and down.

Aroused herself, not least because she knew that she was the inspiration, the catalyst for this show of male desire, she half-consciously sped up her reading so as to be finished with this embarrassingly intimate moment, but as her speed increased, so did the boy's. They kept together, his hand and her voice, and Clarissa couldn't keep from visualising exactly what was going on underneath that desk. Briefly she wondered whether he was circumcised, and she concentrated on how it would feel to have that driving rhythm inside her, pleasuring her moist vaginal cavern as he was so obviously pleasuring himself. Mesmerised, she watched the boy's hand as it guided the invisible staff to its final moment of ecstasy. Donne's words trailed off as she finished the poem, the conclusion of her reading coinciding with the boy's climax, and she noted the exact moment of his orgasm by the way he briefly shut his eyes, tipped back his head and exhaled silently through his mouth. Clarissa imagined the feel of that thick fluid spurting into her hand, could nearly taste its pearlised silkiness on her tongue, and imagined she felt the texture of his opalescent splendour as it rained out upon her body. As the boy opened his eyes and smiled directly into her face, his own expressing both seduction and satisfaction, Clarissa took a deep breath, shook her head nervously a few times, and laid down her poetry book as she turned her attention to the rest of the class.

Visibly shaken – indeed, outwardly more affected by his performance than the boy – Clarissa quickly sketched on the board the assignment she required her students to write over the next five minutes and then turned away from the boy, pretending to study her notes. She did not look up as the students dropped their papers on to her desk and filed out of the door, laughing amongst themselves, but she was acutely aware of the nameless one who wordlessly slid his essay in front of her, then turned and left the room. Her eyes lingered on his receding back, ramrod straight and curiously arrogant, the fullness of his hair, the v-shape formed by his broad shoulders and narrow hips, and silently admired the tightness of his backside. She had a quick flash of how he would look naked from the back – soft, smooth skin, long of leg and sleekly muscled – and then wondered to herself if he was as conscious of her eyes on him as she had been earlier of his eyes on her, so bold, so intense, so openly desirous. Wildly she wondered how she would be able to make it through her next class, or indeed, how she would manage for the next 48 hours until this particular session met again. Clarissa knew that she would not be able to get the image of this impossibly young but impossibly sexy stranger out of her head, and she was already yearning to face him again and to see whether he would sustain this exciting, new, overwhelming erotic intimacy.

It was then that Clarissa's eyes fell upon his single sheet of writing; at the top was his name, Nicholas St Clair, and a few sentences of scrawled summary. Probably not very good, Clarissa couldn't help scoffing to herself, and then she noticed that beneath the boy's assignment lay a single scripted line: 'Enjoyed the reading'. Below that there glowed a small, circular patch of wetness. Clarissa glanced around the empty room, then put the paper to her face and inhaled deeply.

Ah, the sweet scent of his semen.

Back in her house that night, Clarissa replayed the events of the class in her mind, once again seeing the boy's eyes travelling over her body in an open, defiant gesture of desire. Once again she saw the suggestion of his solid bicep through his sweater as his arm moved up and down in strong, steady strokes. The mere image of Nicholas St Clair precipitated a surge of longing that set Clarissa's veins running to fire. She chewed her lower lip and pondered the phone. Should she call Graham? She tilted her head to one side, twirled a coppery strand of hair around her finger, then pushed the telephone aside with a shake of her head, resolving to stick to the terms of their break-up. Her fussy, intellectual, recently-ex boyfriend was definitely *not* what she wanted tonight.

No, tonight she was in the mood for a new man, and so she strode purposefully over to her wardrobe and flicked impatiently through her clothes. She had to get the image of that boy – Nick – out of her mind, and another man inside her body – a hot stranger, not mature, coolly handsome Graham – seemed to be the only way to accomplish this. Tonight Clarissa needed something to distract her from the unnervingly erotic scene she had witnessed in her class today.

Clarissa didn't believe in sleeping with students, although she had no hesitation about exploiting her sexuality in order to gain attention from her class. She was well aware that she could lose her job at the university and her professional standing were it ever discovered that she had seduced one of her students. Clarissa couldn't imagine the horror of that: she had heard rumours while a postgraduate of professors whose careers had been terminated on the grounds of sexual harassment, even those with tenured positions, and she had absolutely no intention of risking her own future simply to satisfy a momentary twinge of lust. In fact, her contract at the university where she hoped to teach for many years was due to expire at the end of the term, and she was determined to remain in good standing with the board so that her position would be renewed. The last thing she wanted to do was jeopardise any chances she had of renewal simply because she fancied one or two of her male students. She could always come back to Graham, or find a substitute, when she was feeling particularly passionate. Indeed, Clarissa doubted very much that a mere nineteen-year-old would have sufficient imagination and experience to pleasure her deeply enough to keep her satisfied, though she'd daydreamed wistfully about the legendary strength and staying power of the very young, daydreams fuelled by her own admittedly dimly remembered sexual adventures of the past. During those times when Graham was unavailable and she had no interest in finding another man, there were always her own skilful, well-tutored fingers to practise and her trusty vibrator, though plastic was often a poor substitute for flesh.

Tonight, however, Clarissa was specifically in search of a man, and to that end she adjusted her jewel-coloured basque, slipping her fingers around her breast in order to fit it more evenly into its wire-rimmed cage. She admired the firmness of her full, round breasts, briefly caressing one rosy nipple, and smiled at her mirrored reflection as it hardened. For the second time that day she studied her nearly-nude body, pleased by the sight of her healthy curves ripened by age, rather than reduced by it. She certainly felt fit enough to compete with any nineteen-year-old girl, and she thrilled to think that it was her 35-year-old face and body that had so inspired Nick to his daring act of orgasm.

Clarissa stepped back to admire the depth of her cleavage, helped along by the padding of her undergarment, then buttoned up a black silk riding jacket so that only the merest bit of violet lace was visible. She eased into her purple suede jeans, whose unusual rich, vibrant colour had induced her to spend half a week's wages on them. As she slid on her black suede boots with the chunky heels, she speculated on her chances of finding a man tonight who wouldn't prove to be a problem for her in the future. Now that she had broken up with Graham, Clarissa was hardly out looking for love; she had a full course load as well as the final steps to go in revising her doctoral dissertation on the erotic in literature so it could be published in book form. She needed a solid achievement in publishing to secure her place at the university, and for this reason the book was taking up a lot of her time. Besides, having recently left an unsatisfying affair, she was hardly in the mood to start a new one, and so a long, hard, satisfying screw was all she was interested in at the moment.

To that end, therefore, she applied scarlet lipstick and black eyeliner, let loose her flyaway, tousled curls, and stepped out into the velvety black night. Everything in this small university town was pretty much within walking distance except for the supermarket and an out-of-town shopping centre, and since faculty were allocated housing within the town centre Clarissa had her pick of the pubs within a two-mile radius of her house. She decided to start with the King's Head – ever a promising name, she thought with a grin – and directed her steps that way, fervently hoping that she wouldn't run into any of her students or colleagues once there. Actually, few of the faculty ventured out into the town's night-life; most had families to spend time with, books to write, or conferences to attend. Even Graham rarely came out on a work night. Students, however, were another problem. Clarissa remembered with an amused smile one night last term when she and Graham had been so impatient that in a rare moment of spontaneity he'd actually seduced her in his car. Just then a group of pupils from her modernism class came walking jauntily by his BMW. Graham and Clarissa were inside, his cock shoved up inside her, her spiked heels placed squarely on the rear passenger window; cold car leather underneath her bare backside. Her head was hanging off the edge of the seat while her body pounded rhythmically against Graham's, but even while upside down and in the throes of vaginal splendour she still recognised snooty Debbie-Marie Townsend staring shocked and amazed at her tutor being well and truly fucked in the back seat of a car.

Clarissa had held her breath around the university for a while after that, petrified that she'd be arrested or fired or something for indecent behaviour, but happily nothing had happened. She smiled to herself as she remembered how Debbie-Marie had avoided her eyes for the remainder of the term, convinced, no doubt, that one word from her and Clarissa would fail her work for the term, while really it was Clarissa who had been grateful that Debbie-Marie had evidently kept her mouth shut. Then, pushing away all thoughts of students – save one – from her mind, Clarissa pulled open the heavy door to the pub and manoeuvred her way inside to the crowded, noisy bar.

Happily, her girlfriend Julian was working tonight, another reason why Clarissa had chosen the Head, as it was known locally, as her starting point – and hopefully her only point of search, if things went well. Julian had a wonderful eye for the kind of men who would please Clarissa, and was quite talented at setting up flirtatious encounters, so Clarissa was relieved there would be someone on hand to help her scout out the possibilities of the night. With the memory of Nick's eyes and hand firmly in her mind, she counted on Julian's ability tonight, and hoped that this wouldn't disappoint her friend, who had been working on seducing her since they first met. However, along with sleeping with students, sleeping with friends was something Clarissa forbade herself on the grounds of principle: unsatisfactory sex often led to broken friendships. She had fixed ideas about the kind of sex she preferred, and would have felt very awkward indeed had Julian been unable to satisfy her properly. Besides, though intrigued, she'd never much fancied the idea of sex with a woman, and doubted she'd be able to go through with it should the situation ever actually arise. Still, Julian kept on trying.

'Hello, my lovely!' shouted Julian over the crush at the bar as soon as she caught sight of Clarissa. 'Are things still finished with Graham?' At Clarissa's nod she smiled and asked, 'And what will it be tonight?'

Though nearly twelve years younger than Clarissa, Julian was one of Clarissa's closest friends. However, they could not have appeared or sounded more different: Julian had exactly that tall, willowy look Clarissa had always despaired of achieving, and she towered over Clarissa by a good five inches. Julian had closely cropped, jet-black hair – which Clarissa knew for a fact was from a bottle, not biology – huge, sweeping dark eyes, olive-toned skin and, much to Clarissa's continued disgust, both a nose-ring and

11

a tattoo of a butterfly on her right buttock, though she assured Clarissa she had neither her nipples nor her navel pierced as yet. Where Clarissa was curvy, Julian was straight, and where Clarissa's education was strictly American Ivy League and Oxbridge D.Phil., Julian was proudly and loudly working class. It bemused Clarissa how someone as hip as Julian and so clearly lacking in restraint or refinement had ended up with such an elegant and aristocratic-sounding name: Julian Eugenia Davenport. Then again, Julian would often mock Clarissa's pedigreed background, and she was the only person Clarissa allowed to mutilate her lovely eighteenth-century name into the hopelessly juvenile-sounding 'Rissa', or worse, 'Ris' – but at least it was better than 'Clary'. In return, Clarissa affectionately referred to her friend as 'Jules'.

Clarissa pushed her way impatiently to the bar, perching herself precariously on the rails lining the bottom of the panelling, and shouted her order at her friend.

'Double shot Jack Daniels, straight up!' It was a running joke between Julian and herself: Clarissa's taste in drink for the evening indicated the kind of man she was hoping to bed for the night. When Clarissa asked for Newcastle Brown, she was really asking to meet a working-class man, preferably one who worked with his hands; vodka and tonic – she hated gin – indicated her interest in a business-man, hopefully in a suit and tie, with a button-fly on his wool gabardine trousers which she could undo with her teeth. If Clarissa called for brandy, which was rare, she was actively seeking one of her own, an educated professional who more often than not disappointed her in bed, but who could at least make her laugh. And the old J.D., of course, signalled her search for a foreigner, preferably a fellow American, of any occupation at all, so long as he was not indigenous to English soil – at a pinch, a Scotsman would do.

'So, any talent?' she queried her friend, accepting her drink and running her eyes expertly across the sea of heads bent over their glasses. 'Anyone worth having a go at?'

Julian concentrated on filling a half-pint glass with

shandy, trying not to sneer since she frequently proclaimed 'real women don't drink lemonade'. She then jerked her head back in the direction of the fireplace where a cluster of men sat puffing cigars and drinking beer. 'Over there,' she said, accepting money and giving change. 'The one with the shoes.'

Clarissa knew exactly what Julian meant: for reasons unclear Julian often preferred men, when she preferred them at all, who wore Italian-made, hand-tooled shoes. The men could look alarmingly ugly or old to Clarissa, but highest-quality footwear was key to firing up Julian's libido, and if they had accessories to match – belt, wallet, purse, condom-carrier – she went wild. Curiously, however, such criteria did not extend to Julian's taste in women; she was essentially unimpressed with women's taste in fashion, choosing instead, perhaps, to focus on their more intimate features.

Now Clarissa thanked her friend and headed over to inspect the man in question. She had no trouble in locating this particular individual, and she didn't have to make it apparent what she was doing. The great thing about applying Julian's standards and putting her search into action was that Clarissa didn't have to peer into men's faces, making it obvious that she was scanning the crowd for the best-looking stud. Instead, she merely had to look at their feet, as though searching for lost change, and in this way locate the ideal partner for the evening. And so it was the pair of tasselled Gucci loafers, neatly crossed at the ankles, that drew her attention tonight. The shoes were a bit of a cliché, she admitted to herself, as though their wearer had simply bought the first, presumably high-priced, brand name he came across; he had obviously paid an obscene amount of money for the double 'Gs' that screamed wealth and undiscriminating conspicuous consumption to the most casual of observers. Still, lurking unobtrusively by the ladies, Clarissa could see by the rest of him that Julian's pick could prove to be an excellent choice: the stranger's legs, encased in sturdy Levi denims, another obvious brand, but always a classic, looked thick

13

and strong, just the way she liked them; Clarissa loathed
the typical British man's toothpick chicken legs. This man
didn't appear too tall, another asset, since Clarissa herself
was only 5 foot 4 inches, and anyone over 5 foot 10 inches
was usually too much of a stretch to reach. This man,
however, appeared to be of a good height and stocky build,
with powerful forearms revealed by rolled-back shirt-
sleeves and broad, set shoulders completely filling the
width of his striped cotton shirt. Clarissa could see a few
jet curls poking out of the shirt's top two buttons opened
at his throat, and then she raised her eyes to his face.
Whatever nationality this man was, his ancestry was certainly Sicilian. He had thick, glossy black hair swept back
from his forehead and lightly gelled into place; heavy
brows placed vertically above his eyes and, even from her
secluded position, Clarissa could note the length of his
lashes, the classic Roman nose, and a full, sculpted, sensual
mouth. That mouth held promise, and Clarissa could
nearly feel it opening on to her own; her body was tingling
so loudly with lust that she would have to make her move
soon, and so, having checked out the possibility, she
positioned herself back at the bar and awaited his inevitable approach. She did not have to wait long.

'Three pints of Pils and a St Clements, please.' She
listened carefully as he placed his order politely, straining
to locate his accent. American he certainly was, probably
from the north-east like herself. She watched as he distrib-
uted the beers among his friends, then returned to the bar
to pick up the remaining drink. He bent to sip his St
Clements, and she tried not to curl her lip in distaste at the
mixture as she loathed orange juice, though she quite liked
bitter lemon. However, she was impressed by an outsider's
knowledge of a typically British soft drink. The man's eyes
met hers over the rim of his glass as he drank – she was,
after all, staring openly at him – and so the time had come
for Clarissa to make her move.

'Excuse me,' she said in her most cultivated Boston
twang, 'but do you have a light?' Yes, Clarissa extended
that tired old chat-up line as she extended her Rothmans

red, but despite its age, or perhaps because of it, it was still the best pick-up line in the world. It had never failed her in the past, nor did it fail her now.

The stranger's eyes passed over Clarissa's body as he clicked open his gold Dunhill lighter, another clichéd accessory, of course, and then smiled in embarrassment as the flame flickered briefly and went out.

'I'm sorry,' he apologised, 'but I don't smoke myself, and so I never remember to refuel the damn thing.'

What, you only carry it for designer status? Clarissa mocked to herself, but she smiled sweetly and said, 'It's just as well; I'm trying to quit anyway,' and tossed her unlit cigarette into the ashtray. The encounter might have ended there, but she held the man with her eyes, noting the chocolate-brown depths of his, and asked, 'May I buy you another drink?'

He hastily drained the last of his mix and handed her the empty glass, saying, 'With pleasure. It's a – '

'I know what it is,' she smiled. 'I heard you at the bar.' She bought refills for them both, trying to ignore Julian's leer, and patted the seat beside her. 'Can your friends spare you for a few minutes?' she asked. 'It's so nice to see another American.' She regarded him for a moment. 'What are you doing here?'

He launched eagerly into an account of how he'd been sent by his American firm to complete a contract in the city, thankfully not in any way associated with her university, and she listened in silence, concealing her impatience, her eyes focusing on his mobile mouth, the width of his shoulders, and his strong, thick-fingered hands. Shut up, she moaned inwardly; I want to fuck you, not hire you! He must have noticed her momentary withdrawal, for he paused in his monologue about multi-tasking microkernels and studied her face.

'I'm boring you,' he said simply. 'I keep forgetting that the history of operating systems is not a story the world thinks should be told.' He emptied his glass and warmly offered, 'Tell me about you.'

She faced him. 'Look,' she said forthrightly – she was

15

nothing if not direct – 'all you need to know is that I'm a single woman living on my own, I'm a responsible professional, I've no diseases or *Fatal Attraction* fantasies, and I'm really in the mood to stay up all night making love to a stranger.'

He stared at her open-mouthed for a moment, then passed a hand over his hair and laughed – a little shamefacedly, Clarissa was charmed to note. 'I guess I should have figured that out by the way you were staring,' he grinned, and then added, 'I like your honesty; I've always admired a woman who speaks her mind.'

She stood and offered her hand. 'Good. Let's go,' she said as he laced his fingers through hers. 'Where are you staying . . . or would you rather come home with me?'

His eyes indicated his trio of colleagues, seemingly oblivious to the two of them. 'It might be best if we avoided my hotel,' he confessed. 'My friends might want a late-night discussion about our company's presentation for tomorrow.' She nodded knowingly and led him quickly out through the back, passing only to wink at Julian as she led him away.

They spoke little on their way to her house other than to exchange names – his, she learned, was Sam – and the most basic of information. Clarissa could feel her desire for him spreading throughout her body, and she didn't want to waste time in talking once they arrived at her house. Neither, apparently, did he, for as soon as her door closed behind them he pinned her forcefully back against its wood panelling and covered her mouth with his, thrusting his tongue deeply inside and pressing her hard against his body. She matched his intensity with her own, twisting her fingers through his glossy black hair and curling her tongue around his. She licked at his lips and sucked on his tongue, running her hands under his shirt so she could stroke the smooth planes of his back. Impatiently he shrugged off his jacket while she rapidly unbuttoned his shirt, actually popping off a button in her haste. She slid her hands over the flatness of his stomach and up over the tautness of his cocoa-brown nipples, marvelling at the crispness of the black curls that covered his chest. Clarissa moved her hands in circles over Sam's muscles while he grasped her tiny waist in his hands, and she whispered huskily against his throat as she kissed it, 'I want you inside me right now – I don't want to wait.'

As she spoke she moved her hand downward to press against the promising bulge in his jeans. She rubbed her palm against its thick protuberance, testing its width and length before deftly unzipping his fly. Out sprang his impressively large penis, a deep rich purple, the head silky smooth under her fingers. Grasping the throbbing, pulsing shaft in her hand, Clarissa smiled to herself, her mouth against his neck; she loved a circumcised man – Americans usually were – and she delighted in the ridged thickness that stood proud and free of the protective British sleeve.

'You feel so good against my body,' she murmured, sucking on his small round nipple, her tongue tracing its puckered edges and pressing against its stiffening tip. She reached up and whispered, 'I want to feel your hands on my bare skin.'

Obligingly he eased her jacket off her shoulders, stooping to run his mouth along the ivory column of her throat. Clarissa sighed with pleasure and tipped back her head, feeling her silken curls tumble around her shoulders. Sam then tugged at the close-fitting fabric of her jeans, knelt and slid them down to her feet along with her satin thong, helped her step out of her boots, and quickly stripped off her socks. He rose, made a futile attempt at unhooking her basque, then smiled sheepishly. 'I think you're going to have to help me with this one,' he muttered and bent to kiss her exposed breasts which jutted forward agreeably as she arched her back, reaching behind to unhook herself from the confining garment. Silk, lace and suede now lay in a jumbled heap on the floor. Sam kicked these impatiently aside along with his jeans before hoisting Clarissa up against the door and positioning himself between her well-toned thighs.

Wrapping her legs around him, Clarissa took a firm hold on his pulsating penis and guided it towards the wet, welcoming mouth of her vagina. She felt moistness flow out of her, and the lips of her vulva seemed to stretch forward in eager anticipation of the plum-coloured member. Sam's penis entered her slowly at first, hesitantly probing its way into her plush, warm wetness, and then with a sudden grunt he thrust himself upwards, his shaft now completely embraced by her supple, clinging sheath. Clarissa gasped audibly in delight, shutting her eyes in rapture as Sam began to move inside her, bracing himself for support. Usually Clarissa preferred a slow build-up to the act of penetration, but her inner fires had been burning so brightly since her morning class that at that moment all she craved was this big, thick shaft pumping up and down in steady strokes inside her. Sam's mouth was now buried at the base of her throat, his palms were flat against the door on either side of her hips, holding her in place, and with every near-complete withdrawal and re-entry of his cock her bottom thumped against the wood. All she concentrated on was the smooth, hard muscles of his buttocks underneath her hands and the slap of his belly against hers as she ground her pelvis against his, feeling him fill her completely. Clarissa sensed that Sam's orgasm was beginning to build and so, mindful of the need to keep pace with him, she slid one hand from around his buttocks to the front of her pubis, slipping her second and third fingers between their bodies and placing them over the retracting hood which had uncovered her rosy, expectant clitoris. She rubbed against that tiny protruding bud in time to Sam's increasingly powerful thrusts, her wetness lubricating her fingers and making them deliciously moist. Clarissa's climax then built very quickly indeed, and as the stiffening of her hyper-sensitive clitoris began to announce the arrival of her orgasm, she withdrew her slippery fingers, fragrant with her inner juices, and shoved them into Sam's mouth so he could taste her pleasure as she cried out repeatedly in the throes of ecstasy. The taste of her on his tongue drove Sam over the edge, and as the crest of Clarissa's orgasm began to recede, the still-vibrating walls of her vagina contracted around Sam's cock so that he too cried aloud and thrust hard within her, raising her several inches further against the door with the force of his body. Clarissa clenched her vaginal muscles around him as he pulsed repeatedly inside her, then smiled a little as she felt his breath hot against her ear. She struggled to catch her own breath as Sam's accelerated heartbeat began to steady, and he slid her down gently until they were both lying fully on the floor.

'Damn, that door's draughty,' he muttered into her neck, still panting a little.

'Sorry, I didn't notice,' Clarissa mumbled against his chest.

Sam stayed the rest of the night, managing an admirable count of three more deeply satisfying couplings before moving off at six in the morning. Clarissa bade him a fond farewell, sorry to see him go, as he was flying back to the States that night, but knowing she'd carry a reminder of him between her aching thighs for the rest of the day. As regretful as she was to see him leave, however, she knew she wouldn't have been tempted into more than a few more nights of rapture with him if he stayed, for she was determined to stay single from now on – for a while, at least. All Clarissa had in mind when she had set out to bed a man that night was to still the desire that flowed between her legs every time she thought of her student's eyes upon her body and his hand upon his cock. Although Sam had proved to be a delightful diversion, once he'd left her house her thoughts turned back to Nick, and she began carefully to plan her lessons – and her wardrobe – for the next few weeks of classes, hoping to capitalise on the erotic material of her course. Thus, although Clarissa still held firm to her resolution against sleeping with students, she had every intention of drawing out the teasing, intimate flirtation the boy had promised her with his eyes. If nothing else, she thought to herself with a smile as she prepared for her morning class, he'll provide me with enough motivation to deliver the most stimulating lectures of my career. With that thought in mind, she removed her copy of Coleridge's 'Christabel' from her shelves and closed her briefcase with a resounding click.

Chapter Two

*U*nfortunately for Clarissa, however, such promise did not hold. Nicholas St Clair faithfully attended every class and completed every assignment, so that Clarissa had to admit grudgingly that his work was actually quite good. He even at times contributed with enthusiasm during seminar discussions, but never once did his eyes meet hers with any of that lingering intensity, nor did he give the briefest of glances over her body. To all outward appearances, he was a thoughtful, committed pupil – respectful even, she supposed. Disappointed, although no doubt a little relieved, Clarissa concentrated on guiding her class through the jocular yet oddly threatening seduction of 'To His Coy Mistress', the earthy sensuality of *Joseph Andrews*, the womanly appeal of Aphra Behn, and the sticky sweetness of the eighteenth-century sentimental novel. Clarissa drew her students' attention to the way masculine desire was represented in these works, and she encouraged them to probe the mysteries of female sexuality which emerged between the lines of these writings. Part scholar, part seductress, Clarissa teased and cajoled her pupils into producing essays of their own which attempted to define the elusive appeal of the erotic, to draw out the sexual symbolisms embedded in the works, and to describe how the poets and novelists imbued the world around them with the hazy veil of sensuality.

It was one such assignment which drew Clarissa's eyes sharply on a particularly damp and windy February day. She was in her office, absently running her thumb along the cool ivory curves of a set of Greek worry beads, when she discovered Nicholas St Clair's paper to be the next in her pile. The name of an angel, she thought to herself, the body of a god – and the age of a boy, the uppermost part of her mind cut in sharply. Nick's paper was entitled 'An Essay on Persuasion', and his subject was 'The Flea', the Donne poem which Clarissa had read out on the first day of class. Much of the essay was a fairly predictable analysis of the poet's use of metre and rhyme, but one line in particular stood out prominently as though etched in bas-relief. Nick was describing how the would-be lover points to the flea that has sucked the blood of woman and man, 'mingling' their fluids in its body. The seducer suggests that because their sexual juices are already joined in the body of the flea, they might as well finish what the flea has started and make love. Nick wrote, 'This poem is all about desire, it's about how far one man will go to seduce a woman, even if it means tricking and deceiving her.'

Comma splice notwithstanding, the sentence spoke to Clarissa forcibly, as though Nick himself were speaking directly to her. The image of Nick trying to seduce her, his open mouth on her naked breast, his cock delving deeply inside her, imprinted itself so powerfully on her mind that her fingers began a downward movement towards her rapidly dampening vagina. She reached under her skirt, slipping her fingers beneath the band of her lace-edged French knickers, stroking aside the crisp auburn curls that guarded her enclosed clitoris. As Clarissa leant back and spread her thighs under her crinkly navy wool crepe skirt, the stiffening little nub poked out its head and she rubbed the pads of her fingers over it gently, bathing it in moisture. She focused her hearing on the swishing liquid sound of her fingers on satiny flesh, and she could smell the scent of her own musky wetness as she pictured the pink inner

21

folds of her velvety lips glistening ripely, blossoming out like the petals of a rose. Clarissa forgot about Nick almost completely in her concentration on the manipulation of her own pleasure; she raised one navy-booted foot and placed it on her desk in order to open herself even more fully to her questing fingers.

As she did so, her heel slid slightly on the slippery balls of her worry beads and, guided by her body rather than her mind, Clarissa reached forward and closed her hand on the knobbly loop. She placed one end firmly against her throbbing, swelling clitoris and inserted several small beads up an inch or so inside the velvet pocket of her vagina. She then rotated one end of the ivory circle against the pulsating nub of her pleasure while easing the other end further up inside, contracting her inner walls around them, relishing the feel of the smooth balls bumping and rippling against her heated flesh. The muscles of her inner cavern contracted around the beads, sucking them in even deeper and then expelling them slightly before gripping them again. She increased the pace of her fingers, rubbing the beads inside and against herself until in a blinding flash of delight Clarissa spasmed against her fingers, the worry beads pressed tightly against her vagina, but she was mindful enough to do so quietly: she was, after all, in her lamplit, cramped, book-lined office.

The details of her location were immediately brought home to her by the tentative rap of knuckles at her door.

'Come in,' she called out briskly, hastily rearranging herself behind her desk and secreting the beads behind her back, reminding herself to rinse them off later. She turned towards the door, hoping it was Nick, intensely desiring to see his face as though she could somehow share with him the pleasure of the last few minutes ... but of course she was disappointed. Facing her was Monica Talbot, another English lecturer and campus gossip at large. She was carrying a sheaf of papers from which she extracted a sheet and dropped it lightly on Clarissa's desk.

'What's this?' Clarissa asked, picking it up curiously. She read the university memo with interest. It announced

22

the codification of a new sexual harassment policy and explicitly stated that any faculty member who was found to be 'behaving in a manner deemed unseemly, unprofessional, or inappropriate to the student–instructor relationship' was to be summarily dismissed, his or her position terminated, regardless of status or tenure. Clarissa's quizzical eyes met Monica's amused ones above the stack of paper.

'So?' Clarissa inquired, indicating the memo. 'Has there been any scandal of late?'

Monica looked even more amused. 'It seems that no less dignified a personage than the head of this department has been dismissed for, shall we say, displaying a little more interest than usual in one of his students' "split infinitives" and his own "dangling modifier".'

Clarissa put the paper over her face and giggled in delight. 'Serves the old bugger right,' she declared with a grin. 'That revolting lecher has been trying to dip his knob into anything in a skirt!'

A look of puzzlement flickered across Monica's face – or was it something else? Clarissa looked at the other woman closely and realised her comment was probably a little unkind; poor Monica undoubtedly hadn't had a pass made at her in years. She wasn't an unattractive woman, she was just ... matronly, Clarissa decided. Although close to Clarissa's own age, Monica suffered from the classically British pear-shaped figure remarkably unenhanced by her dull grey cardigan buttoned tightly over an even duller, shapeless black skirt. She was a kind and generous colleague, showing Clarissa around when she'd first arrived, introducing her to key faculty members, lending her books, and even recommending her courses to registering students. Still, Clarissa always half-surmised that Monica found her body-conscious wardrobe and curvy figure a bit too unorthodox for such a distinguished profession as theirs, as though Clarissa was somehow cheapening the institution of learning by wearing a tight skirt and talking about sex.

Rubbish! she thought to herself now, somehow sensing

Monica's air of disapproval drifting across to her. The greatest literature in the world revolves around sexuality, and I'm not going to downplay that! And can I help it, she added to herself defensively, if I have a shapely body and wear nice clothes? Still, she drew the collar of her blouse tightly against her neck as she regarded the proffered document more closely. Besides, she concluded her interior monologue, it's not as if *I* am sleeping with my students. A stinging jab of conscience, however, prompted her to turn over Nick's essay on Donne, as though merely the sight of his writing could incriminate her. Smiling brightly, she turned back towards Monica.

'I'm sorry,' she said cheerily, 'that was a bit crude of me.'

'Not at all,' laughed Monica – rather forcedly, Clarissa thought to herself – 'you're right; Warburton is a dirty old man. And,' she added importantly, 'he has a truly undistinguished publishing record. It's a wonder he got that appointment at all. No doubt our new head of department will be far more research-worthy.'

Clarissa studied the memo again after Monica left. There was no doubt about it: the university stated in unambiguous terms that there was to be absolutely no sexual impropriety between instructor and student within its hallowed walls. Feeling implicated already, as though her fantasies about Nick had been broadcast over the PA system, Clarissa rose firmly from her seat, shuffled her stack of papers, and prepared to go home.

Once outside, however, where the wind had risen and now whipped around her tightly plaited fiery-red hair, Clarissa contemplated the two-mile walk home with dread. The sky looked like rain and her car was in the garage: always a dismal combination. Even as her mind pictured her usually reliable Honda on the repair-shed floor, its mechanical entrails exposed to the world, huge drops of rain began to pelt from the sky, smacking her in the face, matting down her hair, and running off her nose. Clarissa squinted and ran, holding her books awkwardly against her breasts, heading for the first door she saw. She pulled it open, bracing herself against the ferocious wind, and slammed it shut behind her, panting as she leant against the metal bar which levered across it.

One look round, however, and Clarissa realised with dismay the building she had chosen in her headlong dash to avoid the rain. Even without the huge, black-and-grey menacing shapes, the clinking, clanging and grunting, the jarring and discordant bass thumps, the sweaty and humid air would have informed her exactly where she was: she was in the university gym. Clarissa herself worked her muscles rigorously and routinely a minimum of three times a week, but she had never once tested her strength against the chrome and metal machines at the university weight room; indeed, this was the first time she'd ever set foot in it. Clarissa preferred to sweat anonymously in a gym a few miles outside the town where she saw no one she knew, especially students; she had no compunction whatsoever about strutting her well-shaped buttocks suggestively around the classroom while she read aloud some saucy bit from Smollett, but she had absolutely no intention of showing off the workings of her pectoral and lateral muscles to similarly Lycra-clad students.

Looking around her now, Clarissa's decision to exercise separately from her pupils was reinforced by the mass display of pulsing, bared flesh exhibited enticingly before her. Female and male students, the women in skimpy thongs and bra-tops, the men in string vests or stripped to the waist entirely, milled round her, flooding her senses with their rich bodily scents intensified by the strain of working muscle against chrome. Clarissa felt a bit dizzy with the sight of all of those pumping biceps and heaving torsos, and she was just about to move back towards to the door, rain or no rain, when a movement caught her eye, and she half-turned and saw him.

There was Nick, seated at the chest press in the corner, seemingly oblivious to the rest of the weights room, concentrating on extending and retracting his powerful arms as he pushed the metal bar that levered the weights back and forth in front of him. He was wearing a scant, sleeveless white vest and tight black gym shorts which clung to the well-defined muscles of his long, shapely thighs braced against the pad of the seat. The fringe of brownish-red hair that fell over his forehead was damp with sweat, and that kissable mouth was compressed in a grim line as he frowned in determination, intent on the task of building up the solidity of his already impressive, firmly chiselled chest. Clarissa could nearly taste that smooth skin on her tongue, could imagine what it would feel like to scrape her teeth gently against those solid curves so sharply defined, clearly visible above the deeply scooped neck of his T-shirt. She longed to press her face against his breast, to feel that mass of muscle cushioning her cheek, and to seek out the sweetly erect nipples beneath his vest with her lips. Mesmerised by the back-and-forth movement of his arms, she allowed herself to stare openly at him for a moment and then tried to guess the weight those arms were hauling up and down. She squinted to be sure: it looked like 85 kilos, which greatly impressed Clarissa, who herself could press only 20, and that with enormous effort. She watched the vertical movement of the chrome shaft which carried the weights up and down, and the plunging motion of that metal rod into the hole of the top weight on the stack made her think of the plunging motion Nick's own staff would make as he moved in and out of her body. For the second time in less than an hour Clarissa felt herself moistening in her hidden channel, and the steady rhythm of the steel column reminded her of the rhythm of Nick's arm as he stroked his cock that day in her class. She now stared at him as boldly and openly as he had gazed at her while running his hand up and down his steel-hard pole.

Even as Clarissa's mind visualised that masturbatory moment, Nick's eyes flicked across the room to where she was standing, and for the briefest of pauses his pace seemed to falter. His arms remained at full extension, his legs spread apart as he watched her watching him, and then, incredibly, he smiled. That smile only lasted for an instant, but even so, it was thrillingly intimate: the curve of his mouth suggested comradeship with a hint of complicity, as though Nick were acknowledging that only he and she existed in that tiny space of time. That smile bespoke dazzling erotic promise and, as Clarissa stared at him, she could swear that she saw him mouth the word, 'Soon'.

That smile, however, vanished as quickly as it came, and he bent himself once more to the task at hand. Overwhelmed with desire, Clarissa clung momentarily to the back of the lateral pull-down machine against which she had been leaning, and then mentally shook herself before straightening her back and shifting her load of books. She gave one last glance at Nick as he released the weights and bowed his head in exhaustion, looking physically spent – as though he'd just had a massive orgasm, Clarissa thought to herself, and then hoped she hadn't said the words aloud. She turned her back on the boy and headed out towards the rain, hoping it would quench those internal fires, and she let the heavy door clang noisily shut behind her.

Clarissa now had to acknowledge to herself that she was becoming obsessed with this nineteen-year-old student. It was an obsession strictly sexual, that she knew; she doubted she could ever fall in love with him – indeed, she doubted her capacity to love anyone exclusively at all – but thoughts of this boy haunted her, invaded her, intruded upon her most private moments, occupied her mind at the most inconvenient and inappropriate times. She was consumed with him, with the need to see him if she couldn't touch him, and she cursed the fact that their class met only three times a week, though she vowed to make the most of the classroom dynamics to turn his attention fully, and solely, upon her. She chose the clothes she wore for this class as carefully as she chose the material they read; she splurged on luscious silken blouses and shaped skirts which clung to the curves of her graceful figure. She invested in the sheerest, laciest, silkiest and most sensual lingerie she could find, striving vainly to replace the unattainable feel of Nick's flesh against hers with the richest, most finely textured fabrics available in

the most exclusive lingerie shop in the county. She bought
bras, underwear, stockings and garters in the deepest, most
lustrous colours she saw: ruby, turquoise, jade and violet.
She bought hold-ups, peignoirs, corsets and slips, half-
ashamed of herself for indulging in such a hopeless gesture
of desire. She did not lie to herself about what she wanted
from Nick and she had gone beyond caring about the risks
involved both personally and professionally in fleshing out
her fantasies. Fuelled only by her desperate craving to feel
his body next to hers – and on top of, and underneath, and
side-by-side, and all the variations in between – she
pursued her infatuation with him with calculated intensity,
determined to construct an opportunity for them to meet
privately. Clarissa knew that to gain any peace she had to
experience the pleasure he could give her for real rather
than the phantom satisfaction he had so far afforded her
only in her dreams. She could not deny the hold he had on
her; just thinking about his gaze made her melt between
the thighs, and actually facing him in class created an
unnerving tumult in her belly. She could feel her nipples
tightening and her inner lips blossom and swell even while
she was in the midst of a sober lecture on the impact of the
French Revolution on Romantic poetry. She dared not
speak his name in class for fear that merely shaping her
lips around the word 'Nick' would cause such a wild flush
of passion that the whole class would be able to guess how
she felt about him just by looking at her face.

Such a sexual fixation on this boy, however, did not
dampen Clarissa's interest in other men: indeed, her obsession with Nick seemed to colour the world around her
with the subtle palette of erotic artistry, and the everyday
world of people and objects took on a deeper dimension of
luminescent sexuality. Just as she encouraged her students
to discover sexual symbolism in the literature they read,
Clarissa now found erotic possibility and images of female
and male desire everywhere she looked: her salt and
pepper shakers appeared mouthwateringly phallic, their
smooth wooden shafts seeming to fit naturally into the
curve of her hand. The hairy roots of a carrot she was

peeling spoke to her clearly of curling pubic tendrils, and she couldn't bear to watch anyone eat an oyster or even an orange because of their intimate implications. Even people who wouldn't ordinarily attract her appeared to possess sudden glowing sensual appeal: the thick fingers of the postman as he handed her the mail caused her fleetingly to fantasise about how they would feel inside her; the moustache of the off-licence clerk seemed to highlight his heavy-lipped mouth, looking for all the world like a pelt-lined vagina; the snowy peaks of the milk foaming on Clarissa's morning cappuccino resembled nothing so much as miniature, ripe, swelling breasts which begged to be drawn in and suckled by her mouth. Clarissa was horrified to discover that she had even developed a fascination with what lay beneath the flowing habits of the monks who were members of the theological centre affiliated with her university. The mystery of the devout and celibate ascetic fired her imagination with the possibilities of that first seduction away from the holy, and she had to stop herself sharply before she found herself imagining what could be considered heinously blasphemous scenarios.

Words, too, now seemed to speak directly to Clarissa's overheated libido: words such as 'open', 'spreading', 'juicy', and 'pulse' enticed her with liquid possibility, and it was at times difficult to keep herself from trembling when she had to present a particularly meaningful and explicit passage to her class. Even her own name sounded erotic, no longer merely archaically literary: 'Clarissa' sounded like 'kissing', like 'caress', like 'clitoris', that sibilant 's' sound seeming to call lasciviously to her hyper-attuned senses.

Clarissa's newly enhanced interest in the textured world of the senses – particularly sight, smell and touch – had even inspired her to begin to redecorate her house to reflect the new definition of her sexuality. Now that she and Graham had split up, she felt free to reorganise her living space into an intimate sphere of sensual pleasure. She began by throwing out or giving away emblems of her relationship with Graham: she gave him back his treasured videos of important football matches, his oversized college rugby shirt she used to wear to bed, and his lucky light-refracting prism which he liked to keep on the mantelpiece over her coal-burning fire. She then threw out the chillies she kept on hand to spice up his pasta but which she'd always hated, as she was ultra-sensitive to spicy food, and tipped all his orange juice down the sink. When she'd finally cleared out odd pairs of his mismatched socks, the last dregs of his aftershave and cologne, which she remained quite fond of, and packed away the photos of them together which she half-heartedly promised herself to look through again sometime, she was ready to begin repainting the walls, re-covering her furniture and replacing the old, annoyingly fussy flowered sheets on her bed.

Having rid her house of the delicate, ladylike prints and patterns of her past life, Clarissa chose now to strike new ground with rich, pleasingly discordant colours that both soothed and aroused her and whose names sounded good enough to eat: chocolate, butterscotch, raspberry and cream. She re-covered the sofa in her lemon-yellow front room in deep, plush velvet the colour of a ripe aubergine and added soft overstuffed cushions against which she moulded her body as she lay sprawled with a book at night. She stripped off all the bordered wallpaper with its tiny prints of berries and leaves, and hired painters to drench the walls of her living room, dining room and kitchen with warm, absorbent tones of melon, vanilla and rose. Having divested her living space of all Graham's endearing but unattractive mementoes, she pulled out her neglected store of half-forgotten treasures collected by her eccentric Aunt Mildred during her random and solitary travels around the world. Clarissa examined, dusted off and displayed the eerily eyeless mask of painted porcelain from China, the nubbly-textured tapestry of the dancing Buddha from Thailand, the deliciously smooth polished copy of Rodin's 'The Kiss' carved in black marble, and the impossibly large red wooden clog from Holland in which she planted, incongruously, a leafy bunch of fragrant lemon geraniums.

All of this, of course, Clarissa did with an eye towards

the day when she would finally succeed in attracting Nick to her home. She lit scented candles of cinnamon and musk, she installed dimmers into her lamps to decrease the light to a flattering, diffused glow, and she even restocked her set of CDs, adding jazz, rhythm and blues and soul to her usual collection of heavy metal and rock bands.

Of course, Graham noticed Clarissa's aggressive new approach to interior design when he dropped by to return Clarissa's brandy snifters which she'd insisted on keeping at his place, since she'd already broken several of his annoyingly expensive antique crystal goblets.

'So what's all this?' he asked suspiciously, eyeing the jumble of carpet samples and half-unpacked boxes in Clarissa's spacious front sitting room.

'Come in Graham, it's nice to see you too,' Clarissa responded sweetly, watching with barely concealed amusement as Graham unwound his old college scarf from around his long, slender neck.

She stared at him now, still finding him pleasantly handsome though he no longer appealed to her sexually. In fact, it had been his aristocratic good looks which had first attracted her to him. Although Graham worked in the corporate world, designing industrial lasers for missile guidance systems, he looked the typical academic and, indeed, he had friends in the physics department at the university where Clarissa worked. Graham stood slightly under six feet tall, of medium build, neither thin nor portly, but he had nice wide shoulders and well-muscled thighs thanks to his disciplined regime of long-distance running. He was blond and fair, his eyes a pale blue-green and, though he didn't wear spectacles, he often gave the impression that he should. In fact, he was peering a little even now as he surveyed the mess in Clarissa's front room, squinting his eyes and wrinkling up his nose slightly as though concentrating hard on what lay behind Clarissa's home-decorating enthusiasm.

'Someone's been busy, I see,' he commented with that slightly patronising understatement which always set Clarissa's nerves a-jangle. However, she said nothing, merely accepted her brandy glasses while handing Graham a mug of coffee, and with a shudder gave him back his miniature model of a Sidewinder missile which she'd unearthed the other day behind the couch. Now this was one phallic object which left her distinctly cold, its death-driven cylindrical shape doing absolutely nothing for her libido. In fact, she now realised to herself watching Graham sip his coffee, many things about Graham left her cold these days, particularly his primary passions of quantum mechanics and the FA cup.

Graham seemed to have noticed Clarissa's chilling reflections on their now-defunct relationship because he drew his eyes sharply away from Aunt Millie's porcelain Victorian doll, its pale naked leg jutting jauntily out of a cardboard box, and moved a little closer to Clarissa, asking her casually, 'So, doing a little redecorating?'

Clarissa really didn't want to get into the reasons for her recent enthusiasm for interior design, so she merely pulled the doll out of its box, modestly smoothing the dress down over its cotton eyelet petticoat, and said again, 'Nice to see you, Graham.'

Thankfully, he took that as the farewell it was intended to be, but before he left he turned to her and began, 'You know, Clarissa, I still have those tickets for the production of *Madame Butterfly* that's opening at the – '

'Thanks, but no thanks,' responded Clarissa hastily, nearly pushing him out of the door. 'Watching a lovesick woman committing suicide over a man is hardly my idea of a fun way to spend the evening. The deadline for my book is coming up soon, you know, and I simply have to get back to the chapter on Freud's castration complex and medieval Italian eunuchs.'

That ought to fix him, she thought to herself smugly as Graham finally left her house, wincing on his way out.

It did strike her as odd that, whereas nearly every other man she met now seemed to inflame her in some distinctly sexual way, no matter how peripherally, Graham, out of everyone, seemed to invoke not the slightest bit of interest in her. This really was strange, she thought. Even Julian, whose advances Clarissa had heretofore steadfastly refused, was suddenly imbued with alarmingly irresistible qualities. Although Clarissa still could not imagine herself actually acting on her burgeoning interest in women, the idea of kissing and licking another woman's meltingly warm vagina seemed to hold an element of increasingly thrilling appeal – in theory, at least. In fact, she nearly admitted as much to her friend one Sunday afternoon during a slow lunchtime at the pub.

'So, what were you up to last night, my love?' Julian gaily inquired as Clarissa pulled voraciously at her beer, fighting the urge for a cigarette.

'Work and more work,' she answered glumly, hesitant to reveal to her friend her self-imposed celibacy which she knew Julian would never understand. Despite the intoxicatingly erotic haze through which Clarissa now viewed the world, she determined to remain untouched by hands other than her own until the time when she would finally entice Nicholas St Clair into her bed. She had a pleasingly romantic notion of coming to him purified and cleansed of the feel of all other men, so that the intensity of their final coming together would be heightened all the more by her hyper-sensitive desire, no longer dulled by having become accustomed to a lover's touch. Fuelled by deprivation, Clarissa's body would no longer follow her automatic pattern of response; instead, her long period of abstinence would intensify the pleasure when it would finally be broken by another's mouth, hands and body. Clarissa felt purged and new-born, as though she had sloughed off the memory of all other bodies and had opened herself up to the possibilities of her first sexual encounter. In short, sex had become something new again to Clarissa, and she trembled in eagerness for the pleasure to begin.

But she could never tell Julian this, as she would never understand, and so Clarissa merely extended her glass for a refill of bitter, slightly turned on by the feel of the beer sliding down her throat, and averted her eyes from her friend's sharply inquisitive stare.

'All right then, 'Rissa, we'll forget about your boring old

33

night and instead I'll fill you in on my debauched evening of lust.' Julian leered at Clarissa, the diamond stud in her nose winking brightly as Clarissa sighed, gave in, and lit a cigarette, leaning a little away from Julian as she sat on her stool.

'Unburden yourself, Jules,' she said as she prepared to succumb to yet another of Julian's interminable recitations on the pleasures of multi-gendered sex.

Obviously anxious to tell, Julian leant forward, drank deeply of her beer, and prepared to begin. Usually Clarissa was largely unimpressed by Julian's delighted recountings of her sexual exploits, and she was generally bored by the endings which typically had everyone spiralling simultaneously into orgasmic ecstasies and ejaculations – more fiction than fact, Clarissa usually surmised. Today, however, feeling her own sexual void particularly keenly, she leant forward to listen, her eyes fixed on Julian's darkly animated eyes and glistening red lips.

'It was a cold and stormy night,' Julian began wickedly, her large eyes flashing as she refilled Clarissa's beer and leant forward even further, allowing Clarissa to see down her shirt right past her small bra-less breasts. 'Christie and I were supposed to meet up at the Glory Box for a drink and a "little something" to mark the anniversary of the club's grand opening. The Box has been open for a year now, you know, and there hasn't been a single raid, so there was to be a bit of a party – invited guests only, of course. Naturally I had to put my best gear on, which took a little longer than I expected, I guess, because when I got to the club I could see that my girl Christie had found her way to the Love Chair which had just arrived, and supposedly is the same model as the one at the Vault in the States. So I could see that Christie was, shall we say, already otherwise engaged.'

Julian gave a long, devilish laugh while Clarissa struggled to retain a pleasantly blank expression. The Glory Box was a well-known though supposedly 'underground' sex club situated several miles outside the town, and it was trying to imitate the success of the most famous sex club in New York. Julian was one of the original members – you had to know someone to get in – and she had been coolly turning down requests for admittance from among her friends ever since the club had opened. She had, however, frequently invited Clarissa along, but Clarissa had up till now always refused; perhaps, she thought to herself now, she'd go sometime just to look around.

As if guessing her thoughts, Julian touched her on the wrist and said, 'Maybe soon you'll let me take you – as my guest, of course,' she added hastily, laughing at her always intentional double meaning. When Clarissa failed to return her smile, she continued.

'Anyway, I could see that Christie was trying out the new chair – with the help of a friend, of course. You should see this thing, 'Ris!' Julian enthused. 'It's this marvellous contraption which you can manoeuvre any way you like: the arms and legs move, and there are fastenings so you can trap your guy or girl in whatever position suits your fancy.' She regarded Clarissa with interest for a moment – picturing her, no doubt, ingeniously positioned on this contraption – then continued.

'Well, Christie was all stretched out on this thing, which was propped up vertically, her feet strapped on to the footpads and her hands up over her head, and she was sort of laughing and giggling with this guy I could only see from the back, and it looked as though they were just playing a game. When I got closer, however, I could get a better look and I saw that she was laughing because he was tickling her with a feather while he was slowly unzipping her sexy little PVC catsuit.' That didn't sound like much fun to Clarissa, who outwardly said nothing, merely indicating to Julian that she should continue with her story.

'Well, I could see that beautiful body as this fellow was stripping off her clothes, and though I had often tasted its pleasures myself – ' Julian flashed Clarissa a knowing smile ' – of course it is always a delight to see someone else discovering them as well. So I quietly moved over to the bar where I could get a good look at what was going on, ordered myself a cocktail, and settled back to enjoy the show.'

Clarissa's body was beginning to heat up just a little now as she imagined the girl Christie strapped to the chair, an anonymous stranger slowly peeling off her clothes while Julian sat off to the side looking on.

'What did the guy look like?' Clarissa asked softly, and then, unable to resist, 'and what kind of shoes did he have?'

'Please!' Julian rolled her eyes in mock agony and snorted, '*Trainers!* of all things. Can you *believe* it?' She then looked at Clarissa slyly and added, 'But he had absolutely *gorgeous* long black hair that hung straight down his back practically all the way to his bum – which was beautiful as well, by the way – and a huge, and I mean *huge*, long, thick, really red cock.' She paused to gauge Clarissa's reaction, noticed her rising flush, and added, 'But of course I didn't see that until later.' She reached over, freshened Clarissa's drink, and then continued.

'So I watched while he finished unzipping Christie's catsuit and rolled back the shoulders so it was pulled halfway down the arms, tucked it up under her back, and then he did something funny with the legs, I couldn't see what, so that somehow they unzipped and he rolled them down to her knees, and of course she wasn't wearing anything underneath. Finally she lay there almost completely exposed, only the lower parts of her arms and legs covered up, and this man was running this long pointed feather all over her body, brushing it up under her chin, down along her stomach, all over those slim white thighs, and then v-e-r-y slowly over the tips of her pretty pink nipples. From where I was sitting I could see that she was starting to squirm – she'd certainly stopped laughing by now – and it looked to me like she was trying to spread her legs a little, trying to entice that feather – or something a little more substantial – in there between her thighs. But this guy wasn't having any of it. Just kept on teasing her with that feather until she started to whimper and then he stopped what he was doing; he was just kind of poised over her with his body a few inches from hers and then he smiled at her and said, "Ask nicely, now". And would you like to know what he did when she asked?'

Julian's eyes flashed merrily at Clarissa, whose mouth had suddenly gone dry as if all the moisture in her body was rapidly flowing southward to her pulsating crotch. She shifted position on her stool, gripped it firmly with both hands, swallowed hard and croaked, 'Sure.'

'Well, once Christie managed to get the words out – "Please", I think, was all she said – this guy – I never found out his name so let's just call him Joe, OK?' She waited until Clarissa nodded her head, barely aware of what she was agreeing to but eager for Julian to get on with the story. 'So, Joe bent his head, stuck out his tongue and began ever so lightly to flick it at her nipples. He was really teasing her, getting her all hot and bothered, making her wait for it, and of course she couldn't do anything to help herself, she was all strapped in and tied up. So Joe licked at her nipples for a few minutes, very light and quick, and then – and I'd never seen a guy do *this* before – he flipped his head over, gathered up his hair in a ponytail and flicked *that* at her breasts! He trailed his long hair over his shoulder and brushed it up and down her breasts, and I guess she liked it because she started to wail a little and tried to arch her hips up and kind of push them at his face, so he laughed a little and stepped back, then dropped to his knees and put his head between those lovely thighs. More beer?'

Clarissa looked up sharply and shook her head. 'Go on,' she breathed, trying in vain to rub her straining clitoris against the stool without Julian noticing. Too late – Julian's eyes focused on Clarissa's movement against her seat, so she stopped. Stopping herself touching her moistened pearl which was screaming for some attention was costing Clarissa a considerable effort: she could almost feel that sheaf of hair tickling and stimulating her own breasts, and she felt as constrained and immobile under Julian's watchful eye as Christie must have felt strapped to that deliciously diabolical chair. Undoubtedly, Julian noticed

Clarissa's rising state of excitement but she said nothing, merely continuing with her story.

'So this man – Joe – got down there on the floor and lowered the chair a little so Christie's beautiful pink pussy was right level with his face, and then he spread her out with his fingers and I watched while the great long tongue reached out and began to lick that girl with big, slow strokes, just like a cat licking off its cream.' Julian grinned mischievously then looked down at Clarissa, whose cheeks were stained with a wild flush of colour and whose own sex felt so wet she thought she must be leaving a damp patch on her stool. Julian obviously sensed her arousal, which was hard to miss at this point, for she gently placed her hand over Clarissa's and brought it up to her mouth, slowly drawing Clarissa's fingers apart and spreading out the space between the third and fourth digits. 'Shall I show you what he did?' she asked softly. Clarissa panted and nodded as Julian's shining tongue flicked out and drew a sweet wet path down Clarissa's middle finger and then lapped at the sensitive webbing of flesh at its base. Julian closed her mouth over the juncture between the two fingers and sucked, and Clarissa could have sworn she could feel that mouth between the inner lips of her vagina. She could virtually feel Julian's probing tongue between the pulsing lips of her sex, moving back and forth along the hotly throbbing crevice. With every flick of Julian's tongue between her fingers, Clarissa felt an imaginary stroke between her thighs, and she actually leant back a little on her stool and spread her legs as if allowing Julian greater access.

Julian obviously guessed at what Clarissa was trying to do for she looked at her sympathetically and said, 'And there I was, all on my own on that stool, watching this guy thrusting that lovely thick tongue in and out of Christie's sex while she whimpered and moaned and shook all over. Finally he stood up, sort of wiping off his chin, and unzipped his jeans – he didn't even take them off, for god's sake – and out came that cock long enough to match his tongue. All I could do was sit there and watch while he straddled the chair and guided himself right on into her, and I watched that big red length disappear all the way up into her and I *swear* I could almost feel it all the way up myself.' Julian's eyes suddenly met Clarissa's who was obviously experiencing a similar sensation, and then Julian continued, 'And that man stood there and plunged his shiny wet cock in and out of my lucky girl Christie for what seemed hours until they both came together, or so it seemed to me, because they both kind of shook and howled and grunted and rocked at the same time.' Julian glanced at Clarissa again and concluded, 'And then Joe pulled out of her and I saw him unhook and unstrap her from the chair. I watched while she climbed out of that thing, stretching a little as if she was a bit sore, and then, would you believe it, I watched while they changed places and *she* strapped *him* into the chair.' Julian took a long swallow of her beer, met Clarissa's eyes and then concluded abruptly, 'But that's another story.' She stared at Clarissa and drained her drink, then cast a pitying look at her friend. 'Are you all right, love?' she asked gently.

Clarissa had gone nearly white with the effort of restraining her hands from grinding herself to a screaming, shattering climax; Julian obviously sensed her discomfort, for she tenderly inquired, 'Would you like me to escort you to the ladies?' Clarissa had a sudden, striking image of what would happen should she accept Julian's offer: she pictured Julian's mouth on her nipple, her fingers thrusting into her vagina, her own hands massaging Julian's clitoris. She had a sudden, inexplicable urge to fill her mouth with the taste of the other woman's sex and test its pleasures, tracing the delicate folds with her tongue.

Shakily, she rose and mumbled, 'No thanks, I'll be all right,' tottering her way towards the toilet. Once inside, she locked the door and hurriedly tugged down her jeans and underwear. It took but a few seconds for Clarissa to bring herself to a spiralling climax which arched her back and screwed her eyes shut. Feeling much relieved and refreshed, she rinsed off her hands, reapplied her make-up and sauntered back to the bar, looking for all the world like a woman only in need of a drink. Impressed, Julian took in her newly composed appearance and laughed.

'Good on you, 'Rissa!' she chortled, reaching forward to smooth back an escaping red curl. 'You look like an ice princess!'

Coolly, Clarissa accepted a refill and settled herself back at the bar. She debated whether she should address the issue of Julian's lavatory offer, but then decided it would be best to forget it had happened. She congratulated herself on refusing the advances of her friend, no matter how tempting, her composure only reinforcing her decision not to sleep with her mates. Besides, now that she'd satisfied herself, the mysteries of Julian's orifices held strikingly little appeal. Furthermore, she had Nick to think about: sex with a woman was still sex with another person, and Clarissa stuck firmly to her resolution to hold herself in wait for Nick. Sipping daintily at her beer, however, she wondered gloomily how much longer she had to last.

Chapter Three

*A*s it happened, she didn't have to wait much longer. It started with a kiss; a kiss, unfortunately, that was not actually placed on Clarissa.

The day that it began did not have a particularly auspicious opening. It started with a mildly distressing call from Graham, who telephoned while Clarissa was simultaneously munching unbuttered toast, as she was perennially conscious of her figure, getting dressed for work and choosing a poem to read in class. She hung on to the phone with one hand while trying to roll up a stocking mid-thigh with the other, her eyes frantically scanning her bookshelf as she choked down the last of her slice of brown bread. Thus, Clarissa was only half-listening as Graham attempted once again to persuade her out on a date, this time offering tickets to *La Bohème*, yet another opera where a lovesick woman dies. Clarissa, of course, refused.

Oh just sod off, Clarissa thought to herself angrily while noting in dismay the hole her pointed nail had just poked through her stocking and reaching desperately for a volume of Keats' collected works. Really, what does he see in me anyway? she thought to herself crossly, wiping the last of the crumbs off her naked breasts. She felt guilty about Graham, really she did, but she had no time this morning to listen to his attempts to rekindle their romance, in a hurry as she always was, desperate to get to work so she could count the minutes until Nick walked into her classroom.

However, she said nothing to Graham, merely nodding absently while rummaging through her lingerie drawer and murmuring 'Yes, of course I still do' at appropriate intervals while silently swearing at him.

When Clarissa finally managed to disengage herself from the telephone, only semi-aware that she'd agreed to meet Graham later in the week, she gave a small shriek as she noted the time and made a mad dash at her bathroom door to put on her make-up. The telephone rang again and she dreaded picking it up, fearful it might be Graham again with a newly inspired attack on her conscience, but this time it was her carpet supplier, a startlingly inefficient contractor who continually seemed to be losing the samples she requested, delayed laying her final selections while she trod for weeks on bare floorboards, and, what was most alarming, appeared to be at times downright colour-blind. This time he was calling to check for the third time on the exact shade of the soft dove-grey she wanted to replace the grimy smog-coloured rag that currently covered the floor in her guest bedroom. When Clarissa finally extricated herself from this most disagreeable man, she had a mere 45 minutes before class in which to finish applying her make-up, race to the university, prepare some last-minute hand-outs now that she had chosen her poems, and compose herself into a state of relaxed but seductive calm before her students.

Damn, Clarissa fumed to herself as she expertly guided her car, newly serviced and shining, around the intricate one-way system that cut through the centre of town. Look at me – I'm all sweaty and nervous and rushed; how am I ever going to impress Nick looking like *this*?

Even Clarissa 'looking like *this*' was still Clarissa looking quite pretty, however; her lipstick was a little smeared and askew, but she adjusted it in the car-park, wiping off the last of the toast-crumbs; her hair had curled up even more tightly around her face, framing it in delightful little clusters of ringlets, and her cheeks were stained a wild rosy flush as her heart raced while she ran against the clock.

Finally Clarissa was just about on time to teach, hurling herself at her classroom, shooting out from the library where she'd hastily pulled some books off the shelf, carelessly misfiling the ones she'd dropped on the floor. Annoyingly, the heels of her camel suede shoes kept catching on the sharp edges of the flagstones as she flew across campus, and her movements were further impeded by the constricting seams of her tight brown suede skirt which insisted upon hiking itself up around the tops of her rounded thighs. Pausing briefly to jerk it downwards once again, Clarissa nearly pitched headlong into an embracing couple cuddled closely together at the entrance to the building which housed Clarissa's classroom. As Clarissa looked up from her bent-over position where she was awkwardly attempting to rearrange her hemline, her eyes caught sight of a familiar set of black-leather-clad legs. Time now seemed ludicrously irrelevant as she straightened up fully and moved cautiously off to the side where she hoped she wouldn't be seen.

The girl had her arms underneath Nick's ebony leather jacket, her hands obviously moving over his buttocks and spine, and Clarissa watched enviously as the girl gripped at the tight globes of Nick's clearly defined backside. Clarissa couldn't get a good look at her face, partly because it was obscured by Nick's devouring mouth and partly because half of it was cupped firmly in one of Nick's hands. The other hand was buried in her hair – the shiniest, blondest hair Clarissa had ever seen. It shone nearly white, spilling over the girl's shoulders and halfway down her back, a luminescent halo in the cloud-filled sky, and Clarissa knew she'd recognise that hair anywhere, so instantly remarkable was its sheen. She watched in greedy silence as the couple clung together, mouths and bodies moving, and she felt a white-hot arrow of rage and desire shoot through her heart even as her vaginal lips began to sing in desperate harmony with the passion displayed before her. She stared at Nick's hands which were now enclosing the girl's face and hair almost brutally; Clarissa had never before noticed the graceful, elegant shape of those hands, nor the length and beauty of the long, tapered fingers. Unwilling to break her voyeuristic stance, she had to mentally prod herself into moving away before they saw her, her eyes shining, her cheeks flushing wildly, and her moist ruby lips parted slightly in sympathetic response to the widening ache in her nether mouth. Grateful she hadn't been seen, Clarissa started to move off in an opposite direction when Nick's eyes lazily opened above the girl's head and Clarissa blinked as he fixed her with a deliberate, piercing stare.

His mouth still travelling over the girl's, Nick gazed directly ahead at Clarissa, and it almost seemed as though he were smiling around the girl's mouth crushed beneath his. As Clarissa's eyes met his consuming stare, realisation jolted right through her. My god, she said to herself in amazement, he's staged this whole thing! He's deliberately positioned himself with this girl so they'd be in my way, so I'd be sure to run into them and witness this scene! Clarissa saw with total clarity that this little scenario was set up solely for her benefit: she was convinced that the girl herself was unaware that she was being manipulated just so that Nick could get to Clarissa. No doubt the girl thinks that his kiss is intended solely for her, Clarissa thought to herself with a feeling almost of pity. She, however, knew – *knew* – that the girl was but a substitute, a mere cipher for Clarissa herself; Nick wanted Clarissa to watch him kiss another woman in order to turn her on, to force her to imagine herself in the other girl's place, to see herself in his arms, her body pressed against his, the soft cavern of her mouth being ravished by his forceful, driving tongue.

And as this blaze of insight ripped through Clarissa's mind, her eyes locked with Nick's and she saw that he knew that she knew. Of course that's why he and the girl were stationed by this entranceway: he must have known that this was the door through which Clarissa customarily passed on her way to the classroom. As a thrilling wave of certainty tore through Clarissa's body, she shifted her load of books to her other arm and strode right on past the kissing couple, actually brushing Nick's body on her way, feeling the brief contact of her leg against his ignite her senses and leave her slightly reeling. Once inside the building, she raced to her classroom, hastily extracted his essay on Donne from the stack of graded papers in her pile and scrawled at the bottom: 'Incomplete. See me.'

As she dropped the paper on his desk moments later, when he was the docile seated student and she was once again the commanding English lecturer, she glanced into his face and saw the faint lipstick smudge which lingered at the side of his mouth. Resisting the urge to reach forward and wipe it off with her thumb, she merely smiled instead and swept past him, the rustling nylon of her stocking fleetingly kissing his knee as she breezed on by.

The rest of the class passed in a dream for Clarissa, punctuated only by Nick's brief nod in her direction once his eyes had scanned the note on his essay. That nod alone, however, was enough to moisten Clarissa's sex-lips and liquefy her underwear. She taught that day solely on auto-pilot, virtually deaf to her own voice as she lectured on about Romantic poetry, shamelessly unconcerned with the content of what she was saying. All she could think about was her forthcoming meeting with Nick, for she knew with absolute certainty that he would come to her that day, that afternoon, in her office. She mentally reviewed the list of appointments posted on her door, her schedule continually updated so her students would always know how to find her. As she ran her diary through her mind she also made a mental inventory of what she was wearing underneath her tight suede skirt and cream silk blouse. Relieved to recall that she was encased in smoky grey silk edged in ecru French lace, she seated herself on her desk, crossed one café-au-lait leg over the other, and redirected her attention to the poem currently under her class's contemplation.

Once Clarissa's class was finished, though, the rest of

her day seemed interminable. She suffered through her Victorian literature class, a lunch-time departmental meeting, two sob sessions with tearful students on the verge of failing her course, and a stifling round of mind-numbing pleasantries with some colleagues over tea. And through it all, Clarissa's mind was constantly on Nick, her eyes fixed on the door whenever she was in her office, wondering when he would appear. Now that he wasn't physically before her, she was beginning to doubt he would actually materialise, and she couldn't help but wonder whether she'd only fantasised the desire she was sure she'd seen in his eyes.

By 4:30 that afternoon Clarissa was ready to give up and go home. The sky was almost completely dark, her suspender belt was itching uncomfortably, and she was in such a frustrated state of heightened sexual arousal that all she could think about was a vigorous round with her vibrator followed by a hot shower, cold beer and a brain-dead comedy on video. She heaved a sigh of regret, feeling more than a little ashamed for having humiliated herself by extending such an open invitation – an open-legged invitation, she scolded herself furiously. And to a student! Mortified by her misreading of the signs, Clarissa gathered her books together and rose, when a tap at the door made her freeze.

He was there, lounging in her open doorway, as negligently insolent as he had been on that first day of class. Nick lingered boldly in the frame of the door until she beckoned him inside, too palpitating and weak to speak, and she watched wordlessly as he pushed the door closed and walked slowly towards her desk.

Nipples tightening, belly shimmying, wildly aglow with desire and nerves, Clarissa simply stared at him with a pounding heart, waiting for him to speak. With a grin at her obvious unease, Nick nodded his head and slid his marked essay across to her, indicating her note with an elegant sweep of his artistically long finger.

'Incomplete . . .?' he queried, standing close enough to touch.

Reminding herself that she was his teacher, Clarissa took a step backwards and tried to re-align her priorities. 'Why, y-yes,' she stammered, casting frantically about for an excuse as to why she had summoned him here. In her fantasies he had merely burst into her office, swept her off her feet and crushed her body to his; she certainly hadn't expected having to lecture him on his expository prose style. Now, however, looking into his eyes – she'd never been close enough before to see that they were hazel, like hers – she could only gaze at him and pray that the wetness between her thighs wouldn't start flowing down her leg. Hardly aware of what she was saying, she forced out the words, 'You have left me . . . this essay . . . unfinished.'

He moved closer. 'And in what way have I left you incomplete?'

Damn, he's tall, she thought to herself, having nearly to bend over backwards to look into his face. She noted that the lipstick smudge was gone, and unable to help herself, she raised her finger to his mouth and murmured, 'I see you've wiped off the trace of that kiss.'

Not moving his eyes from hers, Nick placed his thumb over Clarissa's lower lip and slowly stroked the pad of his finger across her mouth, rubbing off her scarlet matte lipstick, then moved his thumb to her upper lip, baring her mouth and wiping off all her carefully applied make-up. He traced the outline of her lips with his thumb and she opened them helplessly, her tongue flicking out, trying to suck at his fingers. Instead he slid them away from her face, framing it between his beautifully sculpted hands and gazing at her intently before unpinning her flaming tresses from their confining but easily undone twist. Feeling the colour of her hair burn hotter, Clarissa allowed him to release her mass of curls which then tumbled waywardly down to her shoulders. Nick cradled her face in his hands once again, and as she saw him bending to kiss her she closed her eyes and waited breathlessly for that crucial first embrace.

Expecting an onslaught, she was caught completely unawares by the gentle, almost hesitant brush of his lips against hers. Nick slipped one arm around Clarissa's waist while with the other he cupped her cheek in his palm, and the feel of his fingers stroking her face nearly caused her to weep at his unexpected tenderness – so different from the roughness with which he'd handled the girl this morning! Because he was so obviously restrained, Clarissa fought to control her own raging desire for him, and in that gap between passion and restraint, she trembled. Finally Clarissa fitted his upper lip between hers, then shifted and enclosed his lower lip, repeating the kiss several times before her tongue eased forward and shyly lapped at his lips. She twined her arms around his neck, straining upwards to reach him, then ran her fingers through his hair as Nick's tongue edged slowly out to meet hers. As their kiss deepened, Clarissa slipped her finger inside his mouth so she could feel his tongue as it rubbed against hers, and she stroked its velvety thickness as it pushed further into her mouth. She clung to him as he lifted her up easily in his strong arms and then deposited her gently on her desk, bending her back slightly so that the distance between their bodies was reduced.

Whimpering with desire for him, Clarissa pushed at the shoulders of Nick's leather jacket until it fell to the floor, and she could now let her hands play freely over the length and breadth of his body. At last she could feel for herself how the strength and firmness of his chest, arms and back surpassed the way she'd imagined them in her dreams. She passed her palms over and around his curves and ridges, glorying in the feel of him under her hands. He thrust his tongue in her ear as she rapidly unbuttoned his shirt and clutched at the hard balls of his biceps underneath the sleeves, being too impatient to lay her fingers on his flesh to bother pulling off the garment completely. Clarissa pressed her groin against Nick's, arching fervently against him as his mouth travelled from the lobe of her ear to the creamy column of her throat. As he kissed her neck he murmured, 'You smell so good, Clarissa,' and the sound of his voice saying her name – embracing it, it seemed – jolted her with a thunderbolt of rapture; she hadn't

48

expected the sudden familiarity and ease of intimacy with which his perception of her shifted from teacher to lover.

Closing her eyes against the kaleidoscope of pleasure that was spinning out along her body and between her legs, Clarissa moved her mouth from Nick's jaw down to the virtually hair-free smoothness of his chest, the softness of his skin in delicious contrast to the manly hardness of muscle beneath. She pressed her face into the cushion of his breast, just as she'd longed to do that day in the gym, and breathed in the wonder of him, his masculine scent of leather and cologne, before locating his pert brown nipple and drawing it lovingly into her mouth. Nick's hands ran up and down her sides, sliding along the deep curves of breasts, waist and hips before scooting under her where she sat and cupping the rounded globes of her buttocks. He held her to him while her mouth lingered at his stiff coffee-coloured tip and her hands traced the tense bands of muscles underneath his arms and along his stomach.

Anxious to explore further, Clarissa wrapped her legs around Nick's waist, drawing him closer as she reached for the powerfully throbbing shaft in his jeans. Usually so adept at fastenings, she was surprised by her clumsy fumblings at the buttons of his fly, her fingers made stiff and awkward by the force of her passion. Once she'd finally freed that awesomely rigid and thick member, however, she drew back to gaze at it, only slightly surprised to discover that he wore no underwear. Nick smilingly followed the downward drift of her eyes as she admired the deep salmon-and-violet hues of his penis, partially shrouded in the thick, slightly spongy cowl of his foreskin. His cock felt hot and hugely substantial in her palm, and Clarissa brought her mouth up to Nick's ear and whispered, 'Put your hand on mine. Show me how you like it.'

In answer he wrapped his hand around hers, his pulsating staff now gripped by both of them, and as he showed her the motion he preferred, holding a steady rhythm as together they worked his cock, she was reminded of the pumping movement of his arm as he'd performed this act alone in her class. Together they moved their hands as one over the steely strength of his shaft, sliding the foreskin up and down and squeezing gently below the royal purple tip. Finally Nick slid his hand away from hers and focused on unbuttoning her blouse while Clarissa leant back on her desk with one hand, the other continuing to pleasure his pink-and-plum-coloured penis.

Pushing Clarissa's blouse and bra straps off her shoulders, Nick bent and pressed his open mouth against the deep cleavage between her breasts, slipping his tongue between the alabaster mounds, his breath warm and moist on her heated flesh. Releasing his cock for the moment, Clarissa returned again to the triangular planes of Nick's back as he nudged her breasts free from their padded enclosures and reared back slightly to admire the small round nipples now scarlet and erect, standing proudly away from their surrounding circles of a deeper rose red. She looked at him looking at her, leaning back on both her hands now so that her breasts arched out seductively above the scrunched-up cups of her cloud-coloured bra. She had a sudden vision of how they must appear to an interested observer, he with his shirt still on but unbuttoned, his cock arcing away from its halo of reddish-brown curls only half-glimpsed through the unfastened opening of his leather jeans. She too was semi-bared to the waist, her blouse floating down around her wrists and hips but still fastened at the cuffs, her bra crumpled and irrelevant beneath the fullness of her free-standing breasts. Nick was situated between her thighs, almost leaning on his elbows as he pressed her back gently and supported her with his hands while he sucked softly on her nipple. Borne up by his arms, Clarissa ran her hands through Nick's hair as he teased her pink crest with his tongue, drawing it in and out of his mouth while she cried out repeatedly, 'Ahhhh . . . ahhhh.'

Eager now to taste more, Clarissa pushed him away slightly, eased off the desk then slid to her knees, gracefully repositioning them both so that Nick now stood braced against her desk and she was head-to-head with his cock, so to speak, her back to the door. She gripped his shaft with her hand and guided it to the lush warmth of her mouth, her lips closing on its thickness, wondering if she had enough room to take it all in. Nick had to widen his stance a little so that his hips were level with her mouth, and he wrapped his hands around her head, helping her to find the pace that he liked while she moved her mouth up and down the length of his pulsating column. She swirled her tongue around the sensitive ridge under the plum-like tip while he continued to nudge her head back and forth along his shaft. Suddenly she took her mouth completely away, smiling at his suppressed growl of surprised frustration before provoking a more pronounced moan of delight as she took his balls in her mouth. She sucked carefully at them one at a time, her tongue playing against the textured softness of the sac that enclosed them. As she enfolded his balls in the heated cavern of her mouth, she reached behind his scrotum with her fingers to stroke that most secret, sensitive space behind the testicles in the way that she knew drove men wild. Nick was no exception, and he nearly cried aloud in pleasure as she felt his balls rise a little upwards in her mouth. Realising that the arrival of his orgasm was close, she turned back to his penis, ready to capture that moment of ecstasy in her throat, but he raised her up roughly, his fingers gripping her arms, and placed her back on to her desk.

Puzzled, Clarissa looked up at his face and said, 'But I want to – '

'I know what you want,' he said almost brusquely, then more quietly he told her, 'but I want to be inside you the first time that I come.' In one swift, sweeping motion he then brushed aside all the clutter on her desk with his arm, much of it falling on to the floor, before easing her back so that she lay on top, her head at one edge of the desk, her melting, fluid vagina at the other.

Nick then pushed up her skirt so it was crushed up around her hips, and he impatiently pulled to one side the now-soaking scrap of lace that covered her swelling crevice. His hands briefly caressed the tops of her thighs where her lace-edged stockings ended, then pressed them apart so that he could gaze at the glistening pink folds of her vulva. Instinctively she sought to close her legs against his intrusive, intimate stare, but Nick gently prised them open again, saying quietly, 'Don't be shy, Clarissa. I want to look at you.' Reaching back, Clarissa grasped at the edge of the desk behind her head, holding on tightly while kicking off her shoes and flexing her bare feet against the deltoid bulge of Nick's shoulders. She felt herself laid out and completely exposed, warmed by the heat of Nick's stare as he consumed those petal-like lips with his eyes. He turned his head towards the bare patch of thigh above her stocking and murmured, 'Damn, you're beautiful, Clarissa.' She then had to bite down hard to keep from screaming aloud as Nick's mouth covered the mouth of her vagina. He entered her, his tongue deep inside her, the lips of his mouth dividing her labia so he could probe inside her satiny depths while he sucked at her inner flesh. His tongue moved in and out of her, mimicking the promise of what his penis was yet to do, and when he finally withdrew to suck gently but firmly at her clitoris, Clarissa frantically stuffed her hand in her mouth as she climaxed convulsively in his.

Panting a little, she disentangled her legs from round his shoulders and sat up, her senses still ringing from the intensity of her orgasm. Rising to his feet, Nick looked at her for a moment as though trying to assess her thoughts, but she left him in no doubt as she slid off the desk and pulled him down with her so that they were lying full length on the pseudo-Persian carpet that covered her floor.

Rolling on top of her, Nick positioned himself between her thighs and, raising himself up on his hands so that he could look into her face, he said, 'I've never heard you say my name. I want to hear you say my name now.' His voice was husky and deep, full of rich, soft warmth.

'Nick,' Clarissa said quietly, the intimacy of the moment making it sound as loud as a thunderclap.

'Tell me that you want me,' he urged. 'Say, "Nick, I want you inside me".'

'I want you inside me, Nick,' Clarissa breathed.

She held on to him tightly and reached down to guide him inside her, holding her breath as he slid slowly into her warm, wet openness. Once fully inside, he held himself still for a moment, and their eyes met in a brief pause while they assessed their mutual fit, feeling the snug grip of her vagina around his pulsing but still motionless penis, and then slowly, tantalisingly, lingeringly, he began to move. Clarissa thought she would nearly faint with the pleasure as Nick's pace slowly increased inside her, and then they were driving against each other, matching their rhythms by instinct as though they'd been making love to each other for years. As their bodies pounded against each other and the tremors of another orgasm began to build deep within Clarissa's belly, she felt tears beginning to form in her eyes. It seemed as though her whole body had become one big pool of fluidity, as though her heated passion for Nick had melted the fibres of her body and she had become total liquid reception. Looking up at his face, Clarissa was stunned to see wetness in his eyes as well – at least, she thought she did, until he lowered his face to hers and kissed her fully, almost roughly, while he drove himself further inside her. As Clarissa's climax gathered in speed and brightness and exploded in a dazzling sunburst of sensation, she felt Nick consolidating his power and his strength, and with a final inward thrust he bore down inside her and she felt the force of his orgasm while her eyes locked with his, the two of them staring silently at each other as Nick exploded within her.

They lay together quietly for a moment and then, half-pushing him off and struggling to sit up, Clarissa winced a little as a slight cramp seized her leg, and then winced even more as she realised the enormity of what she'd just done.

She glanced at him. 'Do you think anyone heard us?' she whispered.

He laughed and ruffled her hair. 'Would you mind if they did?' he asked, smiling up at her.

She tugged at his shirt so that he sat upright and then

she snapped, 'Of course I mind! No one must *ever* know about this!' Glaring at him before burying her face in her hands, Clarissa moaned aloud, 'Oh god, what have I done? How can I ever face you in class after this?'

Gently he pulled her hands away from her face and kissed her. 'Oh, Clarissa,' he breathed against her hair, 'we haven't done anything yet. In fact,' he grinned, 'we've hardly begun.'

Choosing to ignore the promise in those words that was already causing her loins to stir again, Clarissa tugged at him once more and said, 'Hurry up. Get dressed. We've got to get out of here before someone sees us.' She paused, and then pointed to the clutter on her floor which he had so off-handedly swept off her desk. 'But help me clean that mess up first.'

They left the building together silently and there was a brief, awkward moment when Clarissa wondered hysterically whether they should shake hands or something but, unwilling to lose the momentum, she said abruptly, 'Come on. I'll drive you home.'

As he packed his long body into the ridiculously tiny interior of her car, which had always seemed perfectly adequate to her up to now, Nick said almost casually, 'I've wanted to do that since the first day of class.'

She looked at him and stifled a wild impulse to giggle. 'Yes, I know,' she said, indicating his cock with her eyes. He looked at her and their eyes met and suddenly she just laughed and laughed.

They had almost reached the block where Nick shared a flat with a friend when Clarissa asked, unable to bear the uncertainty any longer, 'So, are we going to do this again?'

Absently looking out the window, Nick paused a moment, then said, 'Well, I don't know, Dr Cornwall. I suppose that's up to you.'

Willing him to look at her, Clarissa forced herself to ask lightly, 'And what about the girl I saw you with this morning?'

Now he did look at her, and he smiled a little – rather a

cruel smile, Clarissa thought to herself angrily, as though he were relishing his power over her. 'Jessica?' he asked airily, then briefly held Clarissa's eyes before saying, 'Don't let her bother you.'

'Well, it's not as though I'm jealous or anything,' Clarissa said stiffly, her insides churning. 'I'd just prefer it if you didn't go blabbing to all your little girlfriends about the fact that you've just fucked your English teacher.'

He glanced at her. 'Stop the car,' he said suddenly.

'What?' She stared at him. 'Here?'

'Stop the car!' he repeated and started to reach towards the steering wheel, but she pushed him away and steered shakily towards the shoulder of the road, braking bumpily and skidding to a halt.

'Get out,' he said shortly, already beginning to open his door.

'What?' She couldn't believe she was hearing this. A student bossing his teacher about!

'Get out!' he ordered, then roughly started to pull her over the gearshift towards his open door.

'All right!' she snapped irritably while wondering uneasily what he was trying to do. 'I can get out by myself.'

She stumbled out of her door and looked around, unable to guess at what he wanted. They were standing on the shoulder of a busy side road that led up to the motorway: the street they were standing on had many shops, banks and offices on it. No one else was about at this hour as it was after six, but there were plenty of cars passing, and Clarissa calculated she'd have no problem if she were suddenly forced to run for help.

As though guessing her thoughts, Nick came over to her and said more gently, 'I'm not going to hurt you.' He bent as though to kiss her but as her lips parted to receive his mouth, he turned his head instead and whispered in her ear, 'I just want to fuck you again.'

'Here?' she asked incredulously, wide eyed yet already starting to lubricate. 'Where? On what?'

'On this,' he answered shortly and lifted her up so that she was sitting facing him on the bonnet of her car, and then he was reaching between her legs to snatch off her underwear. Clarissa felt Nick grasp her delicate lace panties between his strong hands and she gasped as she heard the rending sound of lace ripping from lace, and as Nick flung away the remnants of her expensive French knickers she wrenched at the fly of his leather jeans, her fingers now much surer and more competent than they'd been in her office. She curled her hand around his already stiffened penis as his fingers found her velvety vulva, and he smiled to see how open and wet she was, so highly aroused by the evidence of his desire for her.

'Ready for me already, I see,' he grunted with pleasure, and was just about to plunge into her when she stopped him.

'Wait!' she cried, then darted off the bonnet, dashed around to the passenger side of the car, extracted something from within, then rearranged herself on the car. 'Not without *this* first,' she ordered, producing a sensitive, ultra-thin condom.

Nick stepped back a bit, then shrugged his shoulders and said, 'Sure. Whatever.' Then looking at her with a wicked grin he said, 'But *you* put it on.'

Expertly she tore open the packet and shook out the wafer-thin sheath, rapidly unrolling it down over Nick's swaying, protruding cock. 'Usually I do this more slowly and with a little more finesse,' she murmured huskily, her wet, open mouth against his neck, 'but I'm in rather a hurry now, as you can see.'

His penis now safely enclosed, Nick wrapped his big hands round Clarissa's waist and pulled her towards him. 'Come to me now,' he whispered into her ear. 'I want you now.'

She arched up her hips and he glided into her, filling her up and stretching her out. Clarissa looked up at him in the darkness, his face only partially illuminated by the amber streetlights, and she wondered what the drivers of the cars on the road saw. Nick's back was to the street, his body obscuring her from the cars, but she could see movement and headlights over his shoulder, and she could hear the whistle and crunch as tyres sped over tarmac. All she could feel, however, was Nick's cock pulsing as he moved hard and fast within her, gripping her tightly, with his fingers round the soft flesh of her hips. Clarissa felt the cold steel of the car's bonnet under her bare backside, and she revelled in the outrageousness of what they were doing. There was something intoxicating and exhilarating about being half-naked in the open, knowing that anyone could see what they were doing, could see the controlled movements of Nick's semi-nude buttocks as he thrust forcefully inside her. Any passer-by could witness Clarissa's legs entwined round Nick's hips, her skirt hitched up round her waist as she leant back on her hands and arched back her neck. Whereas the sex in her office had been almost tender love-making, this was all sexual desire and urgent, hungry flesh, and Clarissa nearly screamed aloud as her inner walls rippled and vibrated around Nick's pulsating shaft. She watched him pull back so he could see the stem of his penis as it pushed in and out of her, glistening wetly in the moonlight, and then moved forward again, leaning into her as he braced himself with his hands on the car. Never before had Clarissa felt so deliciously licentious, nor so gloriously uninhibited. She wanted the drivers on the road to see her, wanted to exult in her public abandon on the top of her car. She thrust hard against Nick, urging him further inside her, feeling the warm furred sac of his scrotum meeting the hot juncture of her thighs with every stroke of his cock. Her buttocks thumped against the hard cold metal as she opened herself still wider to Nick's rampant pillar of flesh. Soon – too soon – she felt the start of her orgasm thundering forth from deep within her vagina, and as her inner walls gripped convulsively at Nick's cock, he bent down so his head was buried between her shoulder and her neck, and she felt his body shudder as he silently spent himself inside her.

As she watched Nick withdraw and disengage himself from the condom, Clarissa realised that he was right: this had been just the beginning. Having now tasted the incredible head-spinning, mind-blowing pleasure of possessing and being possessed by him, Clarissa wondered how she would ever be able to extricate herself from him. Even now, still feeling the aftershocks of her orgasm vibrating throughout her body, she wanted more of him already, and the burgeoning need she was beginning to feel for this absurdly young man frightened her a little as she sensed the extent of her passion's hold on her and the daring, precipitous risk she was taking in taking him on as her lover.

Nick must have felt her eyes burning into him for he asked her grinningly as he threw the condom away, 'What are you thinking about, 'Ris?'

She looked at him and shook her head briefly, then considered the skyline as she said, 'I think maybe there's a lot that *you* can teach *me*.'

He kissed her lips, ruffled her hair in a friendly way, as one would a child, and merely said, 'We'll see, Clarissa. We'll just see.'

Chapter Four

*A*nd so it began. The next time Clarissa had to face Nick in class, she was terribly nervous. She wasn't sure how she could possibly act the disinterested lecturer when she had passed two sleepless nights mentally reliving the thrill of his body as it so expertly handled hers. Nearly crazed with the anticipation of seeing him again, she was also concerned about the signal she wanted to send. She certainly didn't want the rest of the class to guess at her obsession, nor did she want Nick to see clearly how much she wanted him now that she had had the chance to taste him. So Clarissa dressed extra carefully for class that day, not wanting to appear either too distant or too familiar; her tightest clothes seemed to her to be too much of an invitation, but she didn't want to appear dowdy. Therefore, she chose a lightweight wool apron-front dress that skimmed her curves rather than clung to them, a blouse that buttoned demurely at the throat, and a single choker of pearls. Hoping to strike the right note of attractive but professional university instructor, she held her head high and walked assuredly into the classroom.

She needn't have worried, however; all her care and concern were for naught. Nick wasn't in class. Frustrated and disappointed, Clarissa struggled to concentrate on the day's lesson while straining to keep an ear out for the tread of Nick's boots in the hall, her eyes continually darting to the door, hoping to see his tall, rangy frame. He failed to materialise for the entire 60 minutes, however, and when Clarissa finally dismissed her class she tasted the bitterness of thwarted expectations and silently cursed herself for her impatient desperation to see him. Now that she had experienced Nick's body for herself, she felt bound and tied to him in a way she'd never felt to another lover, and she fought to maintain her equilibrium and to distance herself from the memory of what had happened. As she abandoned the empty room and turned towards the stairs leading to her office, she forced herself to view what had happened as a mistake, promising herself she'd forget about it and somehow try to treat him as just another student.

Later that day, though, when heading towards yet another departmental meeting, she saw him; he was leaning casually against the stairs surrounded by laughing classmates, among them, Clarissa noted unhappily, the blonde-haired girl.

Damn him! she ground out to herself silently. How dare he! It occurred to her that, sensing how desperately keen she'd be to see him, no matter how nervously, he had purposely stayed away as though to torment her further, prolonging her desire to lay eyes on him again. Thorns of angry humiliation invaded her body as she considered the possibility that the sex they'd shared had been no more than an amusing challenge to him, a dare he'd set himself. Horrified by the possibility that he had entertained his friends – perhaps even some of her own students – with the tale of how he'd fucked his English teacher, Clarissa prepared to accost him where he stood, using the power of her position as lecturer, and demand to see him in her office. However, she immediately thought better of it. Her horror deepened as she imagined him defying her authority in front of his friends and refusing to meet with her, and so instead she turned on her heel and strode off in the opposite direction.

He was waiting for her by her car as she approached it

after the meeting, his back leaning against the window, his hands shoved deep in his pockets. He smiled full in her face as she neared the driver's side, and he appeared annoyingly arrogant, as though she had arrived at that place solely to see him rather than to drive herself home. Again it occurred to her that he knew exactly how much he'd angered and hurt her today by staying away from class, as though he were trying to avoid her.

'Hey, Clarissa,' he called out affably, towering over her with his tall, lean body. 'On your way home?'

'Why the hell weren't you in class today?' she nearly shouted at him, unable to appear as cool as he.

He grinned at her, and shrugged offhandedly. 'Oh, that,' he said dismissively, as though it were no matter. 'Sorry I had to skip the lecture today.'

Stung by the brevity of his reply, Clarissa merely unlocked the door to her car, then paused to look at him. Damn, but he's sexy, she thought to herself, unwilling to admit the force of her desire that was already propelling her round to his side of the car to unlock the passenger's door. 'You missed an important class today,' she said crossly, hating to hear herself sounding like a primary school teacher. 'Get in.'

Hardly able to believe herself, Clarissa roughly shoved him inside, slammed his door, then jammed herself into the driver's seat – and immediately stalled the car in her agitation at being so close to him.

'Damn!' she cried, and he laughed aloud and reached over to caress the thin circle of her gloved wrist with his beautifully long fingers.

'Hey,' he said soothingly, 'it's OK.'

She looked at him, and unable to stop herself, reached over to kiss him, her lips briefly enclosing his before her tongue slipped in between them and swept across the inside of his mouth. His unshaven cheek rasped against hers as he drew her towards him and began to reach between her legs when, abruptly mindful that they were still in the faculty car park, she pushed him away and started up the car – successfully this time.

'Are we going to your house?' he asked offhandedly, still keeping his hand up her dress and between her thighs.

'Where else?' she gasped as his fingers inched up the lace banding of her French knickers and began to stroke aside the auburn clutch of curls that covered the lips of her sex. 'Are you offering to take me to yours?'

He merely laughed and continued to stroke, and Clarissa tried to concentrate on her steering as Nick's fingers slyly parted the rapidly unfurling leaves of her blossoming vagina and slipped inside, two of them, to slide in and out of her while his thumb covered her clitoris. Clarissa nearly lost sight of the road as Nick's hand lifted her slightly upwards then down again so she was sitting fully on his palm, two fingers pushing against her plush inner walls while his thumb continued to agitate the ripening bud of her eagerly emerging clitoris. He smiled a little when Clarissa glanced at him, as though merely amused by the quickening pulse of her vagina which was widening and moistening around his fingers, but one quick grope on her part assured Clarissa that he was finding his manipulation of her every bit as exciting as she. He had a taut, promising bulge in the front of his trousers, and she thought she could feel it leap a little under her fingers before she withdrew her hand to resume steering. Clarissa felt a sharp pang of loss when her difficulty in manoeuvring the car around a particularly tight corner caused Nick's fingers to slip momentarily out of her heaving vagina, but he rapidly resumed his position, his increasingly powerful finger-thrusts making her cry out partly in pleasure and partly in panic as the car skid, briefly out of her palpitating control. His eyes fixed on her face, Nick reached over to slip his other hand down the front of Clarissa's blouse, clasping her breast and passing his palm around her stiffening nipple while his lips sought her throat. His warm tongue moved tantalisingly around the milky softness of her flesh, and he shifted position slightly in his seat so that he could bury his mouth at the base of her neck.

Such an intensifying of pleasure proved to be too much for Clarissa, who forcefully shoved Nick away from her while lifting herself off his hand and replacing it firmly in his lap.

'That's enough!' she said primly, trying to conceal the near-climactic ripplings of sensation which continued to reverberate along her now achingly-empty vagina. 'Do you want me to have an accident?'

'Safety first,' he admonished her seriously, then tipped back his head and laughed – not at her expense, she hoped anxiously. Again it struck her that Nick found a certain degree of amusement in her panting response to his touch, as though he savoured the power her desire for him had over her, while he remained curiously detached.

As Clarissa pulled into her driveway, Nick let out a low whistle of appreciation. 'Nice house,' he commented, admiring the neat bed of marigolds and azaleas which bordered her front garden.

Clarissa said nothing but led the way into her cluttered but tidy front sitting room, now thankfully free of boxes, where she deposited her load of books and gestured towards the aubergine-coloured sofa. 'Drink?' she offered.

He nodded. 'Please,' he said, studying the crammed wooden bookshelves, Tiffany lampshade, framed black-and-white modernist prints and, incongruously, a set of cosy family photos skewered lovingly to a ribbon attached to the cheery yellow wall above the menacing hulk of her computer. She watched him examine the intricate ivory curves of her chess set, picking up the pieces and fingering them curiously, as though he'd never seen one before. As Clarissa handed him his foaming glass of beer she watched him puzzling over a replica of an Oxford gargoyle, then moving on to consider a porcelain Chinese vase, causing Clarissa's stomach to tighten in fear that he might drop it. He turned towards her with an inquisitive lift to his eyebrow.

'All yours?' he asked, indicating her curios with a tilt of his head. 'You bought all these yourself?'

'Inheritance,' she said shortly and, she hoped, with finality. Clarissa absolutely did not want to go into the details of her family history with Nick; although not by nature an excessively private person, she felt that she had already shared enough of herself with him, and she wanted to keep as much of her personal life apart from him as possible. She had a deep irrational fear of opening up her life to him as though it were something constructed merely for his amusement. She expected nothing more out of this affair than a mutual giving and taking of pleasure, and she was determined to keep as much of herself as possible separate and inviolable, revealing as little of her life to Nick as the fates allowed.

As if on cue, however, the phone sharply rang, jarring both Clarissa and Nick, and she froze, her gaze locked with his, as the shrill, insistent ringing continued.

'Aren't you going to answer it?' Nick asked, watching Clarissa closely.

'The answering machine will take it,' Clarissa nervously replied, desperately hoping that the caller wouldn't turn out to be someone from work.

As the answerphone clicked on, however, Clarissa realised with deep dismay that it was Graham's voice that came loudly into the room, sounding a bit strained, his accent a little too affected.

'Ah yes, Graham here,' he was saying, his stilted formality grating on Clarissa's ears, as well as his exaggerated pronunciation of the Queen's English. She couldn't help but contrast it unfavourably with Nick's warm, rich Midlands lilt.

'I'm ringing to remind you of our plans for tomorrow night,' Graham continued. Damn! She had forgotten that she'd agreed to meet him. He went on with his message to add conversationally, as though she could answer, 'Please don't arrange anything else, as these bookings are rather hard to come by, and it has been so long since we've been out together, you know.'

He sounds as though he's expecting a reply straight away! Clarissa thought angrily to herself. As though he knows I'm standing here listening to him, but can't be bothered to pick up the phone! – which, of course, was precisely the case.

Nick's eyes met Clarissa's in amusement, and it was with great relief that Clarissa heard Graham finally ring off, vowing to herself to ring him back tomorrow morning and cancel their damned date.

'Husband? Boyfriend?' Nick casually inquired, regarding her over the rim of his glass.

'Neither,' she answered abruptly, then moved away from Nick, nearly backing herself into a corner as though his very presence in her house was making her uncomfortable.

Apparently sensing her discomfort, Nick replaced the mask he was holding on to the carved occasional table and stepped backwards a bit. 'Is my being here making you nervous?' he asked gently. 'Am I invading too much of – ' he laughed ' – your personal space?'

She stared at him, aghast. Really, it was maddening the way he already seemed to know so much about her! Hoping to catch him off-guard, Clarissa deliberately set down her beer and pressed her body firmly against his. 'Invade away,' she invited, her arms reaching up to him.

As he brought his mouth down over hers, Nick lifted Clarissa up easily in his arms and inquired around her probing tongue, 'Where's the bedroom?'

'Through there,' came her muffled reply as she pointed with her arm towards the doorway leading to the stairs. Despite her rising excitement, she maintained enough detachment to be impressed by Nick's ability to co-ordinate kissing her with watching where he was going as he carried her up the narrow, winding staircase and into her surprisingly spacious bedroom. He laid her down on her large, Egyptian-cotton quilt and then stepped back a bit to survey the contents of her room. Clarissa congratulated herself on having finally shed the last of those prissy Laura Ashley patterns that had disfigured her house as Nick's eyes travelled round her room, taking in the muted mauve, teal and strawberry tones of the walls and the intricate scrollwork of her big brass bed. Framed prints of vaginal-looking flowers and erotically contorted dancers covered her walls; there was a beautiful antique oak armoire in the corner, and arched brass lamps were placed strategically about the room. Clarissa sat on the bed removing her pearl choker and watched as Nick wandered over to her low mirrored dressing table with the skirt that covered its legs and ran his fingers over the cut-glass bottles of perfumes, lotions and oils. He held up a particularly ornate atomiser with an old-fashioned black bulb and pressed it slightly, releasing a spray of spicy floral scent.

Clarissa was intrigued, and a little bemused, by Nick's apparent fascination with the way she lived her life. She wouldn't have thought that he'd be interested in how she'd personalised her intimate living-space, and it occurred to her that he was trying to lay claim to her by exploring the margins and details of her house the way he'd explored the folds and crevices of her body. If knowledge was power, then it certainly seemed as though Nick was trying to learn enough about Clarissa to extend the control his body already had over her.

When at last he turned to her on the bed and came to lie beside her, running his hands over her body as he'd run them over her bottles and jars, Clarissa was keen to do something to redress the imbalance of power. She rolled on top of him and began to move her mouth slowly over him, starting with his lips and moving across to thrust her tongue in his ear, and then below to kiss the place where his head joined his neck, turning his jaw away to allow herself greater access. As she moved lower to trail her tongue along the contoured ridges of his pectorals, unbuttoning his shirt along the way, Nick's hands slid down the arch of her spine to cup and squeeze the muscled curves of her rotating buttocks as she undulated her hips against him – but she stopped him.

'Uh-uh,' she said warningly, her mouth against his nipple. 'Don't touch me now.'

He said nothing but merely clasped his hands behind his head while Clarissa's tongue sought out his stiff brown nipple and her hand moved downwards to rub against the protruding bulge in his jeans. She enveloped the organ, rolling her hand around it and moving steadily upwards and downwards in a smooth, slow rhythm. As she did so her left hand finished unbuttoning his shirt, and then she pulled away and commanded, 'Take it off.'

Nick looked at her and grinned, still saying nothing, then neatly stripped off his shirt and dropped it on the floor. 'Now yours,' he said, reaching for the straps of her dress, but she slapped his hands away and said, 'Uh uh – I told you, no touching.' She considered him thoughtfully a moment, then, lifting up her dress so she could comfortably straddle his hips, she deftly unbuckled his belt and drew the leather length rapidly out of the loops of his jeans, saying, 'I see we'll have to do something to prevent your hands from getting in the way.' He glanced at her questioningly and she ordered, 'Roll on to your side,' pushing at his hip and lifting it up to help him oblige. 'Hands behind your back now,' she told him, and then pressed his wrists together and threaded the belt through and around them, securing it by fastening the buckle and then testing its tightness.

'Too tight?' she asked a little anxiously, then fought to regain her control. She had, after all, done this before, but never had it afforded her the thrill it did now, feeling herself exert a form of dominance over this incredibly young man who held her in such thrall.

Nick shrugged, clearly struggling to contain his excitement, as though to show it would be giving something away, and said, 'It's OK.'

Clarissa regarded him a moment, silently admiring the way his muscles bulged underneath the smooth skin of his arms, now tautened and strained by the confining belt. She ran first her fingers, then her mouth along the lines of the arm closest to her, and tongued the sensitive crease inside his elbow. She then drew her mouth down to his wrist and kissed the sensitive flesh before nudging him again on to his back and locating the deep indentation of his navel with her tongue. Clarissa licked up and down the sides of it, savouring the rough, male taste of him and smiling to herself when she heard a low murmured moan of approval. She briefly pressed her cheek against the hollow formed by his stomach beneath his ribcage, then sucked one last time at his salty, textured navel.

Rearing back on to her heels, Clarissa then tugged at Nick's boots and, with some effort, finally pulled them off, careful not to muddy her blouse with the soles. She then eased off his socks and hesitated at his toes, thinking about sucking them, then decided she'd wait until after he'd had a bath – hopefully with her. Instead she bent over the fly of his jeans, briefly bared her teeth at him with a low growl, and then nipped at the fly, gripping the fabric around the top button with her teeth. It had taken her years of practice, but Clarissa was now justly proud of herself for perfecting the art of unbuttoning a man's fly in this manner. Denim was a tough business, but Nick's trousers were well worn and it took but a few firm jerks of her head – like a dog with a particularly juicy bone, she always thought – to release the set of five buttons from their tight little enclosures. Noting that again Nick wore no underwear, Clarissa wondered to herself whether he'd planned on seducing – or being seduced by – her today, or whether it was his usual practice to allow his cock to abrade freely against the front closure of his trousers. She considered asking him, but the shut-eyed look of tremulous anticipation on his face as she slipped off his jeans convinced her such a trivial issue could wait to be resolved.

At last Nick lay naked on the bed, Clarissa sitting beside him fully dressed, and she paused to admire the length of him, his hands tied helplessly behind his back, the skin of his chest and arms pulled tightly enough to display his flexed muscles and his cock dancing a little in expectation, as though trying to attract her attention. Clarissa's eyes absorbed the sight of that long, thick shaft, noting its swelling plum-like tip and already imagining the taste of it on her tongue. She took a firm grip on his penis, feeling it pulse and quicken beneath her fingers, and she smiled down at him, her own body tensing with erotic arousal.

'Comfortable?' she smiled, and was enormously gratified to see him wince a little at her deferral of his pleasure, the tip of his cock already beginning to emit a thick drop of lush, pearlised liquid. Eager to send this boy out of his mind with delight, Clarissa bent over and caught the silken drop on her tongue, swallowing it down and positioning herself between his slim, muscular thighs. 'Mmm,' she purred, looking up at him and nearly mewling with satisfaction, 'let's see if there's more where that came from.'

And then she began in earnest, gripping his cock with her lips and drawing him deeply into her mouth, her tongue slipping under the foreskin and circling round the steely hardness of his shaft. She worked her way around the circumference of his cock, concentrating on keeping her tongue soft and wet, taking in as much of the violet-and-rose coloured length of it as she could. She tried to position it so that the head was enclosed in the tender patch of her mouth where her molars ended and her cheek met her gum, and then she shifted so it was pointing down her throat. She sucked up and down the jutting rod, covering up her teeth with her lips, and she could feel her jaw muscles bulging as Nick's hips jerked in rhythm with her mouth. Clarissa slowly slid his cock out of her mouth and glanced up at Nick, whose face was contorted with pleasure, and she whispered, 'Lie still. Open your legs.'

Obediently his legs spread for her and she took his balls in her mouth, the soft sac reminding her of the texture of moleskin, so sensual and delicate was its feel. Clarissa sucked gently at his testicles, her fingers circling the cushiony pad behind the scrotum, feeling the pulse tick and beat with her movements. Releasing Nick's balls, Clarissa ducked her head lower and stroked that sensitive spot with her tongue then, grasping Nick's thighs and pushing them further apart, she sucked at the core of his body where his legs joined his pelvis. Feeling Nick struggling against the belt that bound his wrists, Clarissa sensed his time was near, so she tugged at his hip, causing him to roll back on to his side. Sliding her fingers down the sweat-moistened cleft between his buttocks, Clarissa found the tiny, tight opening, and, parting the tightly muscled globes of his backside, she inserted her tongue, slowly licking at the pink-and-beige lining of the crease that divided his buttocks. Using the moisture from her mouth as a lubricant, she worked her finger inside, feeling the rectal walls unfolding around it while she continued to suck gently at his anal entrance. Nick gasped aloud in delight – or was it shock? – and Clarissa wondered if he'd ever been penetrated in this way before. She twisted her finger in further, then firmly pushed it in and out while she pressed her mouth against his widening backside one last time. Finally she rolled him on to his back again and moved upward to claim his cock with her mouth. She drew the length of it deeply into her mouth, then slid it back out so that only the head remained between her lips. She withdrew her finger so that she could concentrate on relaxing her jaw as she felt the blood start to pound in the jerking, throbbing shaft, and she knew Nick's climactic moment had come. There was that momentary pause in Nick's movements before his sperm jetted forth into her mouth, and he arched his back and tensed, muttering a single, nearly silent 'ah' of ecstasy. Clarissa stayed absolutely still, simply gathering the fluid in her mouth before withdrawing slowly to swallow it down, wiping off the salty, slightly bitter drops that fell from her chin as she moved away from Nick and bent over to unfasten his belt.

'Wow,' Nick exhaled as he sat up and flexed his aching wrists, grimacing as the blood began to resume its circulation. '*Where* did you learn *that*?'

Clarissa smiled and straightened her clothes, then reached forward to brush Nick's hair back from his eyes. 'Years of practice,' she answered throatily as she leant forward to kiss him, testing to see whether he'd pull away. Not many men could stand to have the taste of themselves revisited on their tongue, but Nick kissed her with force, working his tongue around hers as though extracting every drop of himself from the interior of her mouth. Clarissa was pleased with herself for pleasing him so well, as though this was a competition of sorts to see who could retain erotic dominance over the other.

As if guessing her thoughts – damn, he's good at that, Clarissa thought to herself in annoyance – Nick pushed her back down on the bed and said, 'And now, my dear, it's your turn.'

Unwilling to succumb so easily, despite the vibrant excitement which was rampaging through her body, Clarissa resisted Nick's gentle push, sat back up and lightly jumped off the bed.

'Let's have some supper first,' she suggested cheerily, then absorbed his blank-faced expression. 'Or ... perhaps you'd rather not.' Even though Clarissa was reluctant to share too much of her private life with Nick, that didn't include dinner – or perhaps, she thought, eating together was just too chummy, too much of a boyfriend-girlfriend thing that Nick might not want. I guess it's pretty obvious, thought Clarissa to herself, that he only wants me for sex; perhaps that's the only activity he's willing to share.

His shuttered look rapidly dissolved, however, and was replaced instead by a sly, almost cunning expression. 'Of course, Clarissa,' he grinned. 'I'll eat with you. What are we having?'

Relieved to recall that she had done a week's worth of shopping the night before, Clarissa waited until Nick was dresssed then led the way to the kitchen and directed him to chop up vegetables, blend a salad dressing and peel fruit while she threw together a chicken stir-fry, saffron rice and poured a significant amount of brandy into the fruit salad. Clarissa was a little startled to discover that cooking together was an easy, comfortable affair, cosy even, and she felt that she and Nick worked naturally together in such a domestic environment. She started to instruct him on how to lay the table when, with a wicked glance, he stopped her. 'Let's eat in your bedroom,' he grinned, and searched about for a tray. Clarissa followed him up the stairs with a bottle of champagne, and they set up a little picnic on her bed, feeding each other with chopsticks.

'This is fun,' Clarissa chirped happily, dabbing her napkin gaily at Nick's chin to catch a dribble of soy sauce. She then stopped guiltily and clapped a hand to her mouth. 'I guess I'm not acting very much like a lecturer,' she said, half to herself and half to Nick. 'And don't think I'm looking for anything more involved than this!' she snapped defensively.

Nick laughed and settled back against the pillows. 'Tell me about yourself, Clarissa,' he said, ignoring her previous remark and pouring them more champagne. 'How did you get into teaching?'

Clarissa stared at him for a moment, surprised he was even interested, then decided his question was somehow intended to trap her into revealing enough of herself for him to maintain some sort of hold over her. She was still unable to satisfactorily analyse why it was she wanted him so badly, and she was determined to maintain as much of an emotional distance between them as possible. Clarissa doubted she was more to Nick than just a momentary fling, an amusing sexual diversion heightened by the illicit thrill of her age and position. She suspected that her passion for him ran deeper than his did for her, and so she was anxious not to appear too eager to share confidences or to imply that this was in any way anything other than a casual affair for her either.

So instead of answering his question, Clarissa put the tray on the floor, drew a deep draught of champagne into her mouth and placed her lips on Nick's, letting the liquid flow into his mouth from hers. She kissed his neck while he swallowed, and then his hands were everywhere on her body, under her dress, over her breasts, circling her waist and inching between her thighs, and she gave herself up to the indescribable waves of blissful sensation that were flooding her nerve endings, suddenly inflamed with the need to feel his flesh upon hers. She lunged at the buttons on his shirt, nearly ripping the garment from his body, when his hands caught at her wrists and held them away from him, needing only a fraction of his strength to imprison her.

'Uh uh,' he said, mimicking her earlier admonition. 'No touching, remember?'

Clarissa lay back and closed her eyes while Nick unbuttoned the straps of her dress with one easy flick of his long

fingers, then pulled it over her head, undoing the buttons
at her waist so that the whole thing came off. He then
nipped at the buttons of her blouse as she had done at his
jeans, but her buttons were tiny and tightly fastened, so
with an impatient grunt he undid as many as were
necessary to simply lift that over her head as well. Clarissa
wanted to tell him to be careful, that it was expensive
Italian silk, but she was so mesmerised by the feel of his
fingers on her body she could hardly breathe, let alone
speak. She now lay before him, clad only in her bra,
panties, stockings and suspender belt, and she felt herself
tremble as she awaited his touch, for he had withdrawn
his hands and now simply sat looking at her. She experienced the way his gaze passed over her body as though it
were a tangible, tactile thing; she felt his eyes caress the
heaving swell of her bosom, the striated planes of her
stomach, the fullness of her rounded thighs. She held her
breath in anticipation of the feel of his mouth, fingers,
body, but he merely held himself back, smiling a little as
though he sensed her mounting frustration while he considered what to do with her.

Feeling a little silly, finally, Clarissa started to sit up in
protest when she saw him sip at his glass of champagne as
though he were going to ignore her, but with one easy
sweep of his arm he gently pushed her back down and
then spilled some champagne on to her breasts, causing
her to gasp in surprise and discomfort at the icy cold
liquid. The chill was quickly replaced by his heat, however,
as Nick's tongue plunged into the pool on her chest and
lapped at it slowly, trailing over the cleft of her cleavage
and licking away the last sparkling drops. He grinned at
her again, then expertly unclasped the front closure of her
cream-coloured bra as though he'd received personal
instruction in the ladies' undergarment department. Clarissa helped herself out of the underwired entrapment,
tangling up the straps in her haste, and then felt her breasts
quiver a little as Nick dipped his finger in his glass and
drew intricate patterns on her stiff pink nipples with the
champagne. The delicate alcoholic drops tickled her

breasts, heightening their sensitivity as Nick bent his head and licked at her nipples, drinking in the fizzing wine. He lingered at her breasts for a while, alternating the warm softness of his tongue with the now only slightly cool drops of champagne, and then trickled a path to her navel which he sucked up with his mouth. There was no sound in the room other than the splash of the wine and the swishing sound of Nick's lips; Clarissa was afraid to sigh or pant too loudly lest she break the tingling spell of their passion. Desperate for Nick to do more, yet unwilling to relinquish the feel of his tongue in the well in her stomach, Clarissa was both relieved and disappointed when he finally reached behind her to unhook the itching lace of her frothy red suspender belt. He then unrolled one dusky blue stocking down her right foot, did the same with the left, then dangled them teasingly in front of her, close enough for her to smell the lingering scent of her perfume on the silky fabric.

'Let's see,' he drawled, trailing the edge of one stocking down the length of her stomach. 'Should we use these to tie you up, like you used my belt?' Playfully he grabbed at her wrists, wrapping the nylon tightly around them, then pulled it slowly away, like a conjurer unfolding a magical scarf. 'Or perhaps we should tie up your ankles?' He indicated the scrollwork at the foot of the bed as though he would anchor her feet to that, and then chuckled a little at her reaction as he let the stockings float down to the floor. 'No?' he queried, examining her face. 'Maybe we should leave that for another time?'

Although Clarissa generally enjoyed being tied up, and yes, more than one lover had used her own stockings for that purpose, the idea of lying helpless before Nick, passively awaiting his moves, wasn't something that appealed to her; indeed, the prospect of adding to her vulnerability was much too disconcerting. So it was with great relief and a rush of internal moisture that Clarissa lifted her hips to allow Nick to ease off her panties, obviously deciding against tying her down that day. Once he'd discarded them, consigning them to the heap that was the rest of her clothes, he settled himself on the floor by the side of the bed and grasped her shapely calves, dragging her to him so that her vagina was poised on the edge of the bed directly in front of his mouth.

'Close your eyes,' he commanded against the softness of her inner thigh, kissing the curve where her leg met her body. 'Let this be a surprise.' He then gently pushed her legs apart, placing one foot on the floor and setting the other one next to her pillows so she was spread wide apart. Closing her eyes, Clarissa waited with a beating heart to see what he'd do next; expecting the heat and strength of his tongue, she cried out in shock when she felt something cold, wet and slightly squishy being quietly inserted into her vagina.

'What the *hell* is that?' she demanded, sitting up and nearly kicking Nick in the head, but he quickly rose to his feet and nudged her back down.

'Patience,' he whispered. 'Just wait.' Arranging her back into position, he gently prodded another cold, wet object inside her and then, putting his mouth squarely at the entrance to her vagina, he sucked out whatever he'd put in and then rose above her so she could see his face. He held a slice of melon from the fruit salad between his teeth and Clarissa felt a sudden thrilling jolt as he bent over, slipping the fruit between her lips and watching while she swallowed it, tasting her own sweet-as-honey juices on the piece of honeydew as it went down.

'So *that's* what that was!' she hooted, and then, wildly aroused by such a novel use for fruit, she breathlessly awaited the feel of Nick's warm, wet mouth which contrasted so favourably with the icy chill of the fruit and the sharp, acidic sting of the brandy. Clarissa shivered in exquisite pleasure every time Nick slid in another plump slice or segment of grapefruit, pineapple, melon or strawberry, and she clenched her interior muscles around each piece, coating it with the flavour of her own inner juices. She couldn't tell if the moisture running down her now-luscious crevice and in the cleft between her buttocks was from Nick's mouth, the juice of the fruit, or her own vaginal creaminess. She felt as though the heat of her musky dampness might soften and melt the fruit, so aroused was she, and she thrilled to Nick's obvious enjoyment as he simultaneously devoured her and the dessert she so temptingly offered him from between her thighs. Eventually, the pressure of Nick's mouth against her syrupy vagina was driving her close to the brink of orgasm so she waited until he'd swallowed the last succulent sliver of strawberry and then, turning back the folds of her labia so the shining pearl of her clitoris was clearly visible, she murmured huskily, 'Kiss me here. I want you right here.'

Nick surged forward and laid his tongue against the dewy sweetness of the nub of Clarissa's pleasure, which had also been bathed in the fruity juices which flavoured the rest of her. He licked and sucked at the peaking bud, his long soft tongue sweeping over and around it until Clarissa came in convulsions, her whole body shaking with the force of her climax. The waves of shrieking rapture had barely subsided when Clarissa, desperately craving penetration, lunged at Nick's jeans, tearing at his fly in her frenzy to get at his cock. Laughing, Nick held her off a little with one hand while he reached in his back pocket with the other.

'Whoa,' he said, trying to restrain her. 'Calm down. All in good time. Look what I brought with me.'

Clarissa stared in amazement at the shiny red condom packet he held triumphantly above her, and a heady smile of delight curved her lips.

'Go on,' she said, nodding at the sheath. 'Let me watch you put it on.'

Nick's fingers fumbled with the buttons of his shirt, which he finally drew off, and then he hastily removed his jeans, his cock springing proudly forward as though reaching out towards her body. Clarissa watched while he grasped it in his hand with obvious familiarity and jiggled it a little so that the head fitted securely into the ringed opening of the condom. He pinched the tip of the sheath, expelling the air, then rapidly rolled the condom down until his blushing, swelling penis was entirely enclosed. Clarissa found the sight of him handling his shaft deeply

76

erotic, and as soon as he was safely wrapped up, she reached up to him and pulled him down on the bed so they were body to body, skin to skin, flesh to flesh.

'The first time we've held each other while both completely naked,' Nick mused aloud, and then pressed his body even closer to Clarissa's, saying, 'Let me just experience the feel of you.'

Overwhelmed by his unexpected tenderness – like the time he'd first kissed her in her office – Clarissa felt tears start to well up in her eyes at the same time as she savoured the feeling of Nick's naked body against hers. She kissed his mouth, tasting her fruited flavour which still clung to his tongue, and rubbed against him, trying to tell where her skin left off and his began. When Nick ran his hands along the sides of her body, she could feel the softness of her own skin as though his hands had become hers, and the velvety texture of his chest against her own seemed to mirror the silken softness of her breasts.

Unnerved by this intimate, unlooked-for closeness, she deliberately pushed him off her and rolled him on to his back, throwing her leg across his hips so that she was centred across his cock, kneeling fully astride him, then she leant a little forward, guiding his pulsating staff into the secret depths of her slightly sticky vagina. Once he was fully inside her, she paused for a moment and he held still within her, their eyes meeting, each gauging the other's reaction. Slowly she began to move, sliding up a little and moving back down while he rocked his hips and answered her motions with strong, probing thrusts. Clarissa moved now up and down, now forward and back, rubbing her clitoris against the bone of his pelvis and the base of his cock. She rode him long and slow, her buttocks clutched in his hands, her breasts braced against his chest as she leant forward to kiss him. They moved together in silence, looking into each other's face and listening to each other's breathy, hushed sighs. The bed creaked softly under them as their tempo began gradually to increase, their accelerated rhythm heightening and intensifying their pleasure until Nick was pounding away inside her while Clarissa arched her back and shut her eyes, her knees abraded by the heavy cotton of the quilt, her hands tucked up high beneath Nick's shoulders. As Clarissa's orgasm began to rip through her, she heard Nick's voice through the pounding of the blood in her veins saying, 'Open your eyes, Clarissa. I want you to look at me.'

She looked at him then, a faint flush on his cheeks and his sensual lips slightly apart, and she wanted to hide from the intensity of emotion that swept through her. As Clarissa screamed her pleasure aloud, she felt Nick's own ecstatic spasm, and his body rocked hers as he gave one final thrust, shuddered and lay still.

He lay quietly within her for a moment then, turning away his head, he withdrew completely, gently nudged her off him and disappeared into the bathroom, taking his discarded clothes with him. While he was gone, Clarissa quickly dressed in a pair of leggings and a jumper then dawdled nervously about, unsure of how to act once he re-emerged. She felt naked and exposed, not because of the sex they'd shared, but because she felt that some indefinable emotion had surged forth from within her and was clearly visible on her face. She didn't want Nick to think that this had been anything more than an extraordinarily pleasant evening; after all, she still had to grade his essays and assign his homework. Thus she struggled to maintain somehow a coolly professional demeanour.

When Nick emerged from the bathroom, dressed and obviously ready to go, she hesitated shyly, then forced herself to say lightly, 'Well, I guess I'll see you in class.'

He smiled a little at the absurdity of the situation – at least, she hoped that was the source of the smile – and said, 'I suppose so.'

She followed him down the stairs and then paused at the door as he opened it.

'Well,' she said again, feeling awkward and uneasy – something she never usually felt with a lover. 'See you in class.'

He nodded, smiled and left, shutting the door firmly behind him.

Chapter Five

Nick's abrupt departure from Clarissa's house set the tone and pattern for their sexual encounters over the next few weeks. Clarissa never knew when he would approach her; Nick's desire for her seemed erratic and unpredictable. Days would go by at a stretch where she would see him only in class, and occasionally he would miss entire sessions, as though her classroom lectures no longer mattered to him. When he did show up, more often than not he would simply lean back in his chair against the wall in the back corner of the room, his eyes shut as though he were either sleeping or listening intently, she was never sure which. He seldom looked in her direction while she taught, not once did he meet her eyes, and there was none of that piercing intensity there had been in his face the first day of class when he'd stared at her body while quietly working his cock, something which she still hadn't dared to mention to him directly.

Despite his apparent lack of interest in her lectures, however, Nick's classwork and essays actually seemed to improve a little; his prose style was vigorous and marked with a clearly identifiable voice, and he wrote with energy and passion about the material she introduced, from the lyrical eroticism of Byron to the nearly obscene descriptions of the female body in the poetry of Baudelaire. Indeed, it was becoming increasingly difficult for Clarissa to read Nick's work dispassionately; every sentence of his writing seemed to contain a personal reference to herself – to her body, her sexuality, her passion for him. Reading Nick's work was becoming an intensely intimate act for Clarissa, and she could never be sure if she was merely fantasising that he was actually writing about her rather than the poem, or whether he deliberately intended his work to reflect the sexual relationship which was rapidly developing between himself and his instructor. Regardless, the more she read his work, the more Clarissa was turned on by his writing; the way he wrote about erotic literature seemed an extended expression of the erotic attachment between them. It was always with a sudden jolt that she had to remind herself that she actually had to assign a mark to his essays, and it was only with a conscious effort that she would force herself back into the relatively objective role of his tutor. With a wrench, she marked his essays only upper seconds rather than firsts, for as bound as she felt to him by his writing, there nevertheless remained technical flaws in his style, and his textual analyses at times lacked subtlety and depth, one reason, perhaps, that she assumed they were written so personally.

If Nick really did intend his schoolwork to invite Clarissa's personal, and decidedly non-professional, response, certainly his behaviour when they accidentally met outside the classroom was pointedly cool, aloof even, and he rarely acknowledged her at all, even in her official position of university lecturer. If she chanced to pass him by while he was engaged in conversation with a friend or fellow classmate, she strove to look away, but when she did peek out at him from the corner of her eye, he seemed not to notice her at all. He never once looked in her direction or so much as flicked his eyes her way; she could have been for all the world merely another anonymous lecturer hurrying on her way to class. Clarissa found this elaborate pretence all the more grating on those days when she'd possessed him so completely only the night before, the taste of his semen still fresh in her mouth and her vaginal lips still slightly abraded from his touch. She felt a curious tension within herself during these moments, a certain uneasy friction that rubbed her raw, springing from the contradiction between his public aloofness and their private pleasure.

Yet their pleasure was not always so private; often Clarissa would breeze past him in the corridor, their bodies mere inches apart yet both looking straight ahead, neither appearing to recognise the other. Moments later, however, she could be in her office, marking essays, reviewing an article, talking on the telephone with a colleague, and Nick would casually slip inside the door, quickly twist the lock and sink to his knees, burying his face in her breasts. Clarissa tried to discourage these high-risk office encounters, attempting to set him aside while she finished her business so they could meet separately at her house. In fact, Nick seemed to take a pronounced kind of pleasure in trying to seduce Clarissa in her office as though the prohibited, illicit nature of their relationship was what provided him with the majority of its thrill. At those times when he descended upon her at work, his eyes hot with desire and his cock nearly leaping out of its fly, Clarissa would wonder to herself whether he would even bother with her if she were his age and simply another student.

Indeed, it often seemed to Clarissa as though Nick were merely toying with her; he would let three or four days go by with no contact, and he wouldn't even show up for class, but then out of nowhere he would blaze into her office or knock cagily at her door. When she admitted him – which she always did – he would launch himself at her and fall on her body, enveloping her in his fiery embrace which inevitably started the tremors rumbling within her belly and the blood racing hotly in her veins. Nick would consume her body with his eyes, his hands, his mouth and his penis, and she would consume him in turn, and for those few hours they were together the Vice-Chancellor of the university himself could suddenly materialise officiously at her bedside and Clarissa couldn't give a damn.

And so with a headlong dash Clarissa let all her professionalism and personal goals slide, solely so she could give herself up to the pleasure of sex with Nick. The deadline for the submission of the final draft of her book was rapidly approaching, students' essays were piling up around her, and notices for conferences, calls for papers and research opportunities were shovelled out with the rubbish, for if Clarissa had thought herself obsessed with Nick before, now she regarded anything that remotely interfered in her time with him as a mere distraction.

And yet they really didn't spend that much time together. Given her position and the unequal terms of their relationship, Clarissa never felt comfortable approaching Nick but instead was forced to wait, simmering with sexual tension, for him to advance upon her. It was as if the very height of her position constricted her, limited her freedom of movement, and forbade her from coming to Nick on her own. When he did come to her, he always seemed to have limited time; he never spent the night with her, and he always departed abruptly after their final bout on the bed, floor, staircase, kitchen table or bathroom basin. She had no idea what he did when he wasn't with her, or where he went, and she could almost never tell what he was thinking. Nor had Clarissa ever been to his flat that he shared, and it chafed her to know that he had somehow seduced her into revealing more and more of her life to him, despite her determination to keep herself separate, while he gave nothing away of himself. However, annoyingly, details of her life would continue to slip out: Nick knew where she grew up, what degree she'd received at university, a first, of course, what nights she did her food shopping, and even how much she paid her cleaning lady. Clarissa never knew afterwards how such intimate information, some trivial, some intensely private, had been teased out of her, and she was always angry and amazed at herself for opening herself up to Nick so widely in both a sexual and emotional sense.

And yet she knew virtually nothing about him. She knew that he was originally from Derbyshire, he lived with an old schoolmate who was in the Officer Training Corps, and his favourite rock band was Stone Temple Pilots. Other than that, he remained an enigma. She was especially curious about his sexual past: at what age he'd lost his virginity, which she guessed must have been early, how many women he'd slept with, the most innovative act he'd enjoyed, what was his favourite sexual fantasy. She felt too awkward to inquire, yet it gnawed at her to know that he'd obviously acquired a sexual education somewhere, and she was consumed with envy for the nameless, numberless women who'd possessed his body as she was now doing. Although she said nothing about her private obsession to Nick, she couldn't help but feel that somehow he knew how the gaps in his history continually tormented yet tantalised her. Nor did she feel that she could completely hide from him that she hated the fact that other women had pleasured his body – perhaps better than she.

So one night near the start of the Easter break, hoping to entice him into allowing her access to himself and emboldened by their passionate, exhausting bout under the dining room table – how they got there she couldn't explain – Clarissa nuzzled her way deeper into the crook of his arm and cooed, 'Nick, why are you so perversely secretive about yourself with me?'

He cocked his eyebrow at her in that now-familiar gesture of slightly patronising amusement and inquired, 'And just what would you like to know?' while tasting the enticing protuberance of her pleasure-flushed nipple.

'I don't know,' Clarissa breathed, struggling to retain her train of thought while urging more of her breast into his mouth. 'Why don't you ever invite me to *your* house?'

Nick released her luscious mound from his lips and stared at her blankly for a moment before rapidly rearranging his features into a fondly roguish expression. 'All right, Clarissa,' he graciously assented, 'when would you like a visit chez Nick?'

She rolled away from him and sat up, narrowly avoiding a collision between the crown of her head and the underside of the table top. 'You mean it?' she asked with almost childish delight. 'Can I really come to your flat? You'll actually show me where you live?'

He seemed startled and touched by the enthusiasm of her response and, apparently thinking aloud, he replied, 'Of course,' then suggested, 'How about Thursday? Say, about eight o'clock?' Grinning at the pleased expression on her face, he added, 'Come for dinner. Bring a bottle of wine.'

And with that, he crushed her body to him again, causing Clarissa to yelp with delight as she dived under the polished mahogany table to take his pulsating cock into her open, hungry mouth.

That Thursday night Clarissa dressed extra carefully for her 'date.' At least she knew enough about Nick now to anticipate his preference in lingerie, and so she slid sheer midnight-black hold-ups over her perfumed, freshly waxed legs and shimmied her way into the confines of a lacy blush-coloured corset – no underwear underneath, of course – the subtle pink tones contrasting sweetly with the ebony of her stockings and lending a rosy tint to her creamy white skin. Over this she arranged a sleeveless, mid-thigh Lycra dress that boasted a high neck and plunging scoop in the back; the dress was in a rich shade of mauve that contrasted oddly well with the delicate colour of her corset as well as the fiery red of her wildly cascading hair, yet it was so tight she had to wiggle her bottom repeatedly to ensure that the dress fitted smoothly over her curves without adding bulk or unsightly wrinkles. Stepping into her black strappy high-heeled shoes, she considered her reflection in the mirror, smiling a little at her image of expensive, elegant temptress so different from her usual tailored, professional appearance. I doubt Nick will be expecting me to be as well turned out as this, Clarissa thought smugly to herself as her rose-painted nails twisted her key in the lock. No doubt he'll be fairly scruffy as usual, dressed in jeans and three-day-old stubble. She shivered a little in anticipation of the rasp of that stubble against her tender, pearly skin and folded herself into her car, feeling her stretchy but tight dress inch up to her hips as she did so.

Once she was actually driving the short distance to Nick's flat, however, Clarissa pulled her dress up even higher, almost to her waist, spreading her thighs wide as she stopped at a traffic light, daring herself to lift her leg and hook her heel over the handle that wound up her window. Fully aware that any driver on her right could glance over and receive an eyeful of thigh-high hold-ups and the sharp vee of the pink panel of her corset, Clarissa found herself moistening with the satiny dew of arousal while her nipples tightened provocatively behind the wired panelling of their padded enclosures. She could feel her vaginal channel widening and the nub of her clitoris begin to stiffen in expectation of Nick's knowing caress and as she shifted in her seat, she turned up the volume of the Stone Temple Pilots tape she had bought to feel closer to Nick and pressed down hard on the accelerator.

Arriving at the door to Nick's flat, Clarissa nervously smoothed her dress down demurely over her hips and, bottle of chardonnay chilling her suddenly icy palm, rapped sharply on the door with her knuckles, but there was no reply. Even through the thickness of Nick's front door, however, she could hear the thump of music coming from inside, so she rapped sharply again, then pounded with the flat of her hand against the wood. Fighting back anger and fear – had he dared to stand her up? – she convinced herself that he couldn't hear her knock over the sound of the music, and so she bravely swivelled the brass handle, gently pushing open the door.

Clarissa stepped cautiously inside and quickly assessed the situation. The room she'd just entered was long and narrow and remarkably untidy, littered with books, newspapers, CDs and cassettes, and empty take-away cartons. No wonder he didn't want me to come here, she thought to herself amid the pounding of blood in her head. The boy lives like a pig. Through the pulsing in her head she clearly heard the easily identifiable bass line of the music of The Doors, blaring away from somewhere down the hall.

Aren't you a little young to know this song? Clarissa acidly addressed Nick in her mind. Although her instincts were screaming at her not to follow that sound, Clarissa bravely clicked her way down the tacky linoleum floor, still clutching the bottle of wine as her stomach began to churn nauseatingly inside her. She passed the microscopic bathroom, surprisingly clean kitchen – probably never been cooked in, she sniffed to herself – and one empty bedroom before pausing in trepidation at the entrance to the last room on the right. Reminding herself that she'd come this far and now had no choice but to peek within, she cautiously poked her head round the corner of the door, the noise in her head pounding as loudly as the music on the stereo, then boldly stepped fully inside and gasped in shock at the scene that assaulted her eyes.

The girl was naked, lying width-ways across the high narrow bed, her splash of white-blonde hair tumbling down the side, her eyes blindfolded, her mouth gagged, and her wrists and ankles bound to the legs of the bed. Bizarrely, Clarissa concentrated on determining exactly what it was that was anchoring her limbs, and realised that the girl was restrained by narrow strips of garish red grosgrain ribbon, the kind used for wrapping up Christmas presents. What an unusual use for ribbon, Clarissa stupidly remarked to herself, then forced herself to lift her eyes to confront Nick's cruelly smiling face as he stood, also naked, hip-height to the bed, his feet braced wide apart as he leant forwards, plunging rhythmically into the girl, grinding his pelvis and rotating it slowly against hers. The girl had a pillow rolled up and tucked underneath her hips so her bottom and vagina were thrust up and out, allowing Nick greater access and a deep, steep angle. Clarissa's horror was intensified by the sight of a mirror strategically placed behind Nick's gyrating backside in such a way that it reflected the girl's weaving hips and the movement of Nick's cock as he repeatedly withdrew and re-entered. From her position in the doorway Clarissa could see that Nick had intentionally placed the mirror in this way to face the door so that Clarissa would have a clear, unobstructed view of their bodies meshed together as soon as she stepped inside. She stared, fascinated, at the swollen ruby lips curled lasciviously around the sturdy thick member that divided them with every steady stroke. Clarissa studied the girl's froth of golden fringe that was tangled up with Nick's reddish-brown thatch and the greedy, grasping nether mouth that rippled around Nick's rampant cock. While Clarissa gazed, half-horrified, half madly aroused, at that glistening shaft and juicy red sex, Nick fixed his eyes on her face and removed the girl's gag but left her still blindfolded, completely unaware that Clarissa was a silent, stupefied witness to her frenzied coupling. The girl's limbs thrashed against the confines of the ribbons, and as soon as the gag was taken from her mouth and above the sound of the music Clarissa could clearly hear her hoarsely cry out, 'Yes, Nick! God, you feel so good! I love the way you do it to me!' Clarissa had never seen two people having sex together in the flesh before, so to speak, but now she stood a mere five feet away from the copulating couple, close enough to smell the rich, heady scent of their bodies. She stared dazedly at the sweeping fall of that blond hair that nearly reached to the floor as Jessica arched back her neck and undulated her hips as best as the limited lengths of the ribbons allowed. Clarissa's eyes shifted to the surprisingly erotic sight of the girl's trembling golden breasts crowned by startlingly brown nipples; Clarissa would have expected that a natural blonde such as Jessica – her pubic hair gave her away – would have been pink, like herself. The girl's breasts were high and full, apparently much larger than Clarissa's, but it was hard to be sure as she lay flat; her breasts mounded against her chest. If she would only stand up, Clarissa thought to herself idiotically, I could get a better look. Never before had the sight of another woman's body aroused her so sharply; she almost wished she could walk over and touch those breasts herself, taste their fullness and feel their weight in her mouth.

Seeing the drift of Clarissa's eyes, Nick grinned fully in her face and then bent over the girl's breasts, taking one deeply in his mouth, then drawing back so he could suck loudly at her nipple. It almost seemed as though he were inviting Clarissa to do the same, as though he were kissing Jessica's breasts in the way he knew Clarissa would secretly like to as well, as though he were doing it for her, or as if this whole scenario were a test or a dare of some sort. Thus Clarissa momentarily let go of her angry, hurt jealousy, for she found the sight of Nick's mouth on the girl's nipple and his cock sliding in and out of her so powerfully stimulating she actually moved her own hand to between her legs and rubbed herself in time to the motion of Nick's cock, keeping to the beat of the music. Clarissa hiked her dress up to the tops of her thighs and spread her legs wide, ripping at the poppers of her corset and snapping them apart in one swift motion so she could thrust her fingers into her hot, heaving vagina. She rocked her hips against her self-pleasuring hand in time to the rocking of Nick's pelvis as she gazed at the sight of his tightly muscled buttocks clenching firmly in the mirror. Nick continued to grind away, leaning forward on his hands, his eyes fixed squarely on Clarissa's face, studying her gaze and measuring her reaction. His own pleasure seemed strangely irrelevant in this weird kind of three-some that somehow wasn't a threesome; it was as though Nick was concentrating more on Clarissa's reaction to the scene than he was on his own sexual release – or indeed, even more than on Jessica's pleasure. Clarissa was strongly reminded here of the time she saw Nick kissing Jessica outside her building, and she knew the same subtle power dynamic was at work here, with Nick cunningly manipu-lating her into acknowledging the force of her desire for him. What she – and perhaps he – hadn't counted on was the force of desire Clarissa suddenly now felt for Jessica as well.

Finally, just when Clarissa, and apparently Nick, guessed that Jessica was about to come, he pulled his cock all the way out and swiftly dropped to his knees, inserting his tongue where his penis had just been. From her vantage point in the doorway Clarissa had a clear, uninterrupted view of the fusing of Nick's mouth with the girl's gaping mound. She shifted slightly in the doorframe to appreciate fully the double image of Nick's tongue licking long and slow between those rolling, rippling lips; she could see both what was in front of her and what was reflected in the mirror. Clarissa had never noticed before how those blossoming vaginal folds moved and undulated with the pressure of penis or tongue; those layers of petal-like flesh looked like an inverted kind of mouth that was fluid and mobile, stretching forth and swelling against Nick's lengthy, snakelike tongue. Clarissa's mouth moved silently along with Nick's, as though she too were tonguing that vagina and burying her mouth in its rich, musky wetness. In a strange sort of way she felt that she *was* Nick, or at least that she was experiencing what he was experiencing, that she now knew a little of what he did. Yet she also felt that she was imitating Jessica's pleasure as well, that her own sex and body were reacting the same way that Jessica's were. Thus, as Clarissa's fingers rubbed against the protruding nub of her own hardened clitoris, Nick pulled back the protective little hood at the top of Jessica's vulva to reveal her blushing rosebud of pleasure, and Clarissa actually strained forward a little to get a better look. She knew how sensitive and ripe that clitoris must be judging from her own liquid pearl that was starting to vibrate between her fingers. And so, gazing at Clarissa above those tendrils of spun-gold silk, Nick closed his mouth around Jessica's clitoris and sucked just as Clarissa's own tumultuous orgasm burst forth from inside her. She arched her neck and flung back her head, biting her lip to keep from crying out. She now knew that this scene had been planned solely for her pleasure, that Jessica had been gagged so her moans wouldn't warn Clarissa away, that the music had been playing loudly enough to entice her into the flat, and that Jessica was blindfolded so she couldn't know her real part in this role-playing tableau. Clarissa also knew that by blindfolding Jessica, Nick was protecting her own identity: there was no way Jessica could know that his instructor was looking on. The knowledge of her own manipulation only served to intensify Clarissa's orgasm far beyond simple masturbatory pleasure, and she felt bound to Nick herself by bonds of far greater strength than mere grosgrain ribbon.

As soon as she regained her breath, however, and still clutching the bottle of wine, Clarissa yanked her dress back down over her hips, not bothering to refasten her corset, and turned her back on Jessica's extremely vocal climax, triggered by the motion of Nick's mouth between her spread and constrained thighs. Anxious now to put as much space between herself and that scene as possible, Clarissa turned and ran down the corridor, nearly tripping on the linoleum, as Jessica's screams of ecstasy and Jim Morrison's gravelly voice pursued her all the way out of the door.

Astonished and a little ashamed of herself for responding so violently to that slightly sordid scene, Clarissa vowed to herself on the way home that night to end this ridiculously dangerous affair and to find someone closer to her own age – and someone less likely to ensnare her so intensely in such a tricky emotional and physical scenario. As it was, she was neglecting many of her professional responsibilities: she skipped departmental meetings, merely skimmed her students' essays rather than perusing them with her usual critical exactitude; and, worst of all, she'd been putting off revising the final section of her manuscript ready for publication. And so, turning into her drive with a vicious wrench of her steering wheel, Clarissa started to phrase her farewell speech to Nick in her mind, half-expecting him to appear momentarily to assess her reaction to the tableau he'd so devilishly arranged.

Congratulating herself on her nerves of steel and her unswerving ability to resist Nick's attempts at persuading her to continue their relationship, as she imagined, Clarissa entered her house and marched self-righteously over to her computer. Flicking on the switch and calling up her file entitled 'rude.doc', her file name for her book on the erotic, Clarissa let herself be soothed by the booting-up hum as her Mac called up the document. She changed into a comfortable pair of jeans and made herself a cup of coffee then sat down to work, determined to wipe the image of Nicholas St Clair from her mind and concentrate instead on completing her analysis of Edna Pontellier's burgeoning self-consciousness of her own sexuality in Kate Chopin's *The Awakening*.

Of course, two hours spent writing and thinking about a repressed woman's liberation into unrestrained sexuality did little to distract Clarissa from the scene she'd recently witnessed and, however peripherally, participated in. Instead, she was intrigued, not to mention surprised, by the realisation that her own heightened response to the sight of Nick plunging into Jessica had actually served to sharpen and infuse her critical work with an almost tangible feeling of intimacy. Reading over what she had written, Clarissa was startled to discover that her prose no longer seemed to be in the style of objective academic discourse but rather seemed full of heat, vitality and – there was no other word for it – sex. Working on her draft was actually becoming an arousing sexual experience – she was, after all, writing about sex – and Clarissa was suddenly anxious to go back and re-revise what she'd already written to see if she could make the rest of her book also come erotically alive. With a renewed zest for her work that had been so notably lacking of late, so preoccupied had Clarissa been with the experience of bedding Nick, she prepared to burn the proverbial midnight oil and work throughout the night, something she hadn't done since her postgraduate days.

Driving to the university the next day, tired and a bit bleary-eyed, Clarissa forced herself to admit that it was precisely her passion for Nick which was responsible for her inflammatory new interest in her work. If her writing seemed to sizzle on the page it was because her whole body was continually aflame with the need to feel Nick's body against hers, driving inside her and setting off orgasms of searing intensity. Nevertheless, she steeled herself to confront him as soon as possible and to tell him that very day, as kindly as she could, that it had all been very nice, even the way he'd set her up as voyeur in his bedroom, but it really had to end, and of course she looked forward to seeing him pass her class with very high marks indeed.

Of course, she didn't get the chance. Once again Nick failed to materialise in her class – still screwing Jessica? she thought to herself savagely – nor did he waylay her by her car, in her office, or come pounding on her door demanding a midnight rendezvous. Clarissa fully expected to see him over the weekend, if only so he could amuse himself by goading her about her masturbatory pleasure in what she'd witnessed, but he seemed content to avoid her and let her stew in her copious vaginal juices. For despite her anger at being manipulated the way she had been, and in spite of the sickening stabs of jealousy that twisted through her belly every time she pictured Nick in bed with Jessica, Clarissa knew that he had unlocked some sexual wellspring within her, and the wetter she became while thinking about him, and about Jessica, the more determined she grew to break off this insidiously obsessive affair before it subsumed her identity entirely.

When finally Nick appeared in her class the following Monday, Clarissa had a harder time than usual avoiding his eyes while she guided her class through a particularly sticky and explicit section on Freud. When she haltingly arrived at the discussion of masturbation in the case history *Dora*, something she'd been hoping to avoid, Clarissa actually had to turn her back on her class for a moment as she fought to regain her composure. When at last she turned back, quite red-faced from her inner turmoil, she forced herself to meet Nick's knowing, mocking gaze, for he was now looking at her directly, and the virtual sneer on his face caused her to dismiss the class abruptly twenty minutes early.

As Nick filed past her desk along with the rest of her students, Clarissa did what she'd never dared to do before and called out regally, 'Excuse me, Nick. Could I see you for a moment?' With an infuriatingly arrogant and self-satisfied smile, as though he'd been expecting this, Nick allowed her to pull him aside as she hissed at him urgently, 'I have to see you.'

He merely cocked a brow and grinned – like he's a cocky little bastard, Clarissa thought to herself acidly, but didn't dare pursue the word 'cock' any further, even mentally. 'Tonight?' was all he said.

'Nine o'clock,' she rapped out, then watched him swagger out of the door, admiring despite herself the symmetry of widely spaced shoulders, tapered waist and hips, and incredibly tight and well-muscled backside. Damn, I want that boy in my bed right now, she ground out to herself, then forced herself to focus on dry old Thomas Carlyle in preparation for her Victorian literature class, grateful they weren't yet scheduled to discuss Hardy's *Tess*, so she was spared for the moment from dwelling on that particular novel's lush descriptions of the ripely seductive female form.

As she rose to answer Nick's familiar sly tap at her door that night, however, Clarissa began to doubt to herself whether she did actually possess the required strength to break things off once and for all. She forced herself to admit that she had never before experienced the sexual intensity which Nick's body seemed able to provoke in her, and she was reluctant to deprive herself of such all-encompassing sensual joy. Reminding herself, however, precisely that it was all-encompassing and that she was in rapid danger of relinquishing total control of herself to this frighteningly charismatic boy, she swung open her heavy oak door and admitted Nick inside.

'Hey, Clarissa,' he said almost offhandedly, pausing briefly on the doorstep before venturing into her home. 'What's going on?'

Clarissa caught her breath as she gazed at him, struck anew, as always, by how every fresh meeting with Nick stirred her senses and filled her with an aching need for his touch. He stood towering over her, dressed in a plain blue chambray shirt and faded blue jeans, but his maleness and his potent sexuality were almost overpowering. With a nearly visible effort of will, Clarissa deliberately moved her body away from his and offered lightly, her eyes avoiding his gaze, 'Coffee?'

He accepted the cup with an amused smile, as though he could sense her unease and her desperate pretence at appearing unaffected by his presence. He lowered his body down on to her soft velvet sofa in one fluid motion and asked, stretching out his long legs before him, 'So, what did you need to see me about?'

Although she had rehearsed this speech many times to herself during the preceding days, now that the moment had actually come, Clarissa found it nearly impossible to force the words through her stiff, numb lips. 'I think it's best if we don't see each other any more,' was all she finally managed to say.

Nick stared at her, surprised, for the briefest of moments, then laughed, rose to his feet and set down his cup. 'OK, Dr Cornwall,' he said, maddeningly good humouredly as he reached for the door. 'I suppose I'll just see you around.'

Blankly astonished that he could actually let her go this easily – that it seemed merely to *amuse* Nick that she was ending things – Clarissa acted solely on instinct and blurted out the first thing that came into her head. 'That's *it*?' she cried. 'You're actually *leaving*?'

He looked down at her, an infuriatingly cool smile lifting the corners of his lips. 'That's what you want, isn't it?' he asked. 'Don't you want me to leave? I thought you said it was over.'

Hating herself for her weakness but unable to stop, Clarissa tugged at the arm that was holding open her door and demanded, 'Don't you even want to *talk* about this?' She pulled him back inside and firmly shut the door, turning to face him with her arms crossed defensively in front of her. 'Do *you* want this to end?' she wailed, despising the note of childish desperation she heard in her voice.

He paused for a moment, then gently inquired, 'Is this about the other night, Clarissa? Are you upset because of that thing with Jessica?'

94

I hate it when he doesn't answer my questions! Clarissa thought to herself furiously, but only replied somewhat formally, 'No, of course not. Don't be silly. It's just that I think that this ... this – ' she couldn't think of another word ' – affair has run its course and we'd probably both be better off if we went back to our proper relationship of pupil and teacher. It was all very nice – ' god, I sound like I'm thanking him for tea, she thought despairingly ' – and I'll always remember you fondly – ' fondly! ' – but perhaps this relationship should now be put to rest.'

There, it was out. Nervously, she peered at him and waited to see his response.

And of course, Nick simply did what Nick did best, which was to take her in his arms and press her body into his, completely ignoring what she had just said and instead running his big, beautiful hands over the lines of her body while he bent his head to hers and kissed her willing, open mouth. Unable to resist – indeed, unwilling to want to resist – Clarissa gave herself up to her passion for him and ripped savagely at his clothes, yanking open his shirt and forcing down his jeans while he flipped up her skirt and cast off her panties. With a sudden forceful kick Nick stripped off his trousers then retrieved a condom from one of the pockets and sheathed himself. Then, bending slightly at the knees, stooped to lift Clarissa off her feet, positioning her legs around his waist and lowering her squarely on to his ready cock. Unable to move herself lest she lose her balance and they both topple to the floor, Clarissa could only hold tightly to Nick while he raised and lowered her hips, impaling her on his shaft and releasing her slightly before thrusting into her again. His strength and control were impressive, and even through the fog of Clarissa's desire she observed to herself with a thrill that no man had ever been able to hold her while penetrating her in such a way before. Just as Clarissa began to move towards orgasm, however, Nick pulled her off him with a rapid, unexpected twist and laid her face down on her sofa so that her head was buried in the cushions and her behind rose temptingly above the edge of the seat. She felt him tuck her legs up underneath her and grip her hips and then, with no other warning, Clarissa felt the head of Nick's cock probe questioningly at her puckered back entrance. Clarissa was no stranger to anal pleasures; she quite enjoyed a well-lubricated, latex-sheathed cock entering her rear passage. Nick's shaft began its slow glide into her anal opening. Clarissa held her breath and concentrated on relaxing her muscles, pushing out slightly against the thick staff that edged deeply within her as she felt the thin walls stretch comfortably around him, accommodating his penis which remained temporarily motionless. When finally Nick began to move inside her it was with a gentle caution; Clarissa wanted to tell him that there was no need, that her rear entrance was well seasoned and used to tight friction but, as though guessing her response, or perhaps too aroused to care, Nick's pace and rhythm gradually began to increase, and Clarissa cried out against the pillows as she felt him pound away within her. She clenched her rounded buttocks tightly around his pulsating cock, arching her back and pushing her bottom against him, feeling the unique sensation of tension as her smallest space was filled to capacity, almost feeling Nick's penis deep within her belly. As Nick retreated and re-entered behind, his fingers slid around to her achingly empty vagina and drove inside so that now Clarissa felt filled up completely, the two penetrations moving inside her in harmonised time. She felt as though every nerve centre in her body was located in the space between her hips and her thighs, and just when she thought she couldn't bear it any longer she felt Nick's thumb flick over her clitoris and she came and she came and she came in simultaneous anal, vaginal and clitoral convulsions. Even while Clarissa was screaming her pleasure into the cushions of her sofa, however, Nick was already withdrawing, emptying her in a rush and turning her over on to her back while she panted her way back to reality. He stood poised above her, cock in hand, and then, while she watched, quiet now, he palmed his tense, jutting penis, the head swelling a little further in anticipation of climax.

Watching her watch him, Nick said softly, his voice slightly roughened by his rising excitement, 'You like to watch, don't you, Clarissa? You liked watching me and Jessica together, didn't you? You should have stayed, you know – you could have joined in.'

As though the very image of the three of them together provided all the stimulus he needed, Nick bent over Clarissa, pulled off the condom, and rubbed his cock against her belly as his semen shot out of him, the thick, creamy fluid pooling around the well of her navel and sinking into the milky whiteness of her stomach. As Nick gasped out the last of his climax he put his mouth directly against Clarissa's ear and whispered, 'And soon I'm going to watch you too. I would really love to watch you make it with another man and make him come the way you make me come.'

Wordlessly, Clarissa looked up at him, gazing into those hazel-green eyes that mirrored her own, and she could only nod her head in expectation and agreement.

Chapter Six

*S*everal days later Clarissa sat slumped over her drink at the King's Head, peering suspiciously at the concoction Julian had composed for her of tequila, triple sec and what she swore was cactus juice. Nervously she took an experimental sip, rolled the liquid round in her mouth, then took a bigger gulp as Julian smiled at her encouragingly. It tasted sharp and slightly bitter, with an underlying tang that reminded Clarissa of lime juice. Rapidly acquiring a taste for the obviously potent brew, Clarissa drained her glass, then held it out for more.

'So how's your young stud?' Julian inquired abruptly, breaking the companionable silence. Clarissa knew that her friend was slightly offended that she'd never brought Nick round to be introduced, and she'd tried explaining that theirs wasn't that sort of relationship; they didn't share friends, errands or personal activities, other than sex, of course, and besides, there was the overriding need for secrecy. Still, Julian would occasionally pout, reminding Clarissa of the many times she'd met Julian's friends and lovers at the pub, but Clarissa refused to be drawn into sharing any more confidences other than, yes, she was seeing someone, and she reluctantly admitted that, yes, he was a student. She'd never revealed more than this, slightly put off by Julian's avaricious interest in her sex life and also feeling a little guilty for being so unusually reticent. Normally she'd burst into the pub the day after a night's romp with a stranger and tell all, though without going into the kind of explicit anatomical detail at which Julian excelled. An indefinable something about her affair with Nick, though, made Clarissa wary of disclosing too much information, as though she felt that their relationship was too fragile to be exposed to the eyes of others, even to those of her closest friend. Today, however, fortified – or was it weakened? – by the exotic confection which glowed palely green in her glass, she felt the need to unburden herself, and so she welcomed Julian's sullen intrusion, though she wasn't exactly sure how much she wanted to say.

'Actually, Jules,' she began cautiously, breaking her month-long abstinence and shaking out a cigarette, 'I could use a friendly ear.'

Julian shrugged her shoulders, clearly attempting not to appear too eager, and leant over to offer Clarissa a light. 'So, talk,' she invited, draping her barkeeper's towel rakishly over one shoulder.

Suddenly uncomfortable about voicing what she'd kept so private, and squirming a little inside, Clarissa concentrated her eyes on the burning tip of her cigarette and said slowly, 'I'm not sure what to make of this. I'm not sure how far I want it to go.' She met Julian's eyes and suddenly blurted out, 'I want him like crazy, but I'm afraid of where this is going to take me.'

'Let's start at the beginning,' Julian offered reasonably, tucking her skin-tight white top into the belt of her equally clingy black jeans. 'Who is he, what is his name, how did this start, and how big is his dick?'

Clarissa laughed despite herself and began to tell Julian everything, starting with the first day of class and bringing her right up to the night she saw Nick with Jessica and its aftermath. Swallowing down the remains of her third drink and stabbing her fifth cigarette into the air to punctuate her points, Clarissa finished her tale by saying, 'And the crazy thing is, while I was watching Nick with Jessica, I felt like I was in both of their places – I could feel what

Jessica must have been feeling, because obviously I had an orgasm, but I was also imagining what it would be like to be Nick, doing those things to her that he was doing. I felt like I was both of them at the same time, and I was so turned on that I forgot to be wildly jealous until afterwards.'

She looked up, startled by the sudden ferocious intensity in Julian's eyes as she leant across the bar, gripped Clarissa's hands and asked softly, 'So, you finally admit that you were turned on by a woman?'

Clarissa was drunk, but she wasn't that drunk. 'Well,' she hedged delicately, gently trying to disengage her hands without giving offence, 'I'm not sure if it was Jessica's body itself which turned me on, or just the sight of what Nick was doing to her.' She tried to look away from the flash of disappointment that registered on Julian's face and then said thoughtfully, 'I'm not used to being jealous. Usually I don't care what my lovers get up to when they're not up inside me.' She smiled sadly, then regarded Julian seriously before concluding, 'But I'll tell you, Jules, when I later thought about him screwing that girl with so much obvious enthusiasm, it was as if a white-hot bolt of pain and jealousy slashed right through me, ripping me apart.' She closed her eyes briefly against the agonising image of Nick plundering Jessica's body with his penis and his tongue which, despite her initial arousal, still tormented her every time she thought of it – which, unfortunately, was often.

'I know what you mean,' sighed Julian, straightening up her skinny body and flicking her ebony hair out of her eyes. 'I'll never forget the time I saw Harvey scream as he came; it was while he was enjoying a blow job from Claire, who he always said did that better than me. Normally I wouldn't have minded, but I was sitting on his face at the time and he nearly bit me when he – wow! Would you look at that pair of boots!' And she let out a sharp wolf-whistle as a pair of Texan snakeskins stomped by complete with silver tips at the toes and metal spurs at the back. Clarissa watched with a smirk as Julian's eyes travelled northward, up over the long slim legs, slightly paunchy torso and long, thick brown moustache at the top. The owner of the moustache and boots would have looked right at home sipping Clarissa's south-west American drink, and Julian ran her eyes lustfully over his rangy frame before returning to admire the intricate red-and-gold tooled patterns on his boots.

Unwillingly she dragged her eyes back to Clarissa, who continued musingly, responding to Julian's initial digression. 'And that's another thing: he wants to watch me doing it with another guy.' She caught the arched-brow expression on Julian's face and irritably inquired, 'What? What is it?'

'You mean you've never had a threesome?' her friend asked in surprise.

'Julian, you know I haven't!' Clarissa snapped crossly. 'Why ask such a dumb question?'

'Well, I always supposed that there was something you weren't telling me,' Julian replied somewhat waspishly. 'You should try it sometime – you might like it.'

Clarissa shook her head. 'I doubt it,' she said with less certainty than she was striving for. She extended her glass for a refill and continued, 'But it would almost be worth trying if it made Nick even the tiniest bit jealous. He doesn't seem to care at all what I do when I'm not with him – he never asks about Graham, and apparently I could sleep with the university football team if I wanted to and he wouldn't give a damn, whereas I – ' She broke off abruptly, frowning at the memory of Nick's buttocks tensing and hollowing as he pushed further into Jessica's willing though constrained body. 'Honestly, Jules,' she went on, slurping noisily at her drink, 'I never know what he's thinking, and I can never tell when he's being serious. It's like he only ever comes to me when he feels like it, when it's convenient for him or he's got nothing else to do, and I sometimes seriously wonder whether he even thinks about me at all when we're not together – except when he has to write my essays, of course,' she added glumly. 'I tell you, Jules, the boy is a just an enigma to me. He's so completely other – do you know what I mean?' she asked anxiously, then mused, as though on the brink of some sudden revelation, 'But I suppose that's exactly what it is that drives me towards him so forcefully.' She gulped at her drink. 'Damn this is strong,' she half-muttered to herself, taking another huge swallow. 'Are you sure this is cactus juice?'

Julian showed her the bottle. Sure enough, it had a picture of a cactus underneath a setting sun on the label. Clarissa nodded approvingly before winding up her confession. 'But I'll tell you something else too, Julian,' she said, dragging deeply on her cigarette. 'He still makes me so nervous in class that I'm actually giving the best lectures I've ever given. Even though his eyes are nearly always shut whenever I look at him, or he's looking somewhere else, I can tell he's staring at me whenever I turn my back or look away, like those paintings of people whose eyes seem to follow you but when you look directly at them they're looking slightly off-centre. Well, that's what it's like to look at Nick: he never seems to look straight at me, but I can *feel* his eyes on my ass or on my breasts or on my legs – oh god, I hope he doesn't think my legs are too short and fat.' She drooped despondently for a moment while Julian was obviously trying to frame a denial before brightening as she finished, 'But I try so hard to perform in front of him, to turn him on with my brains as well as my beauty – ' she laughed immodestly ' – that my lectures are truly inspired and *vastly* entertaining.' She smiled triumphantly and then gulped down the last of her drink in a most unladylike manner, licking her lips with relish. 'Damn, that's strong!' she said again, falling back with a thump against her chair.

Julian laughed and patted her hand. 'I told you that was wicked stuff,' she chortled, then happily bustled off to serve a shandy to the pair of snakeskin boots. Even the man's order of what Julian termed a 'sissy' drink didn't seem to dampen her ardour for him, for as Clarissa watched with a snigger Julian batted her illegally long lashes at him and arched her back seductively, her small braless breasts visible through the thin cotton of her shirt. She returned to Clarissa, flushed with flirtatious success, and inquired curiously, 'And how's the dirty book coming along?'

'It is *not* a dirty book,' Clarissa snorted defensively, then added somewhat pretentiously, 'It's a post-modernist, post-structuralist, post-foundationalist analysis of the representation of the erotic, and it's on its way to my editor even as we speak. Don't mock this weighty tome, Jules: I need this book to be really great or I may not have a job here next term.' She stubbed out her cigarette, grimacing as she said, 'Ugh. These things make me nauseous. I swear I'll never smoke again.' She pushed away the ashtray decisively and boasted, 'And that, too, is another pinnacle of my career so far. This is the best damn book ever written – ' strong drink always made her exaggerate ' – and again, that's thanks to Nick. It is so much easier to write about sex when you're having awesome sex, and I really do think that this book is going to benefit my career immensely.'

She squinted blearily at Julian, who suddenly appeared a little fuzzy and out of focus as she summed up, 'So the lad is a great fuck, and makes you a great writer and an even better teacher. So what's the problem?'

Clarissa stood up dazedly and tried to wave her away with one vague hand. It was no use trying to explain to Julian the frightening, intense hold Nick seemed to have over her, nor the desperate unease her passion for him was increasingly causing her. Instead, Clarissa gripped the bar with an unsteady hand and groaned, 'Bleah. I feel drunk. I think I'd better lie down.'

Julian nodded with a sigh, as though she'd expected this, firmly steering Clarissa towards the back door and pressing the spare key to her flat above the bar into her hand. This happened with some regularity: Clarissa would arrive at the pub in total control, drink voraciously of whatever concoction Julian had on hand, then confusedly pilot her way upstairs to sleep off her alcoholic haze in Julian's huge waterbed, too drunk to care about whatever bodily fluids were encrusted in the geometric black-and-white sheets.

After she shut up the bar, Julian would enter her flat, gently shake Clarissa awake and hand her a tall glass of iced water with two aspirins before going off to sleep on the sofa. Whatever sexual interest she might have had in her friend, Julian was too much of a lady to try to force herself on a dead-drunk woman, and when Clarissa awoke in the morning she was always a little embarrassed and shy, but touched by Julian's thoughtful restraint. Tonight promised to be no exception, but as Clarissa stumbled towards the door, she saw Julian steering herself seductively towards the moustache and boots, and through her tequila-induced fog Clarissa was able to wonder to herself whether Julian would even bother to make it home that night.

Indeed, when Clarissa awoke in the morning, a little seasick from Julian's rolling, shifting mattress, not to mention massively hung over, a quick glance at the screamingly empty sofa bed told her that yes, her friend had no doubt got lucky the night before. Smiling and shaking her slightly heavy head, Clarissa started to strip off the nightshirt she customarily borrowed from Julian when a glance at the clock made her shriek with despair. Nine-thirty! She had less than an hour and a half to whip back to her house, shower and dress and coolly present herself in front of her class, all traces of last night's indulgence wiped away. These days dressing for Nick's class seemed to take her at least an hour while she fiddled with her fiery red hair, deliberated over her make-up, and chose and discarded filmy piles of bras, slips, panties and stockings. Now she hastily gathered up her things and flung herself at the door, nearly crashing into a cheerily whistling Julian who was jingling her keys in the lock.

'Hey, Ris, how are you feeling?' Julian called out jauntily as Clarissa pushed past her forcefully.

'Don't mean to be rude but I gotta go!' she called back breathlessly over her shoulder. 'How was the moustache?'

Julian grinned lewdly as Clarissa retreated backwards down the stairs. 'Tasty!' she replied, licking her lips lasciviously. Clarissa laughed and then turned and ran, the minutes on the clock ticking in her head.

Driving to class later with a mere five minutes to spare, she reflected again on the red heat of jealousy which continued to spiral painfully throughout her body, almost a physical thing, whenever she pictured Nick in bed with Jessica. Forcing her mind away from' them with a wrench, she tried to concentrate instead on the sharp shock of pleasure which always awaited her whenever she entered her classroom and saw Nick already seated at his desk, his long legs stretched out before him, his head tipped back against the wall. Although she tried desperately not to look at him, almost to pretend he wasn't there, Clarissa could never resist a quick, furtive peek in his direction the minute she stepped into the room. On the days when he was absent, her stomach would lurch with the sickening drop of disappointment, and she would be anxious to finish the class and hurry back to her office to see if he was waiting for her. But on the days when he did make it to class, she would stride around the room at full power, her sudden insights into the texts seeming to burst spontaneously out of her. She hadn't exaggerated when she'd told Julian that these were the best lectures of her career: her thoughts on the erotic literally seemed to flow right out of her, just as looking at Nick's mouth, hands and body caused the liquid to flow gently between her legs, even in the midst of class.

Thinking about him now, Clarissa felt the familiar leap of anticipation as her insides clenched, and her blood ran fire in her veins at the thought that soon, in less than ten minutes, she would be seeing him. It's funny, Clarissa mused as she pulled into her reserved parking space, I know his body so intimately, and yet I still get so nervous and jumpy when I see him, like I'm nineteen years old again myself. She hoped fervently that this wouldn't be one of those days when he chose to skip her class; she hadn't spoken to him since the night she'd tried to end things, and she was aching and desperate with the need to see him now, if only across a noisy, crowded classroom.

Thankfully, he didn't disappoint her this time. Clarissa

intuitively felt his presence even before she spotted him as she clicked her way nervously into the room. He was there, lounging in the corner, his leather-clad legs sprawled out before him. This time, however, he was looking directly at her; whereas he usually avoided her eyes, as though denying any intimate knowledge of her, today he was staring directly at her, and there was an indefinable something in his eyes which Clarissa couldn't quite decipher. Was it lust? Desire? Or was it something else? Anger? Puzzled, Clarissa allowed herself to gaze fully into his face for a moment, nodding with a slight, almost imperceptible dip of her head, then turned away, certain that she'd made herself clear and he would come to her office after class.

Sure enough, she was seated in her office later that day when a slight tap at her door told her that he had arrived. Clarissa tried to greet Nick as he slithered inside, closing the door behind him, but her welcoming smile faded quickly away as he bent over her where she sat, gripping her hips and lifting her up so that she had to clutch at his shoulders and wrap her legs around his hips for support. He carried her across the room and slammed her body back up against the wall, moulding his mouth to her throat as his tongue slid over her creamy skin, his fingers sliding up to rub at her crotch beneath a skirt that was too short that day for stockings.

'Nick,' Clarissa gasped, her eyes fixed on the door beyond his shoulder. 'Nick, what are you doing?'

'I'm kissing you,' he growled into her ear, his mouth wet and warm against her neck. 'Shall I fuck you here too?'

As desperately as she wanted him, Clarissa was equally desperate to keep her job, and so with a massive effort she managed to push him away while sliding down the wall where he'd propped her until she stood, shakily, on the floor. 'Whew,' she panted, automatically smoothing out her hair and patting down her skirt, 'you're certainly in a passion today, aren't you?'

Suddenly cool and grinning, all traces of heat and desire gone, Nick took a step back and asked with a studiedly indifferent air, 'So, Clarissa, where were you last night?'

So that's it! Clarissa thought to herself with a triumphant inner smile. That's what's been bothering him! She tossed him an equally casual glance to match his as she archly replied, 'With Julian. Why?'

He shrugged offhandedly, then turned to examine the books on her shelves as he answered, 'No reason. I just went to your house last night, that's all.'

Unable to maintain her casually distanced stance, Clarissa couldn't stop herself from howling, 'And you thought I was out getting laid?'

He glanced at her loweringly, his winged brows drawn down in denial, and gruffly asked her, 'Were you?'

She laughed again, delighted by his show of unease. 'Nick, Nick,' she cooed, coming forward to embrace him, 'of course not. I was getting drunk with my friend and telling her about you.' She smiled at him rather provocatively, as though daring him to guess the exact details of her conversation, then drew his head down to hers to kiss those firm, sculpted lips when a loud rap at the door made her freeze for a moment. Quickly she darted behind her desk, frantically motioning Nick to stand before her.

'Clarissa? Are you in there?' It was the high, slightly shrill voice of Monica Talbot, and Clarissa grunted in exasperation, rolling her eyes skywards in a display of dramatic despair.

'Come in, Monica,' she called out, gesturing to Nick that he should leave. 'Tonight,' she silently mouthed at him as he moved towards the door. He glanced at her briefly, then turned to nod and smile charmingly at Monica as she minced her way inside. Monica seemed to experience a slight shock when she saw Nick; it almost seemed as though she stared at him hungrily, her eyes travelling admiringly up and down his long body. Clarissa had to smother a smirk when she saw the other woman openly appraising her lover, and she nearly burst out with a loud snicker as she watched Monica turn to gaze at Nick's tightly enticing backside as he strode out of the door, his boots beating a tattoo on the floor as he went.

When Monica finally turned back to Clarissa, her cheeks

were slightly flushed and, if Clarissa was not mistaken, there was a definite gleam of lust in her eyes which sparkled dreamily out of her slightly befogged spectacles.

'So, Monica, what can I do for you?' Clarissa asked brightly, hoping that her lipstick didn't appear too smudged.

Monica stared at her for a moment then asked, indicating the door with her head, 'A student of yours?'

Clarissa's smile increased in wattage. Lord, if she only knew, she giggled to herself, but merely replied with as professional a demeanour as she could muster, 'One of many. What brings you to my office?'

Nick obviously forgotten, Monica shuffled the papers she was holding and then handed one to Clarissa, who stared at it in silence. It was a letter from the Vice-Chancellor informing the staff that a new head of department had finally been appointed – Professor Malcolm Anderson, who would take up his position from the first of the month. All were cordially invited to attend the welcoming ceremonies, including a formal sit-down dinner to be held during the Easter break in three weeks' time. No mention was made of the unfortunately exiled ex-Professor Warburton.

'Oh, Lord, what's this?' Clarissa groaned, waving the sheet confusedly at Monica. 'What's this guy like? *I've* certainly never heard of him.' She peered at his name again, and then at Monica. 'What's his field of specialism? And do we have to go to this damned dinner?'

'Afraid so,' Monica announced briskly, patting her bun absent-mindedly behind her. 'I believe Professor Anderson's expertise lies in Milton and Renaissance poetry – ' Clarissa groaned again. She hated Renaissance poetry ' – and he's just come over from New Zealand, I think, which may account for the fact that his name isn't immediately familiar to you.' She glanced down at Clarissa, now hunched over the memo, and smiled pityingly at the bowed red head. 'These dinners aren't really so bad, you know; you can request a vegetarian dish if you prefer, and there's usually a great deal of wine, with port and cheese after the speeches – '

'Speeches!' cut in Clarissa in disgust. 'And I suppose it's boy–girl sitting, is it? And no doubt I will be wedged in between the vicar and some ex-old boy who'll want to talk cricket scores and church restoration all evening. Yuk!' she snorted vehemently. 'Why do they have to ruin our Easter break with this thing?' she added, really irate by this time, 'and why can't they appoint a *woman*, for god's sake? Bastards!' She looked glumly at Monica. 'Nuke the lot of them, I say.'

'Now, now,' Monica tut-tutted. 'Your Americanism is showing, Clarissa.' She added with the superior air of one who knew all, 'And I believe the board has scheduled the dinner during the break to allow Professor Anderson time to settle in before the term resumes its usual hectic pace.' She turned as if to go but then paused before remarking to Clarissa, 'You know, with your review coming up at the end of the term, you really do need to make the effort to look as though you are interested in the internal workings of the department.' Clarissa knew Monica was right, but she still resented having to be reminded of her professional duties.

Monica was just about the leave the room when Clarissa called out after her, 'Just one more thing, Monica.' As the woman turned, Clarissa struggled to appear only slightly interested and nonchalant as she casually inquired, 'Any word about what's happened to Warburton?'

She then quailed at the ill-disguised look of contempt and distaste that flashed across Monica's otherwise generally bland features. 'Oh, I heard he got another job somewhere,' Monica said dismissively, waving her hand around vaguely in the air. 'I think he called in some favours from a candidate whose D.Phil. he'd passed decades ago, who is now head of department himself at the *other* university here in the town, and somehow Warburton managed to get himself transplanted to that *other* place practically right across the road.' Monica sniffed derisively; their own university used to be a rather notable polytechnic and had been one of the first to upgrade its status, but it still rankled among many of the faculty that there was another, older, more prestigious university that dominated the town. This was obviously the university to which Warburton had defected – and it was also, Clarissa knew, the university attended by Nick's mysterious flatmate. Staring at Monica now, she wondered to herself with a smile if Nick's military friend was doing any English courses this term. Monica obviously noticed that smile because she bent forward a little as though to examine Clarissa's face more closely and asked her officiously, 'Why do you ask? I thought you were glad to see him go?'

'Oh, yes, of course I was,' Clarissa agreed hastily, unable to stop herself from adding, 'As you said, Monica, his publishing record was quite unremarkable – and, naturally, we can't have faculty members on our staff who abuse and exploit the pedagogical relationship.'

Monica smiled down at Clarissa from the smug heights of the unimpeachably pure. 'Yes, it is Warburton's own fault for getting himself dismissed so scandalously, isn't it?' she purred, settling her bulk more comfortably on its ample frame. 'After all, he had absolutely no business conducting any sort of – harumph – relationship with a student. No business at *all*,' she declared with authority, muttering something about 'his own deserved punishment' and 'penalise him to the utmost' as she swished her way out of the room.

Oh, Monica, what the hell do you know about passion and desire, you stupid old cow! Clarissa barked to herself bitterly, then giggled as she remembered the appraising gleam of lust in Monica's eyes as they'd trailed up and down the length of Nick's body during his swaggering retreat from her room. Sorry, dear, but I don't think you're quite his type, she remarked pleasantly to Monica in her mind, and then turned her attention back to the essay she was marking. Unable to stop herself from shivering, however, Clarissa nearly whispered out loud, her eyes fixed on nothing, but I have never met a man who was more *my* type than Nick. Then she firmly closed the door on that thought and forced herself to concentrate on Victorian social reform and the writings of Elizabeth Gaskell.

As Clarissa walked to the car park later that afternoon, congratulating herself on having made her way through twelve excruciatingly dull essays, she was slightly puzzled to see Nick's tall, rangy frame leaning casually against the side of her car, and she tried anxiously to quell the rush of adrenaline that always accompanied her initial sightings of him. Maybe he wants to cancel our plans for tonight, she thought nervously – or maybe he's just too eager to wait, she then thought hopefully. Riding high on the crest of that thrilling rush of pleasure, she hurried forward to greet him, ready to usher him rapidly into the secure and embracing darkness of her car.

With a grip on her wrist, however, Nick stopped her. 'I'm not coming with you now,' he said, gazing at her intently with his narrow hazel eyes. 'I just wanted to ask you if maybe you'd like to come to my place tonight instead of me coming to you as usual.'

Seeing her stiffen and take a step backwards, he added hastily, with a palms-up gesture of his hands, 'No Jessica, I promise.' Clarissa winced a little at the name, and Nick responded with his customarily uncustomary tenderness. 'It'll be OK this time, Clarissa, really. Come on,' he coaxed with a heart-stopping, knee-weakening smile. 'I'll even clean the flat for you.'

Won over by his unexpected kindness, Clarissa melted into his embrace for a fleeting moment, then nodded and withdrew. 'OK. Nine o'clock. I'll bring the wine.' Momentarily guarded, she glanced at him again and said worriedly, 'No tricks, now. Promise?'

He nodded in response. 'No tricks. I promise.' He stood there looking after her, smiling a little as she climbed into her car, started it up and drove away.

Chapter Seven

Clarissa arrived at Nick's flat later that evening exactly on time. Habitually punctual, she was even more so when nervous, and she was nothing if not uneasy about meeting Nick at his apartment that night. Still stung every time she thought about what had last transpired there, this time she was determined to play it cool, and so she dressed informally but elegantly in a pair of black velvet leggings and a flowing, ruffled, tunic-length white blouse, her flaming tresses pulled back severely into a French braid and a minimum of make-up applied. She couldn't believe that Nick would try anything duplicitous twice, or so she convinced herself, for her desire for him burned as uncontrollably bright as ever. Therefore, she was continually anxious to exonerate Nick in her mind of any mischievous intent so that she could give herself permission to go on indulging her passion for him. Clarissa felt that she was becoming ever more deeply obsessed with Nick, and she worried about the effect of this on her usually ordered and controlled life. Normally so sensitive to the erotic appeal of men, Clarissa found lately to her dismay that other men seemed to hold no attraction for her at all. Indeed, she seemed to have lost all interest in pursuing the admiring glances of strangers, and men no longer appeared to her as sexual, bodily creatures. Nicholas St Clair had eclipsed the appeal of all others, and Clarissa couldn't conceive of the man who could actually attract her attention away from her student, so consumed was she with all thoughts of possessing and being possessed by him.

Even Graham must have noticed her continual distraction, for he had apparently given up trying to re-entice her back into a relationship; in fact, he had been markedly distant of late, calling only infrequently now, and more as if he were simply checking in with her than still emotionally involved with her. However, he was particularly insistent that she accompany him to the Grand National with his boss and a select group of higher-ups in his company during her Easter break which was to start next week. Clarissa did not particularly want to go, as she loathed betting and was distinctly bored by horses, but she'd said yes mainly to shut him up and get him off her back, though she was dreading the occasion. This dread was in part due to the fact that she had absolutely no idea what to wear, and she pointedly refused to wear a hat. She'd tried to put Graham off, telling him that his company's 'function', as he liked to call it, was scheduled the same day as her faculty dinner, but he'd refused to let her off, assuring her that she'd be back in plenty of time to toast the new head of department. Clarissa wasn't at all convinced, and was positive she'd have to enter the senior dining room stinking of horse sweat, but since her attendance seemed so important to Graham, she'd acquiesced with as much grace as she could drum up, which frankly was very little.

Well, that wasn't for several weeks yet, and she certainly didn't want to think about Graham tonight, Clarissa reminded herself as she arrived at Nick's flat. She tapped cautiously at the door, her fingers once again clutched around the slick, smooth bottle of wine, but it was a Bordeaux this time, not a chardonnay, as she couldn't help but admit to a little superstition. Despite her nerves, however, Clarissa felt her sex already beginning to soften and swell in anticipation of Nick's warm, muscular body against hers.

In answer to her knock the man himself appeared, and Clarissa noted with pleasure that he'd showered and changed into clean clothes for her, even going to the trouble of shaving the stubble which typically shadowed his jaw.

'Welcome,' he smiled, stooping to place a soft kiss on the crown of her head and briefly pausing to bury his nose in her scented hair. He then pulled away and cocked his head at her, drawing back to study her figure appreciatively, stroking his fingers down the silky length of ruffles which covered her breasts, smoothing the velvet of her richly textured leggings, and fingering the delicate silk cascade which so becomingly framed her face at the throat. 'You look pretty,' he said, his eyes twinkling, and Clarissa actually found herself blushing at his gentlemanly air of sincerity. 'Come on,' he urged, pulling at her hand and lacing her fingers through his. 'I've got dinner all ready.' He led her into the long, narrow living room, now remarkably tidy and neat and – Clarissa sniffed around and nearly burst out laughing – smelling pleasantly of pot-pourri air freshener. There was a card table set up cosily laid for two with chipped but matching china, quaint tumblers for the wine, and real linen napkins rolled up next to the forks. Clarissa turned with a sigh towards Nick, her eyes shining and her heart thumping in her chest with joy, deeply moved by such a simple gesture of sweetness. 'Oh Nick,' she said gently, touching one finger to his cheek, 'what a lovely thing to do. You actually cooked dinner?'

He looked a little sheepish and smiled a bit self-mockingly before admitting, 'Well, I didn't exactly cook – most of it is pre-packaged – but I hope you'll like what I've prepared.' He started to lead her into the kitchen then stopped, restrained by the tug of her hand. He looked down at her and frowned, flipping his reddish-brown fringe away from his forehead. 'Is something the matter?'

'I just want to tell you how happy you've made me,' Clarissa replied, gazing up into Nick's face. This was certainly a different Nick from the one she had become accustomed to: she was used to him only ever appearing sporadically and at random, as though it was only when

114

the mood struck him. Though he was always fiery and hot when she saw him, he was rarely quiet and affectionate afterwards, often choosing instead to quickly gather up his things, get dressed and leave. To be honest, Clarissa wasn't always sorry to see him go, either; she still felt a little uncomfortable and unsure about exactly what she was doing with this ridiculously young man, and she certainly didn't want him hanging around her house in the morning for her neighbours – or worse, Graham – to see as they collected their milk. Now, however, she was deeply moved by the evident pains he had taken to impress her, even though she couldn't help but be a little suspicious of these sudden househusbandly, domesticated actions.

As if guessing her thoughts, Nick laughingly tugged at her hand and then said apologetically, his face composed, 'Well, it's just that I still feel a little badly about what happened the last time you were here, that's all – not that I ever intended it to hurt you,' he added quickly, lest she see anything malicious in his obvious manipulation of that voyeuristic scene. 'I really did think you'd get a thrill out of it, Clarissa,' he said slowly, studying her face while he spoke. 'I see now that it upset you, of course, and I promise you I'll never set anything up like that again if you really and truly don't want me to.' He then cupped her bottom briefly in his palm, giving her a friendly squeeze before adding slyly, 'Besides, Ris, you know you liked it a little bit, didn't you?' At her embarrassed silence, he peered teasingly into her face and said persuadingly, 'Oh, come on, say it turned you on just the littlest bit, seeing me with her in the bed like that. You know I did it just for you, don't you? You know I did it just to turn you on?'

Yielding, Clarissa glanced at him from the corner of her eye and complied. 'OK, Nick, yes, it kind of turned me on, but can we please just forget about it for now? Let's just eat dinner and drink wine and concentrate on each other, OK?'

But even though Nick seemed to agree to drop it, as Clarissa followed him into the kitchen he stopped suddenly, turned to her and said, 'You see, Clarissa, I think I know what you like.'

Halfway through their main course of prawns mixed with pasta, Clarissa twirled a strand of spaghetti round her fork and enquired casually, 'Where's your roommate, Nick? It's nearly ten o'clock – will he be out for the night?'

Nick shrugged his broad, chiselled shoulders and replied, reaching for the wine, 'Probably. We don't really keep track of each other's movements. More wine?'

She watched him while he leant over to refill her glass, his eyes narrowed in concentration as he poured the wine almost to the tumbler's brim, and then her eyes moved downwards to focus on his hand holding the bottle. She gazed at those long, elegant fingers wrapped round the glass curve, and the sight of the pale gold hairs on Nick's square, thick wrist made Clarissa feel suddenly weak and very, very warm. Hesitantly she reached out her newly manicured nail and traced it along the path of Nick's knuckles, still folded round the wine bottle, then she trailed her finger along the back of his hand and up along his forearm, gently stroking the thin, fine hairs, feeling the need to touch him bursting out inside her. Nick lifted his eyes to Clarissa's as he leant across the table, his face less than a foot from hers. He said nothing, merely raised his slightly arched brows and watched in silence as she released the bottle from his hand and set it firmly on the table, never taking her eyes from his.

'Do you want me, Nick?' Clarissa asked softly.

'You know I do.' His voice was barely above a whisper.

'Say it, then, Nick,' Clarissa said, her voice quiet but steady, her hazel eyes finding their mirror in his.

'I want you, Clarissa.' His voice was thrillingly low and husky, the murmured words deep and sexy in her ears.

'Kiss me, Nick,' she breathed softly, then closed her eyes in hushed expectation, her insides screaming out silently as Nick reached one hand forward to clasp the back of her neck, supporting her cheek with his fingers, drawing her mouth to his. They kissed across the cluttered table, nuzzling each other's faces, their tongues darting across

116

each other's lips, necks and ears, rubbing their cheeks against each other, Nick quietly breathing while Clarissa whimpered and panted and sighed. Oh, yes, this was the man she still wanted, this was the man she still had to have, this was the man whose body seemed designed solely to fit so rapturously with hers. This might not be love, but it was certainly more than simple lust: this was passion, this was fulfilment, this was what the French call *jouissance*, that sensual redefinition of the self that transcended boundaries in its powerful erotic impulse.

Clarissa rose slowly from the table then kicked off her shoes, her body screaming out for his. She knelt at Nick's feet, and swiftly began to unbutton the fly on his fashionably distressed blue jeans.

'Later for that,' he muttered hoarsely against her hair, raising her to her feet and drawing her over to the unfashionably worn and battered sofa. He set her down on it so that she was sitting with her legs wrapped around his waist. 'I think I owe you a little something for what went on the last time you were here,' he said, his voice now muffled by the silky ruchings at her throat. He rapidly unbuttoned her blouse and quickly cast it aside, then deftly unclipped her sheer front-fastening bra. He then paused at her naked, tremulous breasts, gently nipping at their rosy tips and tonguing the creamy twin swells of her bosom. Clarissa thrust her fingers in Nick's hair, tangling them in its satiny thickness, then arched her back in order to push more of her breasts into his open mouth. With his head still bent to her breasts, Nick was somehow able to strip off Clarissa's leggings and panties, his forceful hands easing them down and tossing them aside, never stopping to admire the deep garnet-red colour of her carefully chosen thong.

Clarissa was now completely naked and ready to come from the sheer feel of Nick's mouth on her nipples, but then Nick suddenly shifted position and hoisted her up off the seat of the sofa to its back, so that she was sitting on the top with her back against the wall, her feet planted on the sofa's soft cushions and her hands bracing herself from behind. In this position she could spread her legs wide, allowing Nick total access to the velvet intricacies of her ruby-red mound, meltingly warm and swimming with fragrant juices. Clarissa sighed and leant her head back against the wall, then gasped aloud with the icy shock of sharp, deep pleasure as Nick's hot, strong tongue dipped into her honeyed wetness, and she climaxed almost immediately from the feel of his mouth on her sex.

It seemed that he had only just begun, however, for Nick then moved on to tease the glistening round protuberance of her straining clitoris, almost causing Clarissa to leap straight off the sofa. As his hands reached under her to grasp her buttocks and pull her closer to his mouth, one finger closing in on the tightly puckered entrance to her anus, Clarissa was so close to screaming aloud with the powerful sensations that she nearly didn't hear the sound of a door opening and closing almost directly behind her.

Now she really did scream aloud as a large, dark figure literally passed before her eyes, its features partially covered by an American baseball cap pulled down low over its face, its body almost completely obscured by a heavy green waxed jacket and baggy khaki trousers. Caught between encroaching orgasm and the jolt of sudden awareness that there was now another person actually in the room, Clarissa could only remain helplessly where she sat, her body completely naked and exposed to this stranger's eyes, Nick on his knees before her, his head still thrillingly lodged between her thighs.

The man – or boy, for he seemed to be about Nick's age – did not seem at all surprised to see a stark naked woman perched on the top of his sofa, his roommate's mouth ravishing her succulent vagina, for Clarissa finally understood that this stranger must be Lawrence Hoffman, Nick's mysterious flatmate. Indeed, had the situation not been so absurd and bizarre, Clarissa would merely have extended her hand and introduced herself.

As it was, however, now that she had worked out who this young man was, and had absorbed his and Nick's calm acceptance of each other's presence, she also now knew that this was yet another one of Nick's set-ups. Clarissa finally understood that Nick had lured her to his flat yet again, had obviously arranged for his roommate to show up in order for him to watch the two of them, and that the situation was now in her hands. The question was, what was she going to do about it? Should she push Nick away, reach for her clothes and dash out in a self-righteous show of dignified anger? Or should she acknowledge and respond to the just emerging tingling of arousal, the shiver of delight that ran down her spine at the thought of being the active subject of a deliciously liberating voyeuristic tableau?

Clarissa barely hesitated. She glanced down the length of her body at Nick, who raised his head, indicating Lawrence with his eyes, and simply asked, his voice low and husky, his mouth shining wet with her pleasure, 'Shall I continue?'

And so Clarissa merely nodded once and spread her legs even wider, allowing Nick as much access to her sex as possible, feeling completely abandoned and licentious, and more sexually aroused than she had ever been before in her life. As she felt the tip of Nick's tongue probe its way into her, Clarissa stared defiantly across him over at his flatmate, who had now stripped off his hat and coat and sat quietly at the table, sipping at Nick's wine, watching the two of them on the sofa.

Clarissa stared boldly back at this stranger looking at her, almost beyond caring about the salacious absurdity of it all, hardly able to believe her own brazenness and, yes, the pleasure she was extracting from this most bizarre scenario. What was she doing here, allowing a strange man to look on while her young lover kissed her so voluptuously between her thighs?

And yet she wasn't embarrassed at all; indeed, Clarissa felt she was achieving new heights of self-consciousness and self-awareness, that she was only now coming to a new understanding of the full power of her still-unexplored sexuality. She didn't feel herself objectified by Lawrence's gaze at her naked, exposed body; on the contrary, Clarissa invited his gaze, she welcomed it, and she felt as if *she* were utilising *Lawrence* in order to gain the maximum of sexual pleasure from this scene. Nick, in fact, seemed almost irrelevant at this point, and so, barely even thinking about what she was doing, Clarissa gently nudged Nick aside, gesturing that he should move away from her and over to where his roommate was sitting. Thus Nick seated himself at the table, legs negligently stretched out before him, one arm casually slung over the back of his chair, the other resting lightly on his knee. Then, hardly daring to believe that she was actually doing this, Clarissa beckoned to Lawrence to come over to her, which he did, and silently and obediently he dropped to his knees before her.

Looking down at him in queenly splendour from the top of the sofa where she sat, Clarissa placed her fingers on either side of her blossoming, liquid labia and slowly spread them apart so that the heart of her sex was fully revealed, shining rivulets of clear fluid trickling down between her fingers and pooling on the sofa.

'Look at me,' Clarissa said. She was now fully open and exposed, her vagina spread wide to the gaze of her male audience, and she held her pose for a moment, leaning back and watching the men's reactions to the spectacular display before them.

'Lick me,' she whispered to Lawrence, his tongue already stretching out in eager anticipation, but it was at Nick's face that Clarissa gazed, her eyes gripping his as Lawrence placed his lips on the lips of her sex and his tongue began to lick her vagina in slow, steady strokes. Clarissa balanced her bottom further out on the top of the sofa, thrusting herself fully at the warm, wet mouth that sucked wantonly at her sex, watching Nick watch her. She wasn't interested in whether he was merely aroused by this scene; indeed, Nick's excitement – and Lawrence's, for that matter – seemed nearly irrelevant to Clarissa's own pleasure. What was important to her was more the fact that Nick was a *witness* to what she was experiencing; the intensity in his watching eyes seemed to reflect Clarissa's own desire, and to magnify and enlarge it. Were Nick to respond merely by masturbating to this scene, it would detract from the importance of her role as active subject, because then he would be participating alongside her, rather than concentrating solely upon her; she wanted Nick to concentrate on *her*, not on his own pleasure. And so, having Nick as spectator rather than masturbatory participant helped to bring Clarissa to a stupefying, shattering, mind-altering climax. When it came, Clarissa howled and screamed with the force of her orgasm that seemed to go on and on and on, her gaping, clenching mound clutching spasmodically at Lawrence's writhing, slavish tongue.

When it was finally over, Lawrence backed away quickly, turning his back on both Nick and Clarissa as if in shame, and for a moment there was only silence in the room.

'Well,' Clarissa said lightly, struggling to maintain a sense of decency and propriety despite the sordidness of the scene that had just transpired. 'Perhaps I'd better get dressed.' She was disturbed to discover, however, that she was actually beginning to shake, her fingers and legs trembling so badly that she was unable even to pull on her underwear, her muscles seeming to have suddenly become disassociated from her command.

'Here, let me help you,' Nick offered in a strangely muted voice, and he came quickly forward, easily and efficiently sliding up her thong to its rightful place between her damp, sticky thighs, and buttoning up her blouse over her suddenly shivering, chilled body. Completely ignoring Lawrence, Nick wrapped his long, curved arms round Clarissa in a gesture of protection, placing her head on his shoulder and gently running his hand over the tangle of red hair that had only recently been neatly plaited in place. As Nick cuddled her to his warm body, Clarissa felt closer to him than she ever had before, and she felt her tremors and shakes gradually begin to dissolve. She clung to him for a moment, then with a shaky laugh she pushed him away and slid unsteadily to her feet.

'I think I could use another glass of wine,' she said

briskly, bravely attempting to instil an atmosphere of normality to the room. Nick turned away and went to sit back at the now-empty table.

'I think I'll join you,' Lawrence jumped in hastily, emerging unexpectedly from the kitchen where he'd obviously secreted himself out of a ludicrous sense of modesty. He was holding a corkscrew, a clean tumbler and a fresh bottle of wine.

The three sat in awkward silence for a few minutes, nervously sipping at their drinks, cautiously avoiding each other's eyes. Clarissa seemed to have recovered most of her senses, however, because she abruptly turned towards Lawrence, having decided that she had had enough of this ridiculous pretence at informality.

'I guess you know by now that I am Clarissa,' she said jauntily, extending her hand which was gingerly accepted by Lawrence. She noted with a smile that he was still trying to avoid her eyes and was turning his head away from confronting the sight of her naked legs which she was half-consciously crossing and uncrossing. 'And you must be Lawrence Hoffman, Nick's flatmate. Am I right?' she continued, hearteningly relieved to discover that her usual poise and good-humoured grace had come flooding back to her. She then glanced over at Nick, eyebrows mockingly raised, and said with only the slightest hint of sarcasm, 'Nice set-up, Nick.'

Nick returned her gaze levelly as unsmilingly he countered, 'You liked it, though, didn't you, Clarissa?' At her unashamed nod of consent, Nick leant a little forward in his chair, gripped her hands in his and said softly, 'You see, Clarissa, I do know what you like.' Their eyes held each other's, each smiling a little as they gazed into each other's face, and then the intimacy of the moment was interrupted by a loud 'harumph!' from Lawrence, who reached for his jacket and said, still awkward and uncomfortable, 'Well, then, perhaps I'd better go.'

Clarissa glanced enquiringly at Nick, who merely gestured towards her with his hands and said, 'It's up to you, Ris. Whatever you want.'

She then turned to look at Lawrence. 'No,' she said as if suddenly coming to a decision, surprising even herself. 'Stay. Have another glass of wine.' She indicated the bottle encouragingly. 'Perhaps we should get to know each other a little bit better.' Her eyes flicked downwards to his crotch, where she noticed for the first time that he was sporting a rather large and uncomfortable-looking erection. She actually caught herself admiring it, trying to picture what it would look like when freed from its cumbersome enclosure of zipped khaki trousers, and she wondered whether Lawrence shared his flatmate's disdain for the confining irrelevance of underwear.

When Lawrence caught the downward drift of her eyes, which Clarissa made no attempt to conceal, he couldn't help but laugh, and so the tension between the three of them finally seemed to have broken up a bit. Clarissa now felt fully relaxed, her body glossy and sleek after her mind-numbing orgasm, and she casually decided to herself that perhaps she might experiment, try having some fun with this perverse, odd, but potentially thrilling encounter.

'So, Lawrence,' she began impishly, 'why don't you tell me exactly what schemes you and Nick have devised between the two of you; what twisted, kinky things did the two of you have in mind for tonight?'

Lawrence stared open-mouthed at Nick, clearly not having anticipated Clarissa's sudden cool command of the situation. Nick, however, merely shrugged and looked at Clarissa, asking her almost offhandedly, 'Why, Clarissa, do you have something else in mind that you'd like to try?'

Suddenly inspired, Clarissa leant over to Lawrence and reached out her hand to thoughtfully finger the stitching that bordered the low V-neck of his rough rugby shirt. 'Well, Lawrence – or do you prefer Larry? – Nick tells me that you're in the military. He says that you're training to be an officer while you finish your university degree.' She slowly and deliberately ran her eyes appraisingly up and down his body, then leant back in her chair, raising one naked knee and placing her bare foot laddishly on the table. 'I've heard that military men are supposed to keep

123

their bodies in excellent condition – you know, all that marching, running, climbing and stuff they do is so *rigorous* and is supposed to improve their stamina.' She leant forward now, idly lifting one cold strand of spaghetti from her plate, inserting one end between her lips and teasingly drawing the whole strand into her mouth, saucily eyeing Lawrence the whole time. When he continued to say nothing, merely shuttling his eyes nervously between her and Nick, Clarissa uttered a low laugh from deep within her throat and asked with a show of innocent interest, 'Well, Lawrence, is it true? Do military men have great bodies?' When Lawrence still refused to speak, instead flushing a deep red of embarrassment, Clarissa suddenly sat up straight and said imperiously, gesturing towards his body, 'Come on, Larry, stand up and strip. Show us what you've got.'

Lawrence's mouth gaped as his eyes shifted incredulously between Clarissa's regally smiling face and Nick's inscrutable one. Clarissa could tell, however, that Nick was impressed by her rapid rearrangement of the situation; she could see the admiration in his eyes at the way she had taken control of the scene. He had so clearly tried to set her up, to seduce her into a position of helplessness so that she would be forced to take pleasure from Nick while taking pleasure from the state of being observed by Lawrence. I'd just love to hear what those two naughty boys were plotting together in my absence, Clarissa thought to herself now, half in amusement and half in anger. What exactly did Nick say to Lawrence when describing how he should intrude on our private little moment? Well, she'd never know, for she knew Nick would never tell her. However, she was determined now to reverse the positions of power here. Let *Lawrence* see what it felt like to be manipulated into being the object of another person's pleasure! Clarissa thought triumphantly to herself. And so she gestured again to Lawrence that he should get up out of his chair and stand before her, which he did, twitching a little, his hands nervously clutching at his elbows, but Clarissa also noticed that his erection seemed to have grown even larger, his cock appearing to bulge and strain at the front closure of his trousers.

'Come on, Larry, you've seen my body in all its glory. Now let us see yours,' Clarissa said coaxingly, but with a steely undercurrent of command in her voice.

And so Lawrence, shaking a little but clearly highly excited by Clarissa's erotic invitation, began tremblingly to take off his clothes. Clarissa leant back again into her chair, breathing a little heavily and watching Lawrence closely as he awkwardly pulled his rugby shirt over his head, tangling up the arms in his confusion, and then quickly stripped off his white sleeveless vest, his admirably strong chest now bared to Clarissa's gaze. Nick seemed a little bored by Lawrence's act, almost as though he'd seen it before, but Clarissa hardly paid him any attention at all as she concentrated on watching Lawrence unzip his khaki trousers, now seeming to be in a little more haste, and tug off his close-fitting briefs, obviously unlike Nick in his preference for the comfort of underwear.

When at last Lawrence stood naked before her, Clarissa let out a low whistle of approval and rose from her chair to circle round him in order to admire him from all angles. This clearly had a rousing effect on Lawrence, for his powerfully large organ began to jerk and sway a little, almost as though following Clarissa's circuit around his naked body. Nick still sat quietly in his chair, watching in silence as Clarissa reached out her hand to slide it along the hard, smooth slopes of Lawrence's chest, arms and stomach, and stooping a little to test the strength of the muscles that were etched into his sturdy, stocky thighs. He wasn't bad looking, she decided to herself now, gauging his height at only a few inches more than hers and noting the black, military-style close crop of his hair, his thin lips, narrow cheeks and blunt nose, which looked as though it had once been broken. Of course, he wasn't nearly so handsome as Nick, but Clarissa thought he could do quite nicely for a while. She gazed again at his penis, licking her lips a little in anticipation as she studied the throbbing, veined shaft, its colour a deep purple and its mushroom-shaped head glossy and smooth. Clarissa hastily stripped off her shirt and her thong, then dropped to the floor before Lawrence's cock and brought her mouth right up to its head, opening her lips slightly and sliding it in only a fraction of an inch. With a choked sigh, Lawrence gripped her head hopefully, trying to push her mouth forward and down on to him, but with a cruel laugh of resistance, Clarissa quickly released herself from his grasp and rolled on to her back on the floor, opening her legs and cupping her sex in her hands.

'A little more of this first, I think,' she ordered with a smile, and with a grimace of unsatisfied lust, but obviously willing to obey, Lawrence lowered himself down between her thighs and began once again to play his mouth over Clarissa's ready mound.

She had nearly forgotten about Nick during this little game, and so it was with a slight shock that she saw him appear as if out of nowhere, blissfully nude and rampantly erect. Clarissa gazed up at him in silence as, with a slight exhalation of breath, Nick straddled her shoulders and slowly eased himself down in front of her, coming to rest on his knees on the floor, his cock poised at the entrance to Clarissa's moist, ruby lips. As Lawrence continued to pleasure her with his tongue, Clarissa opened her mouth and slowly drew Nick in, enclosing his hard, muscled buttocks in her hands, steadying his weight in her palms and setting a pace that was both comfortable and tantalising. She rubbed her warm, soft lips along the length of Nick's hotly pulsing shaft, licking the underside with her tongue, searching out the sensitive place under the head and twirling round and round it. As she licked and sucked on his cock, she pictured to herself the image that Lawrence must have before him, if he bothered to look up during his active oral manipulation of her sex. Lawrence should be able to see the sharply defined planes of Nick's back, deeply divided by the snaking length of his spine, and the chiselled globes of his buttocks as his anal entrance was playfully stimulated by Clarissa's fingers. Even through the haze of her pleasure, Clarissa wondered to herself whether Lawrence was enjoying the view – indeed, whether he was aroused by it. She decided to find out for sure, and so she abruptly pushed both men away, silently disengaging herself and reaching for a condom in the back pocket of Nick's discarded jeans which lay nearby. She sat up between the two men and fished out the packet, then wordlessly handed it to Lawrence, who sure enough was massively hard. Clarissa then turned on to all fours, her mouth reaching again for Nick's cock, this time placed directly in front of her, while waiting for Lawrence to position himself at her rear. With Nick's penis once again cradled in her mouth, Clarissa felt the thick protuberance of Lawrence's cock edging its way into the cushioning tunnel of her vagina. When at last he was all the way in, all three paused for a moment, the men politely waiting for Clarissa to set the rhythm, holding themselves still while she hesitantly moved back on to Lawrence's cock, sliding her lips up along the length of Nick's staff, then moving far forward, Lawrence's member nearly completely released but Nick's cock firmly lodged in her throat nearly down to its base. She tried the rhythm again, backwards on to Lawrence, easing Nick out, then back on to Nick, moving away from Lawrence. By now she was comfortable with the pace, and so the two men began to move in time with her, the three of them creating a kind of sensual dance, a pattern of movement and pleasure that was completely new to Clarissa, though she wondered if it was so too for the boys. Her body felt incredibly sharply tuned and hyper-sensitive; the pleasure she felt at having her mouth filled so deliciously with Nick's cock was balanced by her vaginal rapture at the feel of Lawrence's strong, rhythmic thrusts. Clarissa felt, quite literally, to be at the centre of their pleasure, and she found herself wishing she had more than one mouth, more than one sex in order to contain and experience the tremors and thrills which were wracking her body so sweetly.

As Clarissa gracefully arched her back before thrusting her buttocks back hard against Lawrence, she looked up beyond Nick's pulsing organ in her mouth to look into his eyes which were totally focused on her, and she wondered which aroused him more, the feel of his cock in her mouth or the sight of Lawrence pumping away at the back. As if in answer, Nick suddenly withdrew his throbbing shaft, which Clarissa was certain had been about to come, and he reached down to take her face in his hands, motioning Lawrence to stop.

'Let's try something different,' he whispered into her hair. 'I want to be inside you now too.'

Uncertainly Clarissa looked up at him, not sure if she was ready to try what Nick was suggesting. 'Only if you want to, Clarissa,' he said steadily, cupping her chin in his hand. 'We'll only try it if you want to.'

Clarissa looked back questioningly at Lawrence, who said nothing, merely holding his heavy organ tightly in his hand as if it threatened to spontaneously spurt into orgasm if he let it go. Clarissa turned back to Nick and hesitantly nodded her head, whispering a little nervously, 'All right, Nick, if you want to, I'll try it.'

'No, Clarissa,' he corrected her, 'this is just for you. We'll only do this if you want to go ahead.'

'Yes,' she said more decisively this time. 'Yes, I want to try it.'

And so Clarissa fought to stay calm despite the tremors of excitement and nerves that were causing her belly to quiver and roll, her vagina gathering its juices and her back passage already beginning to clench a little in anticipation. She watched with some anxiety as Nick handed Lawrence a fresh, well-lubricated condom to slide over his cock, and as she rolled on to her side Lawrence silently moved to lie behind her, his hands lightly placed on her hips, the tip of his penis already seeking entrance to her rear. Nick came forward to lie in front of Clarissa, his hands resting reassuringly on her shoulders, his eyes holding hers as he lightly kissed her lips. 'Why don't you let Lawrence go first?' he asked softly, glancing over her body at Lawrence, who tightened his grip on her and slowly, every so gently, as though he were nervous too,

128

began to nudge his way inside the tight darkness of Clarissa's puckered anal hole.

Clarissa merely closed her eyes and breathed, feeling as though she could come from the tension alone, fighting to stop herself from pushing Nick away and desperately urging Lawrence on to a fast, wild ride ... but she was keen to try out this deliciously decadent new scenario. When Lawrence was comfortably anchored and still inside her, Nick lifted her top leg and laid it across his hip, his cock at the ready at her vaginal entrance, his legs enclosing her bottom thigh. 'Now look at me, Clarissa,' he said softly, fixing his eyes on hers. 'Just look at me while I move on into you.'

She clung to him then, her eyes gripped by his as Nick adjusted his pelvis to hers, gliding easily inside her and holding himself still once the fit was wholly achieved.

'Now,' he said deeply, huskily, and sexier than Clarissa had ever seen him before. And that was all he said; Clarissa remained completely motionless at first, closing her eyes and concentrating on the pressure of penis against penis as each began to move in matched time. As Lawrence moved in, Nick moved out, and the two young men were soon gliding against each other, the friction being almost more than Clarissa could bear. As she began to join them, her own internal rhythms adjusting instinctively to the motions of the two cocks inside her, she clung deliriously to Nick, her eyes fused in ecstasy with his, not breaking the gaze even when he bent his head to kiss her, his tongue moving inside her mouth to yet another rhythmic beat. Through the haze of Clarissa's sense-drenched pleasure, she pictured to herself the complicated embrace that was passing between the two men who were pressed so closely against her: Nick's arms which enfolded her to him were also pressed against her back, and thus against Lawrence's chest; Nick's long legs must also surely be entwined with Lawrence's as both men positioned themselves on either side of Clarissa for balance and leverage. And of course, their two cocks were rubbing against each other, bringing each other to orgasm just as surely as Clarissa was spiralling upwards to erotic heights of passion she'd never even imagined possible. She felt full, more completely filled up than she had ever felt before, and her entire body was one shivering, trembling, climaxing erogenous zone: her ears were ringing, her nipples were straining, her clitoris was quaking, her vagina was weeping tears of pure pleasure and so, Clarissa was stunned to discover, was she. As her climax seared her with its frightening intensity, the tears flowed from her eyes as the liquid poured from her sex, and she hardly noticed when the men finally came, so consumed was she with the power of her own orgasm.

She must have gone on and on even after the men stopped because she never felt them withdraw, and she didn't even see Lawrence dress or hear him leave, but when she finally stopped screaming and crying and shaking, she and Nick were alone in the flat, its sudden silence wrapping itself around her deafened ears.

When Clarissa opened her eyes and looked up at Nick, she saw that he was lying a little away from her, his head propped up on one hand, looking down into her face with that distanced smile of calculated amusement. He reached out a long, slim finger and trailed it lightly along the curve of her small jaw, then ran it sensuously over her mouth, sliding it inside her lips as they parted. Clarissa sucked briefly on his finger before letting it drop out of her mouth, then sat up and reached for her clothes as if she were beginning to dress. With a tug on her wrist, however, Nick stopped her.

'Don't,' he whispered almost pleadingly as in surprise she let her blouse fall to the floor. 'Stay. Don't go.'

Clarissa was astonished, and deeply touched. 'Nick, are you asking me to spend the night?' she asked gently, feeling her heart turn over. She and Nick had never spent a whole night together before – or did he just want her to stay now so he could be sure that his hold on her was still strong; had what had passed between her and Lawrence made him finally jealous at last?

'Yes,' he answered firmly, 'yes, Clarissa, I want you to stay. Stay the night with me, sleep with me in my bed, even – ' he grinned wickedly ' – walk into class with me tomorrow.'

Not even the thought of class the next day distracted her from the closeness which Clarissa now felt towards her student-lover. 'I can't, Nick,' she said regretfully, rising reluctantly to dress herself. 'You know that I can't – at least, not tonight.'

When she was finally clothed, he began to walk her out but then stopped and leant against the door, blocking it with his body. 'Clarissa – ' he began, then abruptly closed his mouth as if deciding against what he had started to say.

She nudged him. 'What, Nick?' she asked gently. 'What is it?'

He looked round restlessly, his eyes darting about the room, then he looked down at her and said brusquely, 'If you like being with other men, then I want to be there too.'

She gazed at him, open mouthed and incredulous, then began to laugh. 'Is that what this was about?' she shrieked, her laughter bordering upon the hysterical. 'Did you get this whole thing up with your buddy because you're still smarting over last night? You still think I was out getting laid and you're trying to stake some kind of claim on me?'

Nick said nothing, now stubbornly refusing to meet her eyes and suddenly appearing even younger than his nineteen years. 'So?' he asked her sullenly. 'Are you angry with me?'

Now Clarissa really was in the grip of hysteria, the result of nervous tension, depleted emotional energy, and sexual exhaustion. 'Oh, god, Nick,' she gasped out wearily as the final spasms left her, wiping tears off her smudged and tired face. 'I can't be bothered to think about that now. Let's just agree that this was . . . a very pleasant way to spend the evening – ' she laughed at her outrageous understatement ' – and leave it at that, OK? I'll see you in class tomorrow, all right?' She suddenly peered at him, her voice unintentionally sharpening. 'You will be in class tomorrow, won't you? It's the last class before the break, you know.'

He nodded down at her, smiling at her almost tenderly, she thought, then moved aside to let her pass through his door. 'Good night, my love,' he whispered as she passed – or at least, that's what she thought he had said. Did he really call her 'my love'? she wondered to herself. She couldn't be sure.

Chapter Eight

Clarissa woke up the next morning in her bed, stretched experimentally, then sighed to herself in unashamed pleasure as she felt the tell-tale residual soreness and ache in her vagina and between her buttocks. She felt glossy, sleek and voluptuously sexy today. She rolled over on to her stomach, buried her face in her arms, and inhaled deeply: she could still detect traces of the now-familiar scent of Nick's body which clung to her smooth, silky skin. Clarissa breathed in and smiled again, running her fingers down the curves of her arms, feeling along the contours of her biceps, smaller versions of Nick's, and visualising her workout in the gym later that afternoon. She felt extraordinarily good this morning, and her scheduled session in the gym couldn't have come at a better time. She'd had to skip several sessions lately because of her work load, but she was keen to get back into routine. She traced along the patterns of her stomach muscles, testing their strength and shape, then flexed her firm buttocks under her fingers, picturing herself flat out on that blasted leg curl machine and straining to complete those particularly loathsome lunges which were so difficult to do correctly, yet which produced such marvellously tight results. Clarissa's strenuous workout the night before – she smiled dreamily at the remembrance – made her particularly keen to exercise in a different way today. She was so incredibly conscious of the powers of her body, sensitised to every movement of her muscles and reflex of her nerves, she couldn't wait to extend the repertoire of the range and scope of her body's capabilities.

But first class. Clarissa rose to get ready for the day, then groaned out loud, thinking of the preparation she still had to do for the remaining weeks of the course. Next week was the start of Easter break, and she was very grateful indeed for the opportunity to devote an entire three weeks to catching up on marking her students' essays and completing the background reading she needed to strengthen her final class lectures. She was also beginning to fret about how her book on the erotic was faring under her editor's annoyingly meticulous and critical eye. Please, no more revisions, Clarissa urged silently. She'd heard nothing from the usually reliable Heidi since she'd sent her manuscript in, and she fervently hoped that this wasn't a bad sign. She really didn't feel that there was much else she could give to the book – not since the burst of enthusiasm she'd displayed in revising it after that sordid scene with Jessica and Nick.

Nick. Clarissa paused under the pounding spray of the shower, massaging her expensive salon shampoo into her hair while contemplating the events of last night, feeling once again the lingering soreness in her most private parts. Well, she'd always been curious about how threesomes worked, and now she knew for sure, she mused to herself, combing the conditioner out of the heavy silk of her hair while turning up the cold water just a notch. As Clarissa rinsed off and stepped out of the glass cubicle of her shower, she wondered again about the meaning of Nick's oddly sullen and jealous behaviour as she was leaving last night. He'd got what he wanted, hadn't he? He'd arranged the whole scenario between himself, Clarissa and Lawrence, so why did he seem so distressed for that brief, fleeting moment when he'd begged her to stay? If he was still sleeping with Jessica, which Clarissa thought was a distinct possibility, then he had hardly any right to insist on intruding on her affairs with other men.

Clarissa pondered the question while absently stroking the cool metallic shape of her perfume bottle, seductively moulded to suggest the twin globes of a particularly ripe pair of female buttocks. As she pulled on the luxurious soft folds of her wool crepe trouser suit, she decided to shrug off the issue of Nick's peculiarly possessive stance and instead concentrate on today's lectures, the last before the break began.

While Clarissa arranged the sharp points of the wide collar of her cream silk blouse over that of her black wool jacket, she wondered to herself whether she'd even see Nick over the break. She shivered at the thought of going an entire three weeks without seeing or touching him; surely he'd stay up during that time rather than go back to stay with his parents, whoever they were? Clarissa smirked to herself as she studied her reflection in the mirror, the glorious red sheen of her hair set off so brilliantly by the rich deep black of her suit, the jacket long and slim, the trousers fluid and wide. I'm probably closer to Nick's mother's age than his, she laughed to herself, leaning over to blot her claret-stained lips. But I bet his mother wouldn't behave the way I did last night! She tugged at her jacket one last time: the violet hues of her amethyst-coloured bra could clearly be seen through her blouse, she knew, but she planned on wearing her jacket all day, so no one would be able to see it. She was just about to grab a banana for breakfast and leave when the sharp jangle of the phone stopped her.

'Hello,' she said abstractedly, frowning at the unsightly brown spot on her banana.

'Hey, 'Rissa, we're up early this morning!' Julian's loud London tones boomed out at her from the telephone.

Clarissa held the phone away from her ear, turning her frown from the banana to the receiver, then put it close to her mouth and shouted out angrily, 'Do you have to be so goddamned cheery in the morning?'

'Sorry, Ris, no time to chat,' Julian replied breezily. 'I'm off to open up downstairs for the early-rising boozers. I'm just calling to see if you want to join me at the Glory Box tonight for the Visitors' Open.'

'The what?' Clarissa squinted into the air, trying to figure out what on earth Julian was babbling on about. 'The who?'

'The Visitors' Open,' her friend explained patiently, clearly trying to focus Clarissa's attention. 'You know, where members can bring invited guests for a kind of look-see, to check the place out and decide if they want to join the club, so to speak.'

'Oh, I see.' Clarissa went silent for a moment, trying to decide if this was her kind of thing. She decided that it wasn't and had just opened her mouth to say so, when visions of last night's decadence flashed before her eyes. She saw herself, naked and gasping, lewdly positioned between Nick and Lawrence, one cock in her mouth, the other in her hotly throbbing sex, and decided that yes, perhaps an underground sex club might be very much her thing after all.

'Hello? Ris, you still there?' Julian must have tapped the phone impatiently with her keys or something because there was suddenly an unpleasant clanging noise in Clarissa's ear.

'Yes, I'm here, Jules.' Clarissa closed her eyes briefly, then plunged on ahead. 'Yes, of course, I'd love to come.' She studied her painted nails, wondering what in hell she'd just committed herself to.

'Great!' Julian was jubilant. 'I was hoping you'd say yes. Come to the pub around ten. We'll down a few pints and go on from there, OK?'

Great, another late night, Clarissa thought grimly to herself. Just what I need. 'Sure Jules. Ten. I'll see you then . . . Right . . . Bye.'

She put the telephone down and stared at herself in the mirror. A sex club. Was this a good thing? She patted her loose, jumbled curls reflectively, picked up her banana and briefcase and headed for the door. Time to concentrate on how to face Nick in class after last night's shameless debauchery.

Once again, however, Nick turned out to disappoint her. He failed to show up for class, even though it was the last one before the break, and even after the extraordinary events of the night before. Clarissa was distressed by the surge of frustrated longing that rose up within her as she confronted Nick's vacant chair in class, its very emptiness seeming to mock her with Nick's absence. In vain she tried to concentrate on the slippery, difficult densities of James Joyce's *Ulysses*, a text tough enough to talk about when she was at her best – and certainly beyond her students' comprehension – but absolutely murder on her nerves today, when she was clearly so distracted. Although the class was only studying an excerpt, including Molly Brown's famous soliloquy on the joys of oral sex, Clarissa simply didn't have the strength to go through it, and so, with as much grace as she could summon, she dismissed her class with a smile, wishing them a happy Easter and admonishing them to study the text harder when they returned next month.

Where was he? Clarissa demanded angrily to herself as she stomped her way down the hall, the sensuous lines of her trousers whipping against each other as she walked. She had half a mind to ring him – it would be easy enough to pull his file from the student records department – but then she decided not to. She wasn't about to degrade herself by running after her student; if she had to wait and let him come to her, then so be it. Not for the first time Clarissa chafed at the restraints imposed on her by her position of power; if she were just another college student, she would have no problem turning up at Nick's doorstep or telephoning him whenever she felt like it. For a moment Clarissa allowed herself the luxury of that fantasy, the absolute freedom of knocking on Nick's door regardless of who might see her, the bliss of kissing him openly, in public, on campus.

But no. She couldn't ignore the fact that she was so much

older and she was his teacher; she wasn't about to humili-
ate herself by chasing after some nineteen-year-old student
just so that she could have a good lay.

Firm in her resolve, however, it was nevertheless with
an unpleasant shock that she caught sight of Nick later that
afternoon, leaning casually against the wall by her office
and chatting amiably with a group of three other students,
one male and, Clarissa noted with dismay, two absolutely
stunning female students. There was no way Nick couldn't
see Clarissa as she turned the corner down the hall from
where he was standing, shook out her keys and opened the
door to her office but, though Clarissa actually dared
herself to stare him full in the face, he continued breezily
to ignore her. She deliberately slammed the door to her
office loudly enough for him to hear, then sank down in
the chair at her desk, miserably dropping her head into her
hands and prodding agitatedly at her temples. This was
just like the day after the first time they'd slept together!
she thought despairingly to herself. Clearly last night's
closeness meant nothing to him. Just a momentary lapse
into tenderness, she concluded, mortified. She tried to pull
herself together so that she could get some work done,
telling herself he would still come round as usual, but she
was panicked at the idea that the day would come and go
with no Nick, and she wouldn't set eyes on him until after
the break, three unendurably long weeks away. Maybe
tonight's club date with Julian will turn out to be an
inspired idea, Clarissa told herself wearily, rearranging the
essays on her desk. Certainly the exotic and unusual scenes
she would be witness to tonight should take her mind off
Nick.

Of course, Nick did turn up later that day, and Clarissa
was positively alight with joy when she finally heard
Nick's familiar rhythmic strut outside her office. She
couldn't control the eagerness in her voice when she called
out a welcome 'Come in!' to his light tap at the door.

Nick snaked his long body slowly around her door,
leaving it wide open, then leant casually against her desk,

picking up and glancing over papers on a conference entitled 'The Grotesque Body'.

'So, Clarissa,' he said by way of greeting, dropping the paper back on her desk, 'what are your plans over the break? Doing anything in about three weeks' time?'

Clarissa strove to appear as casual as he. 'Not much,' she shrugged indifferently while cautiously observing him from under lowered lids. 'You?'

'Listen,' Nick said, leaning over her desk so their faces were almost touching. 'I'm going away tomorrow for a while – ' of course he doesn't say where, Clarissa noted acidly to herself ' – but three weeks from today, the last night of the break, there's a party at my cousin's house. I'll be back by then – say you'll come with me.' When he saw her hesitate he added quickly, 'No one from the university will be there. Promise.'

Clarissa stared at him silently for a moment. He'll be gone for three weeks? A whole three weeks without him? And no mention of last night? Was this his version of goodbye? Well, at least meeting his cousin would be meeting a part of his family. Then it struck her: the day of the party was the day she'd arranged to go to the races with Graham. Well, she'd just have to cancel. This sounded a lot more fun. And damn! it was also the night of that horrid faculty dinner.

'I'm sorry Nick,' Clarissa began slowly, reluctantly, 'but I have to go to a faculty dinner that night and I don't think that I – '

Swiftly he cut her off. ''Rissa, the party won't even be started until long after your dinner is over, I'm sure,' he said with a smile, then added quietly, 'Please say yes. I'd really like you to come.'

She stared at him for a moment, softened by his unexpected warmth. 'A party. At your cousin's house. Of course I'll come.' Even as she said the words, however, Clarissa could feel her mind ticking away in suspicion. Would this party prove to be yet another one of Nick's set-ups? Would there be some tricky new sexual scenario waiting for her there like the one she participated in last night?

139

As if sensing her thoughts, Nick stood facing her expectantly where she sat, waiting for her to speak.

'Nick,' Clarissa began carefully, unsure of what she was about to say. 'Look, about last night . . .'

'Yes . . . ?' Nick arched a brow, and waited.

But Clarissa could think of nothing to say. She could only gaze up at him, wide eyed and full of desire and, almost without thinking, she found herself reaching up for him, her arms round his neck, drawing his head down to hers so that their lips met, feeling his mouth open on to hers, her tongue slipping out to rub along Nick's, his hands beginning to feel along the seamed lines of her jacket, searching out the round curves of her breasts . . .

'Clarissa? What on earth are you doing?'

Graham! Frantically, Clarissa pushed herself away from Nick, out of his embrace, her face scarlet, her chest heaving, escaping tendrils of hair curling heatedly around her face. Oh god, the door was open! Unwillingly, Clarissa dragged her eyes upwards to face Graham's which had gone curiously blank, his face smoothly composed, giving nothing away. How much had he seen?

Plenty, it seemed. Graham's eyes flicked contemptuously up and down Nick's rangy and – Clarissa couldn't help but say it to herself – decidedly superior frame. 'Is this one of your students?' he asked pointedly.

Clarissa was grateful for Nick's quick, considerate retreat. 'Thank you for your help on my essay, Dr Cornwall,' he said politely and with no evident trace of irony or sarcasm. 'I think I'll be going now. Have a good break.' And with that, he sauntered his way out of the door, leaving her alone with Graham, wondering what to say next.

'So.' She cleared her throat nervously. Was her lipstick smudged? 'This is a nice surprise,' she said as pleasantly as possible. 'What are you doing here?'

'I came to arrange for some recruitment officers from the company to come over to the physics department after the break. You remember, I told you on the phone the other day,' Graham explained easily, conversationally, all traces

140

of contempt and suspicion gone. 'We're always interested in interviewing bright young graduates fresh from their degree courses in physics.' He eyed Clarissa sharply before adding, 'And I thought I'd drop by and take you to a late lunch if you were – ahem – free.'

Lunch with Graham! Clarissa could think of few things less appealing at the moment. With the taste of Nick's kiss still fresh in her mouth, Clarissa couldn't help but compare him most favourably to Graham. She looked at Graham now with distaste. His blond hair was swept back off his forehead – she'd never noticed before how rapidly it seemed to be thinning – his paisley tie was neatly knotted, his white shirt freshly pressed, and his expensive camel cashmere coat was arranged tidily over his arm. He was the very epitome of cool corporate professional; hard to believe he's in the military, the same butch business as Larry Hoffman, Clarissa thought sourly to herself.

'Sorry, Graham,' she said sweetly, but through her teeth. 'I've already had lunch. But thanks anyway,' she added thoughtfully.

'Ah.' Graham shook out his neatly folded coat and prepared to put it on, then stopped. 'About the horse races – ' he began, but she cut him off.

'Sorry, Graham,' she said again, even more saccharine this time, 'but I'm afraid I really won't be able to make it after all. I'm sorry, but other things have come up.'

Graham took a step nearer to her, his face peering uncomfortably close to hers. 'Something came up?' he repeated nastily. 'For instance with that student whose tongue I just saw stuck down your throat?'

It wasn't like Graham to talk so crudely, Clarissa thought to herself in disbelief. What in the world was the matter with him?

'That's none of your business now, is it?' she said crisply, rising to her feet and clearly indicating that he should go. 'You'll just have to take along some other little woman to impress your boss with.'

For some reason this seemed to hit a nerve with Graham. He gripped her wrist in a gesture of aggression that was so

141

completely unlike him, Clarissa stared in shock for a moment before thinking to brush him off. 'Let go of me!' she cried.

Instead he gripped her wrist tighter, drawing her off her feet and right up to his face. 'Listen, Clarissa, you'd better come with me to this *very* important company function. I have a lot of friends in this university, you know, not all of whom would be pleased to hear about your ... shall we say ... extracurricular activities.' He sneered. She had never been more turned off by Graham than she was now, seeing him behave in such an ugly, aggressive, dominating manner.

Horrified, Clarissa shook him off and took two steps backwards, away from him. 'Are you threatening me?' she breathed out in disgust. 'How dare you?' And yet, she couldn't help a trace of fear from appearing in her voice. Graham must have heard it too, for he responded with a quick turn-about of attitude.

Suddenly he was re-composed, as though he'd sensed that he'd gained the upper hand. With a satisfied smile he smoothed his expensive coat down over his chest, turned on his heel to go, then stopped at the door and pointed a finger directly at Clarissa.

'Horse racing,' he said shortly, then strode out of the door, slamming it shut behind him.

Pedalling furiously on the exercise bike at the gym later that evening, Clarissa blew her hair off her face and wiped the sweat off her nose in disgust. She was really wallowing in her black mood now, a mood compounded by the fact that she loathed the exercise bike, vastly preferring the derrière-tightening powers of the far more demanding stair climber. All those machines were now in use, unfortunately, so she was condemned to the bike, where the seat rubbed uncomfortably against her crotch, still sore from last night and gaining in discomfort with every rotation of her feet strapped to the pedals. Clarissa couldn't help but replay the scene with Graham repeatedly in her head, growing more irate and ill tempered with every review.

How dare he speak to her in that way, threatening her with exposure if she balked at attending the Grand bloody National with him! Clarissa ground her teeth in fury, increasing the rate on the bike with a jab of her index finger at the speed button. Great! Now she'd just broken a nail as well! What the hell had got into him?

When they'd first met, Clarissa had been impressed with Graham's tenderness and polite manners, his courteousness as well as his intellect, wit, and connoisseur's collection of single malt whiskies. She'd thought he was just what she needed: a gentleman as well as a grown-up, well educated and enthusiastic about his job, an apparent reflection of herself, though Clarissa could never quite reconcile herself either to the fact that he was so corporate-minded or that he worked in the industrial–military complex. However, he was presentable, easy to be with, undemanding, generous and gracious, though at times a little patronising. But as the relationship wore on, Clarissa began to grow a little bored with his polished charm and corporate interests; she longed for someone a little more loose, a little less restrained, someone who could understand her craze for American action films, heavy metal rock and the occasional Mills and Boon. She might be an academic, Clarissa now snorted to herself as she reached to switch off the damned bike, but at least she wasn't stuffy, uptight or pretentious. Graham, with all his expense-account aspirations and public-school breeding, was beginning to get on her nerves. What she was beginning to long for – what she thought she had found in Nick – was not someone too similar to herself but someone vastly different, someone who, as she'd told Julian, was completely *other* than herself. And so, apparently reaching a kind of tacit mutual agreement, she and Graham had decided to call it quits.

As Clarissa hefted the five-kilo weights in each hand, alternating her bicep curls while remembering to tuck in her pelvis, she reflected now on the way Graham had changed. Always gentle, always considerate, in bed as well as out, he had seemed an odd kind of man to be the type to design software for military weapons. As a lover he was patently skilled in technique; he could locate her G-spot with the greatest of ease, something Clarissa had rather doubted she possessed until she'd met Graham, and he was adept at coaxing forth both the readily accessible clitoral orgasm as well as the more elusive vaginal climax. Nick was the only other man who had been able to perform the same feat, though Clarissa now speculated that the climaxes she achieved with Nick were due to the inflammatory chemistry between them, whereas Graham had simply consulted a sex manual at some point in his life.

Whatever. Clarissa shrugged, seated herself at the chest press, sliding the pin into the twenty-kilo spot, and decided to let the matter of Graham rest. She was simply not going to go to the Grand National, whatever he threatened; she was confident this whole predicament would simply dissipate once he'd come to his senses. For now she determined just to finish her workout and meet Julian later at the pub as planned, setting aside all thoughts of Graham and his recent unpleasantness.

When Clarissa finally turned up at the Head, she was uncharacteristically late, having wasted twenty minutes in fretting over what to wear. She just didn't know what would be suitable attire for a sex club, especially as she was attending solely in the capacity of tourist, and she had forgotten to ask Julian's advice earlier that morning. In desperation she'd finally decided on the trouser suit she'd worn that day, with clean underwear and a fresh blouse underneath of course, but arriving at the pub now, she wasn't at all certain that she'd made the right choice.

'Wow, look at you!' Julian whistled out from her place at the back of the bar. '*Very* butch indeed!'

Clarissa located her favourite spot by the cash register and leant cautiously over the wet bar. 'Why don't you just say it a little louder, Jules?' she snapped out in irritation. 'I think there are a few people at the back who didn't quite hear you.'

'You'll get loads of invitations tonight looking like that, lady,' Julian teased Clarissa, sliding her finger along the panel of Clarissa's wide black lapel. 'Seriously, Ris,' Julian said, though her black eyes were sparkling, 'you might want to consider changing your clothes. I'm not sure you want to be sending out the signals this little ensemble seems to invite.'

'But what should I wear?' Clarissa began to wail. Really, this was too much! Maybe she'd just better go home.

'Skin,' Julian said decisively.

'Julian, I am *not* going naked – ' Clarissa cut in hastily, but her friend merely laughed out loud and shook her head.

'I meant *leather*, you dope!' she chortled, stroking Clarissa's cheek affectionately. 'Come on upstairs. I've got something I think will suit you. Bill, can you take over now?' she called out over her shoulder.

Once up in Julian's flat, Clarissa hung back, a little shy, as Julian began energetically to strip off her clothes. 'I've got to get changed too,' she declared breathlessly, ripping her tatty striped jumper over her head. Clarissa then backed away in horror as Julian dramatically shook out a studded black leather outfit at her, complete with cut-outs, straps and neck harness.

'Uh, uh,' Clarissa declared emphatically, turning for the door. 'No way. I'm out of here.'

'Not for you, for me, silly!' Julian chortled again, clearly enchanted by Clarissa's evident naïveté. '*You* may not be hoping to score tonight, but *I* certainly am!' And so Clarissa could do nothing but watch in amazement as Julian tugged, snapped and coaxed the clinging black leather up her long, cigarette-slim legs, over her boyish midriff, along her skinny arms, and fastened the harness round her long thin neck. When Julian was dressed – if that's what it could be called – Clarissa could do nothing but stand back and gaze in amazement. Julian was wearing a skin-tight catsuit that had gaps cut away at the sides of her waist and also at her stomach to reveal a newly-pierced navel, the gold ring winking brightly at Clarissa. Julian's breasts were covered – just – in wired demi-cups that pressed them together, creating a manufactured depth of cleavage which, frankly,

Clarissa hadn't believed Julian was capable of until now. The suit was also cut out above the breasts to form a halter at the throat, and straps ran down from her shoulders to removable sleeves attached at her elbows. The sleeves, if that's what they were called, began mid-arm and ended at the base of the fingers, where the leather was formed into little rings, leaving the backs of the hands bare. All in all it was, Clarissa decided, a most complicated piece of attire, and she wasn't even entirely sure it was legal. Sharp little silver studs were placed in a pattern around the breasts and the crotch which was, Julian pointed out, zipped shut – 'at least for the moment,' she laughed wickedly. High, sharp-heeled boots completed the outfit, and Julian did indeed look fearsome, and when Clarissa saw her pull out a long coiled whip from the back of the cupboard she turned once again for the door until Julian stopped her.

'Tonight,' she said with authority, cracking the whip with a snap, 'this is just for show. Tonight, Rissa, my dear,' Julian promised with a grin, 'I will be a mere spectator, your humble tourguide, and this whip will not touch another's flesh, I swear.'

'I thought you said you wanted to score,' Clarissa said suspiciously, eyeing the whip nervously.

'Only if you do, my love.' Julian's grin became positively satanic. At Clarissa's rapid shake of her head, though, she dropped the whip and the devilish look and came forward to tap Clarissa gently on the arm. 'Just kidding, love. Now, let's get you dressed,' she said, suddenly very business-like. She indicated Clarissa's clothes with her head. 'Strip.' At her friend's blank stare, Julian smiled gently and added, 'It's OK. I won't look.'

'Don't be silly.' Clarissa was quick to appear casual and nonchalant, and indeed she wasn't at all distressed by the thought of being naked in front of Julian; on the contrary, they'd often seen each other's bodies when Clarissa spent the night. She wasn't at all sure, however, what Julian had in mind for her to wear. 'No leather, though, OK?'

Julian regarded her thoughtfully for a moment in silence, then threw something red and shiny at her which, Clarissa was relieved to discover, was nothing more exotic than a short PVC skirt and matching zipped, long-sleeved top. 'Go ahead, put them on,' Julian suggested impatiently.

Hesitantly, Clarissa stepped into the cool, slick skirt and tugged it up to her waist. 'Help, I can't breathe!' she gasped, barely managing to fasten the skirt at the back.

Julian laughed again and shook her head. 'Relax, it'll stretch,' she assured her friend.

Clarissa doubted it. She hoped she wouldn't sweat too much – she could just imagine how uncomfortable *that* would be. She studied the short length of the skirt in the mirror. It just reached to the tops of her toned, round thighs, the hem of the skirt hitting the fullest part of her leg. 'Damn, this thing is short, Jules,' Clarissa grunted out, tugging the skirt down. 'How does this fit *you*, with those stork-like legs of yours?'

Julian grinned even wider. 'Crotch-level!' she said proudly. She gestured towards the top. 'Come on, put this on.'

With the slim skirt already straining at her hips and thighs, Clarissa couldn't imagine how the top would fit. Though six inches shorter than her friend, she was also several inches wider in circumference, and she doubted whether this tight top would meet. To her alarm, she discovered that the top didn't actually zip. The zips were only for show; instead it was attached only by easily undone velcro fastenings. She looked inquiringly at Julian.

'Easy access,' her friend explained cheerfully. Clarissa snorted in disgust but there was nothing for it but to put the thing on. However, she immediately saw that the top was cut much too low to allow her to wear a bra; the turquoise lace of her undergarment could clearly be seen. With a shrug and an attempt at casual indifference, she calmly unhooked the offending item, dropped it negligently on the floor, then did up the top over her now-naked breasts. The cool, smooth PVC felt deliciously supple and sensuous against her bare skin, and Clarissa shivered a little in delight.

'Feels good, doesn't it?' Julian said knowingly, then

became brisk and business-like again. 'Now for the stockings.' She dangled a strappy black suspender belt seductively from her finger, but Clarissa shook her head at once. 'Oh no. Uh-uh. There's no room for anything else to be strapped on under this skirt.'

'Oh, all right.' With a show of resignation, Julian dropped the belt and instead produced a pair of lace-topped hold-ups. 'Better?' she asked sulkily.

With misgivings, Clarissa unrolled the stockings up over her legs. Yes, just as she'd guessed, the tops of the stockings left a gap an inch wide between their lace tops and the hem of her skirt, but she knew she had no choice. 'They'll just have to do,' she grudgingly announced, then pulled on the low-heeled ankle boots she'd been wearing earlier that day.

'Ready?' Julian asked, adding the last of her black kohl liner around her eyes. She looked over at her friend, winked and said, 'OK, I think we're definitely ready now.' She joined Clarissa who was peering nervously at herself in the mirror, and the two women stared at their reflections, Julian in her fearsome leather and Clarissa in her shiny PVC. They stared in silence for a moment, and then Julian tugged at her friend's short red skirt. 'Come on,' she said. 'You drive.'

It was a standing joke between them: Julian continued to fail her driving test with shaming regularity, and Clarissa liked to feel in control anyway, so she was glad to have the excuse to be the designated driver. As she shook out her keys from her ridiculously tiny bag, she followed Julian out of the flat, feeling tremors in her belly, whether from anxiety or excitement, she couldn't be sure. Perhaps it was both.

Chapter Nine

When they arrived at the club it was already after eleven. Clarissa had driven past the Glory Box once or twice in the daylight but now, seeing it at night, she was a little taken aback by its eerie and sinister appearance. Situated on the outskirts of the town, in a somewhat rough neighbourhood, the club was housed in a large stone building which was rumoured to have once been a church, though Clarissa thought the story was more for effect than for veracity's sake. There was a tattoo parlour upstairs, denoted by a hanging black sign, and it was evidently still open, Clarissa assumed this was to accommodate any new customers, spontaneously inspired to imitate the artistic flesh on continuous display at the club.

As Clarissa made her way inside next to her friend, she clutched at Julian's arm – being sure to avoid the one that carried the whip – and whispered urgently, 'Don't leave me.'

Julian patted her shoulder comfortingly in response. 'Don't worry,' she replied. 'I won't.'

Once inside, however, Clarissa was relieved to discover that in the outer part, at least, the Glory Box resembled nothing more ominous than a busy, lively bar. The outer room was brightly lit, people were dancing to the cheery pop music burbling out from the impressively loud sound system, and the large oakwood bar was flanked by apparently normal women and men, though many were wearing costumes to outrank Julian's in weirdness. There were, of course, lots of leather, studs and flesh, but there were also feathers, devils' horns and tails, half-masks, vampire capes, and even one woman incongruously dressed in a full-length blue silk taffeta ballgown. Julian gently directed Clarissa's astonished gaze away from a heavily tattooed bald man wearing a showgirl's costume from the 1920s, and deftly pinned a blinking red badge on to the shoulder of Clarissa's PVC top.

Clarissa looked down in annoyance. 'More red?' she frowned, twisting the badge up to look at it. 'It just doesn't go with my hair.'

Julian laughed and explained, 'Red, baby, means "no". Your badge tells people you're not here to play, only to have a look round. Strictly a tourist and off-limits to others.' Attempting to appear terribly casual, Julian then made as if to pin a green badge on to herself.

'What are you doing?' Clarissa cried out in alarm, and leant forward as though to rip the thing off. 'Uh-uh. Absolutely not. You are unavailable here too. I am *not* going to lose you in this crowd just so that you can go and – and whip somebody or something!'

'Please?' Julian whined, clutching her badge tightly in her hand. 'Or at least can I wear a yellow one? One that says I *might* be available?'

'No,' Clarissa said firmly. She prised the green badge out of Julian's hand, reached for a red one from the basket on the bar, then paused in indecision. Where was there room to pin it on Julian's outfit? Gingerly she positioned it on the strap at Julian's shoulder, then sprang the catch and pinned it on.

'There,' she said, stepping back hastily. 'Let's go and get a drink.'

Sipping at her Sex on the Beach – one of the more tamely named cocktails on offer – Clarissa followed Julian as she slowly made her way through the crowd, stopping here and there to greet lovers and friends and always politely remembering to introduce Clarissa, who tried not to look embarrassed or shocked as she smiled gravely back at Julian's odd collection of friends, some of whom Clarissa had met briefly before at the King's Head. Within a few minutes and on to her second cocktail, Clarissa began to relax. Despite the clothes the club members wore, she soon discovered that they were, for the most part, warm, friendly people who obviously sensed her nervousness and strove to put her at her ease. Some even made jokes about their appearance, some of the queens camping it up for her benefit, encouraging her to laugh with them as they good-humouredly paraded themselves before her. Most of the people here were wearing flashing green badges, it was true, proclaiming their availability, but they were respectful and courteous to Clarissa, whose red badge now seemed to her almost a silly, unnecessary encumbrance. With her drink in her hand and Julian protectively by her side, Clarissa felt entirely comfortable, and she found she was enjoying herself immensely. Last night with Lawrence and Nick seemed a million miles away, as did Graham with his stuffy corporate demands and his ugly threats of exposure. In fact, as Clarissa moved through the swaying, dancing crowd who were bumping and grinding energetically to the music, she actually found herself eyeing up a few men, enticed by the appealing contrast of the hardness of their leather and the vulnerability of the bare flesh strategically exposed in compelling and unpredictable places: the muscle of the upper arm, a triangle view of the back, a bare patch of upper thigh.

Clarissa was barely managing to stop herself from staring overtly at one particularly sexy black man, his ebony beauty enhanced by his simple white vest and Levi's jeans, when Julian elbowed her sharply in the side. 'Come on,' she ordered sternly, pulling Clarissa away. 'Stop drooling.'

'Where are we going?' Clarissa was reluctant to leave the cheery outer bar with its boy-band music and flashing disco lights. 'Can't we stay and dance a little?'

'We can come back later,' Julian urged, pulling hard at

Clarissa's PVC-sleeved arm. Clarissa cast a longing, backwards glance at the attractive young man, just in time to see him kiss a horned red devil rather passionately on the mouth, then shrugged and followed Julian out. She quickly found herself in a long, narrow, mirrored corridor; the bar's music had grown fainter and fainter until there was only an eerie silence, and the two women went round a corner until they came upon a harsh wooden door, studded with nails and adorned by a big black ring made of metal.

Julian banged the ring loudly against the door. Clarissa could hear the sound of keys jangling on the opposite side and she moved closer to Julian, who maddeningly backed away to stand behind her short friend. 'Where are we?' Clarissa whispered nervously.

'The dungeon,' Julian whispered back with a macabre laugh, and Clarissa went rigid as the door was slowly pulled open. She was greeted by a monstrously big bald man with rolls of fat round his huge neck and multiple piercings in his ears, nose and eyebrows; he was dressed in a peculiar leather tunic that reached to his bare hairy knees and looked like it was straight out of Roman times, right down to the sword in a scabbard at his waist.

The man stared at Clarissa menacingly, his eyes boring meanly into her face for a moment. Clarissa quailed under those cruel, brutal eyes, half-expecting him to bark out a 'Hark! Who goes there?' before she turned tail and ran. Amazingly, however, the man's eyes shifted to Julian, who had hung behind a bit but who now stepped forward with an evil glint in her eyes.

The man's face suddenly lit up like Trafalgar Square; his face was wreathed in smiles as he inexplicably sank to his knees at Julian's feet. 'Mistress!' he cried, bending forward to kiss her booted foot.

With a frightening lash of her whip, Julian kicked the man aside, still slobbering at her heel, and gestured for Clarissa to move forward. 'Away slave!' she cried out imperiously, and the 'slave' – or bouncer, Clarissa surmised – scrambled hastily away from Julian's boot, then rose rapidly to his feet with an agility one wouldn't have thought possible, considering his vast size.

Now Clarissa really was frightened; she scuttled behind her friend, anxiously trying to hide, but with an amused snort Julian pushed her forward and guided her down the narrow wooden steps. They weren't kidding when they called this place an underground club, Clarissa muttered grimly to herself, concentrating on gripping the cold metal rail for support as she descended the rickety staircase. She finally came to the bottom and just stood for a moment looking round, her mouth dropping open in astonishment.

'Behold the dungeon!' Julian intoned dramatically.

And what a dungeon it was. Clarissa stared in disbelief, half-consciously repeating to herself a stanza from Dante's *Inferno*, a text which seemed uniquely suited to this place.

The huge, cavernous room – if room it could be called – did indeed look medieval. Darkly lit, with a high vaulted ceiling, no windows that Clarissa could see, and sconces set far back in the recesses of the stone walls, the place was filled with people manacled to walls, tied on to revolving wheels, bent over double atop strange wood-and-leather contraptions, and attached precariously to nets affixed to scaffolds. The air was pumping with the discordant rhythm of some rock music, but even above the erratic bass line Clarissa could hear the wails and groans as whips cracked, leather creaked and machinery turned.

Leaving Julian's protective side for the moment, Clarissa went forward into the dungeon, making a close inspection of the place, determined to begin at one end and slowly make her way to the other end of the room. The nearer she got to the pairings and groups she saw around her, the clearer it was becoming that the wails and groans were of pleasure, not pain, though it was a strange kind of pleasure and one she couldn't ever imagine herself enjoying.

Clarissa paused at the corner, staring at a woman bent double over a low vaulting horse, her hands and feet bound to the four legs that supported it; she was completely clothed in a frilly Victorian petticoat except for her bottom, where her drawers had been pulled down to her knees to expose the round pink globes of her buttocks. A caped man strode back and forth before her, his polished black boots clicking loudly on the floor as he tested the strength and flexibility of a thin birch cane.

Clarissa turned inquiringly to Julian. 'Will they mind me coming over to have a look at them?' she asked worriedly, unwilling to intrude on others' private moments of pleasure, no matter how peculiarly wrought.

Julian shook her head with a smile. 'Not at all. Quite the opposite, really.' She gestured towards the room with a wide sweep of her arm. 'The whole point about these folks doing their thing here is exactly that it *is* in the open, it *is* in public. They *want* you to look at them, they want you to watch them get off: part of the pleasure is being seen.' Julian thought for a moment, then shrugged. 'I don't know: it's as if having someone else watch them makes what they're doing seem more *real* to them.'

Clarissa thought about her experience of the night before, about how having Lawrence and Nick watching her made her pleasure all the more intense, and she nodded her head in agreement. If her eyes upon the participants here could deepen and intensify their pleasure in the same way, she was more than happy to oblige. She stepped closer. Indeed, though neither the woman nor the man appeared to look in her direction, or even to notice her at all, she saw that their actions became that much more exaggerated, their movements more pronounced, as though they were deliberately trying to attract her attention. The woman writhed against her constraints more forcibly, which only resulted in inching her drawers further down her legs, while the man straightened up his shoulders and stomped loudly on the floor.

'You see,' Julian indicated with the handle of her whip, 'part of the appeal of this place is its drama, its sense of theatre as well as ritual; these people are making a scene. They're not quite like actors, of course, because what they experience is real, but part of the atmosphere of the dungeon is all about *performance*. What we do here is set apart from the everyday world – ' Clarissa couldn't help

154

but notice that all-inclusive 'we' ' – and everyone here wants everyone else to see them as special, as each acting out their own private fantasy inside the public arena. Besides,' she added carefully, watching Clarissa's reaction, 'being out in the open makes it safe. There are witnesses around to make sure that nothing gets too ... um ... shall we say, out of hand. This is a very controlled environment: no one can get carried away. There are too many people watching. Nothing happens here that the participants don't want to happen, and having all these people around makes sure of that, protects them in a way. Now watch.'

Clarissa had never heard Julian speak so eloquently before, nor with such insight, and she regarded her friend with new interest for a moment before turning back to the tableau laid out before her.

'Kiss the cane that will beat you,' the man said to the woman, loudly enough for Clarissa to hear. He came over to lay the birch rod against the woman's mouth. 'Show the cane that you desire its kiss; show the world your willingness to submit.'

Obediently – indeed, eagerly – the woman pressed her lips to the cane, imprinting it with the lipstick red of her kiss before laying her head down against the hard leather of the horse, closing her eyes and quietly drawing in her breath.

Crack! went the cane, and Clarissa nearly jumped an inch off the ground at the startling loudness of the noise – who would have thought that such a whippity-thin stick would make that kind of sound? She peered in amazement at the woman's behind. And who would have thought that a little thing like the birch could leave such a painfully raised and red mark? Clarissa held her breath and winced as the man raised his arm to strike again, watching through scrunched-up eyes as the woman bucked and writhed against her bonds, crying out, 'No more! Please! No more!'

'Why doesn't he stop?' Clarissa hissed angrily at Julian, about to stop the man herself. 'She said "no", didn't she?'

Julian shook her head and laid a warning hand on Clarissa's arm. 'Just wait,' she said in a low voice.

155

Again the man raised his arm to strike, and this time Clarissa winced even harder as she saw the man carefully aim for that tender part of the woman's thighs directly below the buttocks. Yet she couldn't tear her eyes away; as much as it hurt her to watch, and as much pain as the woman seemed to suffer, there was yet something about this classic tableau of dominance and submission that Clarissa found perversely fascinating to watch. Again and again the woman cried out, and again and again the man struck, sometimes on her buttocks, sometimes on her thighs, and once or twice aiming directly at her sex itself. He was sweating now, really going at it; he'd slipped out of the cape to roll up the sleeves of his fine lawn shirt tucked into tuxedo trousers, pools of his perspiration staining the expensive cotton of his shirt, marking it with his exertions. The woman, however, seemed to be thrusting herself towards the cane that beat her, rather than twisting away from it. Indeed, when Clarissa leant a little forward to get a closer look at that gleaming pink mound, she actually saw traces of clear sticky fluid running down and darkening the frilly white flounces of the woman's Victorian drawers. Clearly she seemed to enjoy this, and clearly it seemed to be turning her on, and Clarissa was now beginning to learn that there might be a peculiar kind of pleasure in pain for some, that the very linguistic dichotomy between 'pleasure' and 'pain' might not hold. She was beginning to muse over this thought while watching the birch land on the particularly sensitive crease between the buttocks when the woman gave one loud, high-pitched wail as though in orgasm, then raised her head and howled out 'Green!' The man then abruptly dropped the cane on the ground; the beating had suddenly stopped.

Puzzled, but dimly beginning to understand, Clarissa turned towards Julian and asked, 'Green . . .?'

Julian nodded towards the couple, the man now kneeling behind the bound woman and tenderly kissing the welts his cane had so cruelly raised.

'You're allowed to say "no" in the context of the game without meaning the role-playing to stop,' Julian

156

explained, watching the man gently caress the reddened and marked behind. 'Saying "no" and having it ignored is all part of the fun; it teaches the slave self-control and endurance. There's also something awfully thrilling about having a select part of your anatomy singled out for such attention and, believe it or not, devotion. You see, Clarissa,' Julian said slowly, as though thinking this through for herself, 'a scene of this kind, or head-trip or mind-game or whatever you want to call it, is all about *desire*. The slave feels the total focus of the master's attention: he wants her so badly he'll do anything to show her how much, even hurt her. The slave's pain is proof of how much the master wants her. What he's doing is showing his desire for her.'

Clarissa turned to Julian in disgust. 'That's ridiculous,' she snorted dismissively. 'How absolutely horrible. I don't buy it for a minute.'

'Don't go condemning other people's fantasies just because you don't understand them, Clarissa,' Julian admonished her solemnly, then shrugged and added, 'besides, when you've decided you've had enough and you need to call it quits, you call out a pre-arranged word that's entirely neutral, but you both understand the code. There are still ways to say no and to mean it. You see,' Julian continued earnestly, obviously keen for Clarissa to understand, 'the relationship between the master and slave, or whatever you want to call them, is like a contract: both parties use this kind of role-playing to build up their trust in each other. It actually *enlarges* relationships,' Julian said, looking directly at her friend, then she laughed. 'Maybe you should try it with your young stud.' She laughed again at Clarissa's shudder and horrified expression, then nudged her in the direction of the couple. 'You might even have your chance now,' she murmured quietly.

Clarissa turned. The woman was kissing the rod again, presumably thanking it for the pleasure it had given her, but the man was staring intently at Clarissa. When the woman gave a sigh and laid her head back down, eyes closed in bliss, the man gestured with the cane towards

Clarissa, and the invitation in his eyes was unmistakable: perhaps she would like to try it herself?

When she widened her eyes and shook her head in horror, pointing frantically at her flashing red badge, the man merely threw back his head and bellowed with laughter, then looked back at Clarissa, smiled gallantly under his pencil-thin moustache, clicked his heels and bowed. At his howl the woman opened her eyes and smiled dreamily at Clarissa, then closed her eyes in bliss again, arching her back a little and mewling with pleasure.

Clarissa turned back to Julian. 'I don't know,' she said, wrinkling her nose in distaste. 'It all seems so *humiliating*, so, so . . . *violent.*'

'No, it's not!' Julian countered quickly, anxious to set Clarissa right. 'Don't you see? – it's got nothing to do with violence at all. It *is* about pain, yes, but it's also about trust, like I said, and role-playing and ritual and scene. These women don't want to be beaten or raped in the outside world! They don't want *real* force, non-consensual sex; they don't want to be coerced into participating in someone *else's* violent fantasies. They're interested in learning to control their bodies and their responses, and they find it liberating to revert back to childhood helplessness, but it's all carefully controlled by mutual consent – otherwise they wouldn't be allowed in here.'

'But why does it always have to be women being beaten by men?' Clarissa argued. 'Aren't women disempowered enough in the real world? It all seems so stereotyped, such a cliché!'

Julian smiled. 'Let's go look at something else,' she suggested. She guided Clarissa along a little until they arrived at a niche in the wall with open-worked wall-high wooden brackets set around it. Inside the niche a man was attached to a huge wooden wheel, the kind that perhaps once drew water, his hands and ankles spread out so he looked like a human X. He was naked save for a pathetically small skin pouch over his genitals, perhaps suede, perhaps moleskin, held in place with a string around his waist. The wheel was slowly spinning round, the man along with it, and Clarissa worried that it would stop with him pointing head-downwards, resulting in such a rush of blood he might pass out. Such fears were laid to rest, however, when the wheel came to a stop with the man upright so that he could look his tormentor in the eyes. She was a big, tall, beautifully black-skinned woman in jewel-coloured African dress, her hair in a hundred different braids studded with beads and streaming down her back. Her dress was brief, leaving the woman's powerfully muscled, smooth, coffee-coloured arms and legs bare and her bulges and curves sharply outlined. She turned to wave cheerily at Julian, obviously knowing her well, and eyed the whip speculatively. 'May I . . .?' she asked politely, dropping her small crop on the floor and gesturing towards the whip. With a smile Julian handed it over while Clarissa noted with interest the man's sudden sharp intake of breath, whether from fear or desire, Clarissa couldn't tell. She stood well back, watching while the woman took careful aim, drew back the whip, then let it lash out, striking against the man's chest.

Clarissa gasped in horror at the huge welt that rose up across his breast, imagining how painful that welt must feel. She gazed in outrage at the woman, who merrily returned her look, then drew Clarissa's eyes down to the man's crotch, his prick now straining and jutting at the tight skin pouch. With infinite skill and expertise, the woman drew the whip lovingly across the man's belly and slid the end of it under his pouch, deftly making a loop of the lash and catching the string of the pouch in the middle. With a swift flick of her wrist she pulled on the whip, the string snapped apart and the pouch fell at the man's feet, revealing his proudly erect penis in all its reddened and distended glory. Carefully the woman twined the whip around his cock, catching it in the leather embrace, and gently tugged upwards, the man's cock now completely enclosed in leather coils. She masturbated his cock in this way for a few moments, gripping it in the leather and pulling the whip upwards, then with a twist she pulled the whip free, releasing the man's prick. He gasped with shock and moaned out in desperation, eager for more stimulation. Clarissa watched while the man opened his mouth and wailed, 'Please, mistress!' but the woman struck him smartly against the chest again and barked out, 'You are not to speak, slave!' She then handed the whip back to Julian with a smile of thanks, and rearranged her features into an expression of severity. She fitted a scary-looking black rubber mask over the man's face with slits for the eyes and nose, but no mouth through which he could speak. Clarissa couldn't imagine how terrifying the interior of that mask must be: heavy, shrouded, enclosed, leaving the victim feeling yet more vulnerable, the covering up of the face making the nakedness of the body seem that much more evident. The man apparently, however, felt nothing but pleasure, for his erection seemed to gain in length and breadth, pulsating madly, with a drop of clear juice trembling ecstatically at the head. Clarissa stared at this man, wondering what it was about this particular scenario that aroused him so, being strapped naked to a revolving wheel, a heavy rubber mask over his head while a big black woman struck him repeatedly with a whip. Clarissa shrugged her shoulders, muttered quietly to herself, 'Well, whatever rocks your world,' then turned to Julian.

'Can we try something else?' she asked.

Julian thrust the whip at her. 'Here, try this,' she offered.

Clarissa took a step back, not sure of Julian's intent. 'I'm not about to whip anyone . . .' she began, but Julian cut her off with a laugh.

'No, my dear, I don't think you're quite ready for that,' she said cheerily, urging the whip into Clarissa's hand. 'But maybe you'd like to try a stroke or two, just to see how it feels?'

Uncertainly Clarissa reached out and took hold of the whip. She fingered the handle meditatively: it felt heavy and smooth, with grooves worn into the thick base from the fingers that had wrapped themselves round it. The handle was warm from Julian's hand and fitted naturally into Clarissa's palm; it felt, in fact, almost as though she was holding a man's cock, and she couldn't help but cup her hand and rub it up and down the handle a few times as if by instinct. She then aimed the whip at the wall and, while Julian looked on in amusement, awkwardly flicked her wrist at the stone. The whip was heavy, far heavier than she'd expected, and did nothing more than slap limply at the floor. Hastily Clarissa dropped the whip and turned sheepishly back to Julian.

'I don't really think this is my thing,' she said apologetically.

Julian merely laughed. 'No, you're way too vanilla for this scene, I think,' she smiled, and guided Clarissa away from the wheel where the woman was now reaching behind to roughly thrust the handle of the crop between the bound man's buttocks. *Ouch!* thought Clarissa to herself as she followed Julian further into the room, imagining the thrust of that crop into her own anus, still tender from the night before.

She was about to follow Julian over to what she thought must be the Love Chair, occupied by a shrieking woman being devilishly paddled by another woman, when she saw something out of the corner of her eye that made her pause. She walked over to a puzzlingly compelling tableau in the middle of the dungeon, Julian following inquiringly behind, and stood off to one side so she couldn't be seen. Clarissa's attention had been caught by the sight of a grey-haired man bent double over a low wooden trestle that obscured his face, his head hanging down by his hands on one side, his trousers pulled down to reveal a large pink bottom on the other. The woman behind him was energetically spanking his behind with some kind of instrument, Clarissa couldn't see what, while chastising him about something in a voice which Clarissa couldn't quite place. She seemed oddly familiar somehow, though Clarissa was pretty certain she'd never met this woman before. She was clad in classic dominatrix gear: a black mask across the top half of her face, conical breasts atop a black leather-and-metal corset, fishnet stockings gartered up over her plump white thighs, and fetishistic black patent leather boots with cruelly pointed toes and impossibly high heels. Her dark hair was pulled into a top knot from which swung a long ponytail, and her arms and hands were gloved up to the elbows.

Clarissa wasn't quite sure exactly what it was about this particular scenario which drew her so sharply, so she crept a little closer, near enough to hear what the woman was calling out as she whacked at the man's bottom with what Clarissa now saw was a long-handled silver-backed hairbrush.

'And *this* is for writing that slimy, whiny reference for that perfectly awful student, Melissa Dodwell!' Thwack! 'And *this* is for giving a first-class degree to Melissa Dodwell when you know perfectly well she only deserved a second!' Thwack! 'And *this* is for admitting to lusting after Melissa Dodwell, just because she's young, blonde and beautiful!' Thwack thwack thwack! 'Do you have anything to say for yourself?' Thwack!

'No, mistress, I mean yes, mistress,' the quite red-bottomed man panted out. 'I am sorry, mistress. I didn't mean to, mistress!'

'You have been a *very* naughty boy, haven't you? Say you've been a naughty boy!' And the woman aimed a particularly painful-looking smack directly at the poor man's scrotum, hanging sadly down under his flabby loose buttocks.

That voice! Could it be ... Monica Talbot? Clarissa sidled up even closer and peered intently at the woman. Good god, it was she! At close range Clarissa heard her addressing him as Warburton. She scurried away to the bar at the far end of the dungeon lest Monica should spot her ogling. Julian followed in hot pursuit, catching up with Clarissa as she ordered the first thing that came to mind, a double Come Shot, without even bothering to ask what was in it.

'Clarissa? Do you know Mistress Monica?' asked Julian worriedly as Clarissa downed her drink in three thirsty gulps, then held out her glass for more.

'Know her? I *work* with her!' Clarissa choked out, a piece

of ice lodged in her throat. 'And Warburton – he was my boss – before he was fired!'

Frantically Julian clapped a hand over Clarissa's mouth. 'Hush! Don't say it so loud! No one here is supposed to say any names! Anonymity is key!' Her eyes blazed intently into Clarissa's, who suddenly burst out laughing, guffawing so hard she nearly snorted her drink out through her nose.

So it all made sense now. So *that's* why Monica had such a funny look on her face when Clarissa had called Warburton a 'lecherous old bugger'. And no wonder Monica had looked after Nick with such shameless lust all over her face. So the poor old bat did have a sex life after all. Then another thought occurred to Clarissa, one so astonishing she nearly dashed back to Monica to ask her herself. Was *that* why she had been so interested in the sight of Nick's retreating backside yesterday in her office? (Unbelievable! Had that only been yesterday?) Did Monica want to smack Nick's tight, athletic bottom, which must seem a real treat after Warburton's large paunchy one? Clarissa hurriedly drained the rest of her drink, feeling distinctly light headed. This place seemed to be getting to her now. She looked round her intently, absorbing the images of women tied to the wall, men bent over trestles, women kissing women, men penetrating each other's mouths and anuses, and various people of indeterminate gender being constrained and contorted above, below or alongside strange-looking machinery. All around there was naked flesh, intricate tattoos, piercings of cocks, nipples, labia and scrotums; the more Clarissa studied the world of the dungeon, the more limited and tame her own sexual history seemed to her ... and the more Julian seemed an integral part of this dimly lit, subterranean and unfathomably other world.

Clarissa turned now to Julian, a sudden light blazing in her eyes. She gestured towards Julian's flashing red badge. 'Take it off,' she told her friend shortly, swallowing down the rest of her drink. 'Take off your red badge.'

Julian paused, staring. 'Are you sure, Ris? I'm happy just to stay with you – '

'Take it off, Julian,' Clarissa said again, even more brusquely this time. The surprised look on her friend's face suddenly softened her. 'Yes, I'm sure, Jules,' she said more quietly. 'I think you've baby-sat me long enough. Besides,' she suddenly blushed, unsure of how to say what she felt. 'Besides, I want to . . .'

'What is it, Clarissa?' Julian prodded her gently. 'What is it you want to do?'

'I want . . . I want to watch you,' Clarissa whispered in embarrassment, hanging her head away from her friend.

Julian stared at her for a moment, then smiled. 'You want to watch me with a woman?' she asked, her eyes alight with black fire. 'Are you sure about this?'

Clarissa turned to look her in the face. 'I'm sure,' she said bravely, then reached out a warning hand. 'But please, Julian,' she begged, knowing her friend would understand. 'No pain, OK?'

Julian regarded Clarissa for a moment in silence, then nodded. 'OK,' she said finally. 'No pain.' She positioned Clarissa firmly on the stool. 'You wait here for a moment.'

Clarissa watched while Julian went off into the crowd, melting in amongst all the other leather and skin until she was momentarily lost from view. Clarissa then spied her leaning seductively against a wall, talking earnestly and rapidly to another dark-haired woman – almost a Julian look-alike, Clarissa mused to herself, staring at the stranger. She was tall and slim like Julian, with cropped black hair and a nose ring, but this woman was dressed a little more conventionally in a sheer stretchy white top pulled off her shoulders and ending at her midriff, and a short leopard-print skirt, with black mid-calf boots on her bare legs. Clarissa saw Julian laugh and whisper something in her ear, stroking the woman's black hair before reaching into the other woman's bag and looking inquiringly within. Whatever she saw there seemed to satisfy her, for she said something loudly and laughed again, then gestured for Clarissa to join them.

A little nervously Clarissa made her way over and smiled numbly at the woman, who appeared quite friendly and at her ease. Julian introduced her as Christie, then said to Clarissa, as matter of fact as though discussing her occupation, 'Christie's into bondage.'

'Oh, I see,' Clarissa said as politely as possible. She stared at the woman, wondering if this was the same Christie Julian had talked about before, the one who had been tickled by the man with his feather, and decided that it was. She was now very curious indeed to see how she interacted with Julian.

'I see the Love Chair is free,' announced Julian, gesturing towards that piece of furniture. 'Perhaps you'd like to come with us?' she offered to Clarissa, adding, 'Maybe you'd like to see the chair in action?'

Clarissa couldn't help but notice that Christie was trembling a little – with delight, she assumed – as they approached the chair. Clarissa inspected it carefully. It was indeed as Julian had described: loaded with complicated movable parts and restraints. She hung back and watched as Christie seated herself in the chair, closing her eyes in rapture as Julian slid down her top so her small round breasts were completely exposed and pushed up her skirt to reveal to the world that Christie wore no underwear.

'Ready?' Julian asked expectantly. At Christie's breathless nod, she raised the woman's hands above her head and fastened them in place with a click of the cuffs, then carefully spread out her legs, anchoring her feet in the restraints at the bottom. Clarissa took a good long look at Julian's friend, her clothing rolled up into a band around her waist, the rest of her completely naked except for her boots, her hands positioned above her head, her legs wide apart. Already Clarissa could see the telltale wetness beginning to seep out from between the rapidly unfurling lips, and she could see by Christie's shut-eyed expression that she was rapt with anticipation.

Clarissa felt her own inner juices begin to heat and flow; she was becoming tingingly aroused by the scenario being played out before her. She tried to ignore it, hoping it would go away, not wanting to embarrass herself in front of Julian, who merely glanced at Clarissa once and grinned before turning her attention fully to Christie.

Once the woman was strapped securely into place, Julian reached into Christie's bag to take out whatever had caused her such excitement. Clarissa's eyes widened in horror when she saw it. It was a strap-on dildo, something she'd never seen before, but its use and identity were immediately apparent even to the unschooled eye. It was of monstrous proportions, shiny black and made out of some kind of durable plastic, she supposed, attached to a panel of material with straps to fit around the waist. Despite her horror at its size, Clarissa felt her own vaginal lips beginning to moisten and swell at the sight, and she found herself swallowing repeatedly as she waited to see what would happen next.

'Open your eyes, Christie,' Julian was saying softly, dangling the thing before her friend's face. 'Open your eyes and take a good look at what I'm going to put inside you.'

Christie opened her eyes and let out a low moan. Now this really is play-acting, Clarissa thought to herself sharply, despite her rising excitement. Of course the woman knows what it looks like! It was in her bag, after all!

Christie, however, now seemed completely caught up in the game because she looked at the artificial phallus before her with longing and surprise, and she began to writhe against her bonds as though she were trying to lunge herself at it.

'Now, now,' Julian admonished her teasingly, slowly drawing the tip of the dildo down Christie's nose and rubbing it gently along the lines of her mouth. 'I want you to taste this big cock,' she whispered as Christie's mouth opened helplessly and her tongue crept out to lick along its length. 'I want you to make this thing really wet and slippery so it'll just slide right on up that juicy pink pussy of yours.'

Clarissa had certainly never heard Julian talk like this

before, never seen her so overtly sexual and domineering before, and she began to whimper a little herself with frustrated desire as Christie drew the thick plastic cock into her mouth and groaned out loud as Julian began to slide it in and out, Christie's saliva running out of her mouth and down the sides of her chin as the dildo filled her mouth completely.

'That's right, baby, suck on it hard now,' Julian was crooning, the fingers of her free hand trailing up Christie's thigh and settling between her legs to stroke at her open, wet sex. 'I can feel you starting to cream,' she whispered, her fingers tugging and spreading out Christie's moist labia. Christie whimpered and moaned even louder, her lips working steadily at the big black dildo lodged between them. 'You really want this right in here, don't you?' Julian was saying, moving aside a little so Clarissa could get a good look at the curly black thatch now soaked with dew and the entrance to the hidden tunnel that was gaping widely. 'You're very wet now, Christie, aren't you?' Julian whispered, easing two of her fingers inside that engorged, liquid sex and beginning to push them in and out. 'You're all open and ready for what it is I'm going to give you.'

With that she swiftly withdrew the dildo from Christie's open, gasping mouth and removed her fingers from her sex. Julian then fastened the dildo at her studded crotch and wound the straps between her legs and around her waist, then gripped the handles of the chair and leant over Christie, positioning herself at the ready. 'Now,' she whispered in Christie's ear, but loudly enough for Clarissa to hear, and then she pushed forward with her hips as Clarissa watched in fascination. The long black dildo disappeared into the hidden depths of Christie's vagina before slowly emerging back into view, coated with the richly scented fluids of Christie's obvious pleasure. Julian drew in her breath, then plunged again, her black leather-clad frame nearly obscuring the bound woman from sight: she was leaning nearly completely over her, her legs between Christie's bare ones, her hands wrapped around the arms of the chair, her head bent down over Christie's

167

shoulder as she withdrew the cock, pausing to note its shiny slick surface so wet with Christie's juice. She then arched her hips forward again, sending the dildo straight up inside the other woman's vagina. While Christie gasped and screamed and moaned, Julian was shut-eyed and grim-faced, reminding Clarissa startlingly of Nick, who was also always so silent in his pleasure apart from the occasional husky intake of breath. Clarissa wondered what it was that Julian was feeling as she pushed that cock in and out; was the base of the dildo rubbing against her clitoris through the heavy sheath of leather at her crotch? Was Julian feeling direct clitoral stimulation herself as she ploughed deeply within Christie's spasming sex? Was that why she seemed to be intently pursuing her own womanly pleasure even as she gave such obvious pleasure to Christie? Or was she imagining that she was a man, feeling what a man felt, imagining that this piece of plastic was really her own flesh, that it was her own penis probing the satiny depths of Christie's greedy vagina?

Clarissa had no way of knowing and doubted she'd ever ask. She simply stood and watched in breathless awe as Julian thrust with the cock again and again while Christie twisted and writhed against her bonds, apparently working herself into a frenzy.

While Julian worked the dildo deeper and deeper into Christie's sex, swivelling her hips and grinding her crotch against the other woman's, Christie howled and screeched and moaned, her head whipping back and forth against the headrest of the Love Chair, her mound oozing juice, the plastic cock making little sucking noises as it plunged wetly into that soft, slippery sex. Christie continued to gasp and shriek, her mouth straining open, her eyes screwed shut, her bound hands spasmodically clenching and unclenching with every powerful thrust. She braced her feet harder against the cuffs that restrained them and arched her hips upward, offering herself even more fully to Julian's cock, and then seemed to wrench one final orgasm from the depths of her fluttering sex, screaming out ecstasy in a voice gone hoarse with her exertions. Eventually she ceased her writhings and screams and instead merely lay limply against the chair as Julian slowed her deep, hard thrusts and then finally came to a stop, sweating and panting a little.

Julian then turned her head to look at Clarissa while still leaning against Christie; Clarissa stood open mouthed, her own sex fluttering wildly between her legs though her throat had gone completely dry. Christie looked completely spent, her head thrown back, her eyes closed and a little smile playing tiredly around the corners of her mouth. Clarissa decided she had seen enough here and it was time to leave; she didn't want to intrude on anyone else's pleasure here tonight, no matter how public it was; she was desperate now to go out and find her own. She came closer to Julian and whispered to her softly, unwilling to disturb the two women, 'I'm going now.'

Julian merely smiled gently at her and mouthed out the words, 'So long,' before closing her eyes and resting her head against Christie's long neck.

Clarissa turned and walked away, slowly ascending the narrow stairs, smiling quietly at the big bald bouncer, no longer so scary, still at the door. She walked along the silent mirrored corridor and into the front disco bar where couples slow-danced together under muted blue lights. Clarissa dropped her badge back into its basket on the bar and walked outside into the cool night air, grateful for the breeze sweeping along her flushed cheeks. She had only one thought in her head now and that was to get to Nick, to see him tonight before he left the next day. She was desperate to see him, even more so than when her craving for him first began. She glanced at her watch. Three in the morning. Was it too late? Would he still be up? She didn't know, and she didn't care. She got into her car, started up the engine and sped off.

When Clarissa arrived at Nick's block of flats she immediately saw that lights were on, and she even thought she could hear music pouring out through the window. She sat in her car, clutching her steering wheel, suddenly indecisive. Should she go in? What if he didn't want to see her? Clarissa's insides chilled at the thought; she pictured him coolly turning on his heel and saying he was busy. She peered up at his window. Was Jessica up there? Well, there was only one way to find out: if she was brave enough to face the dungeon at the Glory Box, she was certainly brave enough to face Nick. Clarissa shouldered her courage, got out of the car and went up to knock on the door of Nick's flat.

Once at his door, Clarissa did not allow herself the luxury of hesitation but instead made herself knock firmly and sharply, wondering if she could be heard over the sound of the Who coming out clearly from within. She pounded again, frantic now that no one would hear, and was just contemplating the efficacy of kicking at the door when it suddenly opened and Clarissa nearly stumbled and fell inside.

She found herself gazing into a young stranger's eyes, blonde, beautiful, and definitely male. 'Is Nick here?' she asked as coolly as she could, straining to see over the stranger's shoulder into the crowded living room.

'Who are you?' the boy asked her rudely, studying her shiny red suit and panting, nearly exposed bosom.

'None of your business,' she answered back as rudely as he. 'Is Nick here?' she repeated a little more loudly, determined not to be intimidated.

The boy shrugged and stepped back, leaving the door only slightly open. 'Nick! For you!' he called out over his shoulder.

Clarissa closed her eyes in joy. He was home! Then fear clutched at her heart. She half-expected to see him emerge from the depths of his bedroom, eyes smoky with sex, stripped to the waist and grasping a near-naked girl at his side. She could certainly hear female voices, she thought perhaps she saw a glimpse of Jessica's blonde hair, and she was pretty damn sure that wasn't a joss stick she was smelling.

'Who is it?' she heard Nick call out gruffly. At the sound

of his voice, so desperately longed for, she nearly melted, clinging to the door for support. She didn't hear the muffled reply, but suddenly the door swung wide open and there he was, dazzling Clarissa with his potent male beauty. His reddish-brown hair was flipped negligently over his forehead, his strong jaw was stubbled and unshaven, his jeans were ripped and his shirt half-unbuttoned but she didn't care; Clarissa was instead aroused anew by his seductive, erotic power.

When Nick recognised his visitor, which seemed to take him a minute, a slow smile spread over his face, and he gripped her wrists and held them away from her, stepping back to take in her somewhat outlandish appearance.

'Well, Clarissa,' he drawled out, 'this is a nice surprise.' He then cocked his head at her. 'And what *are* you wearing?'

'Come outside with me,' she whispered, reaching up to his face and twisting her wrist so his hand was locked in hers. She pulled him easily out of the door and down the stairs after her while he laughed at her evident haste.

'Whoa,' he said, slowing to a stop when they reached the chill night air outside. 'What is this? We're having a party up there, you know. I can't just leave.'

'A party?' she asked tremulously, unable to keep the dismay out of her voice. 'And you didn't invite me?'

'Hey, come on, Clarissa, it's cold out here,' Nick said uncomfortably, gazing down at her. When he saw her evident distress he said more gently, 'They're all university people, you know. You wouldn't have liked it. Besides,' he added appeasingly, 'you're coming with me to my cousin's party in three weeks' time, remember?' When she finally nodded back at him, he ran his finger along the swell of her bosom, outlined by the low cut of her top. 'Hey, I like this, but what's with the outfit? Where were you tonight?'

'Never mind, Nick,' Clarissa said softly, backing herself up against the cold stone wall of his building and pulling him along with her. 'I just wanted to see you. This won't take a minute.' She reached up to pull his mouth down to hers, to kiss him. She had to have him, and she had to have

171

him now. 'I want you, Nick,' Clarissa whispered huskily, snaking one leg round his thigh, and handing him a condom. 'I need to feel you inside me right now.'

'Didn't you get enough of this last night?' Nick uttered a low laugh, then pressed her body back into the cold stone of the wall. In one swift move he thrust up her skirt and grasped her panties between his hands, ripping them apart and sending the remnants sailing over his shoulder. He released himself rom his jeans, then tore open the condom wrapper and eased the rubber sheath over his cock before hoisting Clarissa up against the wall and wrapping her legs securely round his hips. Clarissa was already well wet and ready for him, and she cried out with lust as she felt him position himself at the entrance to her hotly eager sex. Without another word she reached down to guide him inside her; whereas usually she liked to keep her eyes open and watch his face while they moved, tonight she simply closed her eyes and leant forward into his neck while Nick pressed her back into the side of the building. Nick then placed his hands for support on the wall and drove himself hard and fast inside her, barely moving out of her with each withdrawal yet seeming to move higher and further up inside with every thrust of his cock. Clarissa clung on to Nick's firm, hard shoulders, digging her nails into him and feeling the rough stone chafing against her bare skin where her top rode up to expose her naked back. Nick then stopped moving for a moment and leant Clarissa back against the wall, balancing her precariously on his hips and thighs while his big hands gripped the sides of her top and ripped it open, baring her naked breasts to the world – how he knew it was fastened with Velcro, she would never know. He lowered his head and just stared at her breasts for a moment, handling them and squeezing them together, admiring their full creaminess before bending his head to run his mouth hungrily over her nipples, drawing her breast into his mouth and sucking on it while she ground herself against his groin, his cock temporarily motionless inside her. When at last she couldn't stand it any more she slid her breast out of his mouth and whimpered out urgently, 'Come on, Nick, now. I need to feel you moving inside me now.'

And so Nick leant himself into her, bracing his hands against the wall and rocking her body with his as he thrust ever harder and deeper within her. This was no black plastic dildo moving within her. This was hot, pumping flesh, the heat of Nick's passion causing the blood to pound inside her as his cock arced and reared against the sheathing embrace of her molten interior walls. They were moving together now, their hips clashing against each other, belly slapping against belly, the base of Nick's cock agitating into ecstasy Clarissa's protruding clitoral nub. Just when Clarissa was about to scream out loud with the pleasure of her climax, regardless of who could hear her, she dimly felt his hand come up behind her head to cradle it gently in his palm, protecting her scalp from further abrasion where it banged against the wall. Nick then used his flexed knuckles to support Clarissa's head and prevent it from slamming against the stone as she howled out her pleasure to the wind, the orgasm seeming to sear all through her body, joining with Nick's as he released himself in her quivering, contracting vagina. They held on to each other tightly as each other's heartbeat slowly returned to normal, their sharp ragged breaths gradually becoming more regular, the perspiration drying on their bodies as the chill of the wind blew over them.

'Whew,' Clarissa blew out as Nick gently lowered her to the ground, and she stumbled a little, still dizzy from the intensity of her orgasm. 'Thanks for that,' she said lightly, trying to laugh off the effects of their passion as though to deny the depth of emotions which still raged throughout her pulsating body.

Nick said nothing, only looking slightly away from her as he quickly refastened his jeans and buttoned up his shirt which had become completely unfastened during their wild ride against the wall. He then raised his eyes to look at her. 'OK?' he asked cryptically, lifting his brows as though questioning Clarissa about something, but when she didn't respond, he simply shrugged and headed back towards the stairs to his flat.

'Wait!' she called out after him, confused by his unfriendly silence. 'Where are you going?'

He turned to her. 'Back to the party,' he said simply, as though that should be obvious.

She stared at him a moment, unsure of what to say. 'Oh. OK,' were the inspired words that came to her lips. Then, more sure of herself, 'So I will see you in a couple of weeks, right?'

He came back to her then, smiling a little as he reached out to touch her tousled red curls. 'Right. I'll drop in when I'm back and give you the details about the party.'

He turned to go again but she grabbed his hand and tugged on it. 'Nick?' she asked, smiling at him a bit worriedly. 'Aren't you going to kiss me goodbye?'

He bent down to her then, his mouth finding hers, his tongue sweeping inside as his hands wrapped themselves around her body, holding her close to him. He kissed her for a long, full moment, then slowly released her as though reluctant to let her go. He looked her in the face for a moment, smiling softly at her, then tousled her hair again before turning back to the stairs. 'Be well, Clarissa,' he called out to her over his shoulder.

'Come back soon, Nick,' she called back softly, but loudly enough for him to hear. He didn't turn back, only nodded his head, then ran lightly up the stairs and was gone from view.

Chapter Ten

The following three weeks passed very slowly indeed for Clarissa. At the start of the break she briefly debated flying back to the States for an impromptu visit, then quickly rejected the idea, determined to plough through her pile of work instead. As homesick as she was, and as appealing as the idea was of spending time with her family and friends, she knew that her time would be much better spent where she was, in chilly England. Although Clarissa had been living in England for over five years, once she'd finished her doctoral dissertation she'd contemplated moving back home to the American Northeast. However, when she had been offered a job at her university, it had naturally evolved that England would remain her home. She still thought longingly at times about returning to live in the States, but such thoughts had receded since her affair began with Nick, and nostalgic images of America no longer floated so tantalisingly before her. Since meeting Nick, Clarissa had felt more rooted to England than ever; at times it seemed as though she couldn't even imagine being the same person once their affair was over. Nicholas St Clair remained a powerful incentive for Clarissa to remain exactly where she was; even these three weeks without him seemed to stretch into an eternity.

She was certainly kept busy, however; the proofs of her

book had finally arrived, her editor having given it the all clear, and the book's distribution date was set for the end of May, several days before the term ended and the week before Clarissa's annual review before the university board. Just in time for the vice-chancellor to buy a copy of my book and pick out all the dirty parts, she thought to herself with amusement. Clarissa was proud of her work, and she was hopeful that it would be a successful cross-over book, appealing to academic and non-academic readers alike, similar to Susan Faludi's *Backlash*. In order to secure her position at the university she needed a solid achievement in research, and she fervently hoped that her book on the erotic was it.

So, in between correcting the proofs, grading students' essays and finally sending out some long-delayed proposals for conference papers and publishing contracts, Clarissa was kept very busy indeed. She was also extremely grateful that she had a few weeks' grace before she had to face Monica Talbot at work; how she was going to look 'mistress' in the eye without giggling was a problem she had to work on. Clarissa was fairly confident she hadn't been spotted by Monica at the club, which could only work in her favour; she certainly didn't want Monica to think that she, Clarissa, was a dominatrix-in-training.

Clarissa had also been given a lot of time to speculate on exactly what had transpired that had caused Warburton to be 'sent down': she certainly couldn't imagine that the whiny, red-bottomed man she'd seen at the dungeon was capable of gross sexual misdemeanour with an undergraduate. For all she knew, it might well have been nothing more sinister than a misconstrued suggestion, a certain impropriety of gesture or word. Although Clarissa vehemently opposed the naked exploitation of power and the insidious violation of true harassment, such as the exchange of sex for high marks, she also understood that sometimes a relatively innocent remark could be mistakenly interpreted as something more threatening. It was certainly entirely possible that something completely consensual had passed between Warburton and his student;

he was, after all, still fairly distinguished looking, for those who found the father figure appealing, and certainly his standing within the academic community could carry some aphrodisiacal appeal to an impressionable young woman. Nevertheless, Warburton's contract had obviously been terminated because his relationship with his student, no matter how consensual, was evidently still outside the bounds of accepted professorial behaviour. Clarissa shivered. If that was the case, then her own position was precarious indeed; if the university were willing to fire a head of department for some slight sexual impropriety with a student, then one discreet but well-placed word from Graham to one of any number of people in power could be enough to discredit Clarissa entirely and cause her to lose her job in an instant, possibly her entire career.

Clarissa squared her shoulders where she sat at her desk, drumming her Montblanc pen on a stack of students' essays. Well, she simply was not going to be bullied into taking up with Graham again, no matter what he threatened. It was her word against his, and everyone knew he was Clarissa's ex-boyfriend; he'd certainly have cause for petty grievances once their relationship had broken up. Besides, Clarissa thought, reaching for comfort where she could, no one has any proof about me and Nick; no one else has seen us together. She tried to talk herself out of her paranoid fantasies, convincing herself there was no way Graham would stoop so low as to spread rumours about her unprofessional conduct as a way to get back at her for not coming to the races.

In fact, when Graham rang the day before she was due to go, she refused to pick up the telephone, recognising his ring as if by instinct and passively sitting by and allowing the answering machine to record his call. He left a brief, tense message reminding Clarissa to meet him at work, not even bothering to apologise for not picking her up but blithely assuming that she would be cowed into giving in to his demands. He expected her to present herself at the appointed time at his office to be transported to the company's hospitality tent by limousine along with all the other higher-ups and their dates. Clarissa shuddered. No way, she declared to herself firmly. There's no way he's forcing me into a hat and gloves in order to stand around and watch some smelly horses while he tries to impress his boss and his smarmy clients with his docile little girlfriend. No, Clarissa decided, if Graham couldn't be bothered to pick her up at his house and escort her, or even wait until she answered her phone to talk to her directly, she couldn't be bothered to remind him that she wasn't going. That'll teach him to make threats and act aggressively, Clarissa thought smugly to herself. Let him stew over *that* at his bloody company do! She refused to believe that Graham would actually make good his threats, despite all her fabricated scenarios; he had always been too much of a gentleman in the past for Clarissa to think he would actually do anything quite so underhanded and nasty.

And that took care of Graham. No, the real person Clarissa had been dreading facing after her night at the Glory Box was, of course, Julian. Clarissa was a little shy and nervous about stopping by the King's Head the day after her visit to the dungeon for she felt she had now seen a side Julian usually kept hidden from her. Though Julian frequently talked about her sexual exploits, her typically hyperbolic verbosity usually made them sound more like details from a fantasy novel than experiences in real life. However, after having seen Julian actually perform, as it were – and at her own request – Clarissa felt a little unsure about how she could preserve their friendship without hampering it with the embarrassment of unlooked-for intimacy. This was exactly why she generally tried to avoid sex with her friends, Clarissa had thought crossly to herself as she'd prepared to assemble her courage and steel herself for the inevitable moment of meeting her friend face to face. Intimacy can so often ruin a friendship, as paradoxical as that may sound, and after having seen Julian having sex, as it were, with Christie, Clarissa now felt almost as though she'd slept with Julian herself.

However, she need not have worried. Clarissa should

have trusted Julian's grace and good nature to put her at her ease when she finally braved her way into the King's Head the night after the club.

'Hello there, love, and what'll it be tonight?' Julian called out in her usual cocky, cheery manner, without a trace of unease or awkwardness.

'Whisky,' mumbled Clarissa, sliding on to her stool unable to meet her friend's eye.

'What, not a Come Shot?' Julian asked with a smile. Relieved that Julian wasn't going to try to pretend that nothing had happened but was ready to address the issue head-on, Clarissa raised her eyes, looked Julian full in the face and burst out laughing. All right, so she'd seen Julian thrusting a big black strap-on dildo up some woman's vagina – so what? They were still mates after all. Clarissa accepted her drink as easily as she ever had and conversationally enquired, 'Did you and Christie make it home OK last night?'

'Oh, we made it at home all right,' Julian laughed, winking lewdly, and Clarissa totally relaxed, the last vestiges of embarrassment completely dissolved.

So that left Nick. Of course Clarissa hadn't heard from him the whole time he was gone, nor had she expected to, but he was continually in her thoughts; she'd even driven past his flat a few times, ashamed of herself for her schoolgirl obsession and terrified someone might recognise her, but of course she didn't see him. So here it was, the day of the party, a few hours before she was due at the faculty dinner, and the day she was supposed to be at the Grand National. Of course Graham would have noticed her absence by now, and was probably fuming over it, but so far he hadn't called to see why she hadn't appeared ... and still no word from Nick. Had he forgotten he was supposed to see her that night? That he was supposed to drop in on her that day? Had he even made it back at all?

As if to seek an answer, Clarissa gazed round the walls of her study, actually a back bedroom she'd had converted during her recent redecorating mania. She'd had the walls painted a soothing 'crème de cocoa' which complemented

179

the rich chocolate tones of her antique oak desk, polished to a glossy reflecting sheen. Clarissa had installed an expensive new CD system, and the lush, trilling beauty of Beethoven's Seventh Symphony floated out over the speakers, the poignant sweetness of the second movement washing over her and seeming to mimic her longing for Nick. Frustrated, she sifted through her pile of marked essays, retrieving Nick's paper from the bottom for, as always, it was the first one she'd graded. Clarissa reread his essay on Byron yet again, as though searching in his writing for coded references to herself that would indicate Nick's state of mind and his feelings about their affair. Her eyes traced again Nick's lines about desire and loss, about erotic arousal and lack of fulfilment, and it did begin to seem as if she were reading about herself, as if Nick had captured her mood in his writing and had actually composed an essay about *her*, Clarissa, and not Byron at all. Clarissa read again Nick's words about the impossibility of satisfying desire and about the Romantic search for unity, perennially doomed, in Byron's case, to despair, when the doorbell suddenly sounded, causing Clarissa nearly to jump out of her chair.

Still clutching Nick's essay in her hand, she raced downstairs to answer the door, suddenly fearful that it might be Graham outside. She drew back the bolt and opened the door to reveal Nick himself standing on her front step.

'Sorry about the bell,' he said casually, leaning against the door, 'but I don't think you heard me knock.' Even from outside he could hear Beethoven from upstairs, for he grinned and indicated the music with his finger. 'Bit noisy up there, eh?' he laughed softly, then straightened up. 'Can I come in?'

'Oh – of course.' Clarissa finally prodded herself out of her surprise at seeing him and moved aside to let Nick in. Even when she knew to expect him, it always came as a little shock to her when he actually showed up; as she had no way of tracking his movements, Clarissa always thought of Nick as a shadow, a phantom, who would suddenly appear and then vanish as mysteriously and spontaneously as when he'd arrived.

She peered at him now, his essay still clutched in her hand. 'How did you get here?' she asked curiously, watching while Nick fingered the open book on her sofa. She frequently wondered how he got back and forth to her house: he often said he'd walked, though it was over two miles each way, but it never seemed to bother him. Sometimes, like many of her students, he rode a bike.

'A friend dropped me off,' he said shortly, then glanced over at Clarissa and added, 'and she's picking me up again soon, so I really can't stay long.'

She? Clarissa thought acerbically to herself, but forced herself to say nothing. Instead she merely looked at Nick expectantly, waiting to see what he would say next.

'Hey, is that my essay?' he asked with a hint of eagerness, reaching for the rolled-up paper in her hand. They seldom ever spoke about class, both tending to treat it as something that existed outside their relationship, but today, apparently, Nick's curiosity got the better of him. Clarissa briefly thought about teasing him a little and withholding the paper from his grasp, then shrugged and decided that such games were for children. Instead she simply handed him his essay, watching while his eyes sped over her comments.

Suddenly the phone rang just as Beethoven ended, and without thinking, Clarissa picked it up.

'Hello?' she said, watching Nick smile at the upper second mark she'd awarded his essay.

'Clarissa?' Graham asked, and even on the telephone she could hear the tension in his voice. 'Is something the matter? Why aren't you here?'

Clarissa could guess that he was not alone, as she could hear voices in the background, and he was obviously suppressing his anger at the blatant way she had stood him up. Well, she'd told him she wasn't going, Clarissa fumed inwardly. Why hadn't he believed her?

'I told you I wouldn't be able to make it, Graham,' she

said as calmly as she could, watching Nick while he scanned her bookshelf, appearing not to be listening.

'Everyone is waiting for you,' Graham ground out, his voice low and menacing.

'Tough,' Clarissa replied crisply, tempted simply to bang down the phone. 'Just tell them I'm not coming.'

'Clarissa,' Graham began, patently struggling to gain control, 'I thought you understood that – '

But she cut him off. 'I said, I'm not coming!' she nearly shouted, and then abruptly hung up.

Nick turned to her, one eyebrow mockingly raised. 'Trouble?' he enquired, laying his essay down on her end-table.

'No,' she answered briskly, struggling to look relaxed. 'So where is this party?' she asked as lightly as possible, handing him her pen.

Nick scribbled down directions on the back of his essay. Puzzled, Clarissa stared at them. The address he had given her was far out of the town, almost in another county, and a good 30 minutes' drive from her house. 'This looks like it's way off the main road,' she mused aloud.

'The house is set pretty far back from the road, but you shouldn't miss it,' Nick told her with a mysterious grin, adding, 'There'll be a lot of cars and people – it's going to be a really great party. You'll have a good time, Clarissa, I promise.' He was looking at her intently, his hazel eyes staring into hers. She gazed up at him, Graham all but forgotten, and moved a little closer. 'I missed you, you know,' Nick murmured, bending over to lay his lips along her hair, but when she reached up to press her mouth against the base of his throat, he gently moved her away and straightened up. 'Not now, Rissa,' he told her, smiling a little at her eagerness. 'Save it for tonight.'

As if on cue, a horn sounded outside. Nick moved easily towards the door, his eyes still on Clarissa. 'Try not to be too late,' he said, reaching for the doorknob.

'About ten or so, I should think,' Clarissa said in response, still desperate to touch him but forcing herself to stand still. She watched while Nick turned and left her house, running lightly down her steps to the shapely low Porsche in her drive. Clarissa didn't want to appear to be snooping, so she shut the door quickly – too quickly, alas, to get a good look at the driver of the car. Then Nick was gone.

Clarissa spent the rest of the day marking essays and tidying up her house, nervously trying to avoid thinking about what Nick might be doing until the party. She was relieved, after all, that she had to go to this dinner first; it might help kill time. She chose her clothes carefully, knowing she'd be too anxious to get to Nick to return home for a quick change after the dinner. She hesitated over a black silk sheath – too funereal; a short scarlet suit – too flashy; and a tartan wool jumper dress – too casual, before finally deciding upon a conservatively cut but richly hued merino wool dress in a deep forest green, not a colour Clarissa would normally choose, but she'd been swayed by the fine wool fabric of the dress. The wool clung discreetly in all the right places but without looking tarty or cheap. She clasped a heavy black belt with a curiously shaped buckle around her hips and stood back to admire the view. Her curly red hair, stunningly set off by the green, was arranged in a tidy braid at the back, sheer black stockings flattered the muscles in her calves, and demure pearl earrings gleamed brightly in her ears. Clarissa had just blotted her muted bordeaux matte lipstick and stuffed the tube in her black evening bag when the downstairs doorbell rang. Fearing the worst, Clarissa slowly descended the stairs, squaring her shoulders and clenching her fists.

'You'd better have a bloody good explanation for this!' Graham shouted aloud as he rudely pushed past her and strode into the centre of her front sitting room. 'Where the hell were you?'

Clarissa stepped back and took a deep breath. 'Graham, I told you I wouldn't be able to make it,' she said steadily, trying to appear calm and in control, in obvious contrast to Graham. 'I thought I'd made myself clear.'

'How could you do this to me?' Graham cried out, ignoring Clarissa's reasoned response. 'Do you know how much you've humiliated me? What a fool I looked, standing there dateless while all the other men were paired up? Stood up by my own – my own...' He faltered and fell silent for a moment while Clarissa faced him in white-hot anger.

'Your own *what?*' she asked him coldly, astonished at his overbearing manner. 'I'm not your wife, I'm not your girlfriend, and at this point I'm not even your friend. I refuse to be paraded in front of your pompous boss and stuffy little clients like some guarantee of your big studly prowess just so you can – '

What on earth had she said? Graham advanced on her with so much rage in his face she shrank back for a moment, actually afraid he would strike her. Clarissa had no idea what it was she'd said that seemed to affect him so shockingly.

'What are you going to do, Graham, hit me?' she asked icily, regaining her ground. For indeed, Graham seemed to tower over her, fist raised as though aiming for a blow, but as Clarissa confronted him with no trace of fear or anxiety, he let his fist drop and then turned towards the door.

'We're not finished yet, you and I,' Graham said warningly, shaking a finger at her. 'This is not over yet.'

Clarissa watched wearily as he turned and left, slamming the door behind him so forcefully it shuddered on its shiny brass hinges. Clarissa then blinked her eyes and shook her head as she heard Graham's BMW speed away, its tyres screaming against the tarmac as he viciously ground his gears.

What the hell was that all about? Clarissa asked herself in amazement, then decided to shrug it off as she slid on her coat, choosing to leave the matter for the moment. There was nothing she could do about Graham now, she reasoned, so she might as well go on to this damned dinner and deal with the matter of Graham and his anger tomorrow, when he'd had some time to cool down.

Of course, when Clarissa arrived at the Senior Dining

Room 20 minutes later, the first person she saw was 'Mistress' Monica Talbot, evidently monopolising some wizened little man as she bore imposingly down on him. Probably boring the man to death, Clarissa thought to herself, then nearly giggled aloud, unless she wants to whip him first, of course! Happily, Monica didn't seem to suffer from the slightest trace of embarrassment as she briefly paused in her monologue to flap her fingers at Clarissa before resuming her verbal hold on her no-doubt reluctant audience. From Monica's casual and indifferent stance, Clarissa could only surmise that she hadn't been spotted after all in the Dungeon, and that Monica had no way of knowing that Clarissa had been a witness to her severe chastisement of poor Professor Warburton's pink bottom.

The speeches turned out to be just as dull as Clarissa had imagined, as did the new head of department, Professor Anderson, and Clarissa, scowling, wondered angrily again why the board couldn't have hired a woman. She looked around her; the English department was composed largely of men, ten of them to four women, and she happened to be wedged between the loquacious Bob Evans from media studies – what he was doing there, she didn't know – and, just as she'd feared, the local vicar who also served on the board of governors. Clarissa sighed and pushed her slimy salmon mousse around on her plate, only half-listening as Bob and the vicar enthusiastically compared local cricket and football scores. Clarissa sincerely hoped that she was scoring some points with the board by being seen at this hellishly tedious meal, and she was just about to contemplate manufacturing some excuse to leave when she heard something across the table that made her freeze.

'Yes, it is a shame about that recent scandal with Warburton and that Dodwell girl,' the Chaucer expert was remarking rather loudly to the English secretary. 'Fancy actually laying one's career on the line just because some nubile young thing happens to turn goggle eyes one's way!'

Goggle eyes? At *Warburton?* Clarissa was finding this gossipy exchange a little hard to believe, but she was dying to hear more, so she leant as far forward as she dared while tipping her head towards the vicar as though hanging on his every word.

'Yes, and they say the reason she left was to follow him to his new university,' the secretary giggled, helping herself to more wine. 'In fact, Warburton himself wrote her a recommendation so she could transfer to his college; I actually saw a copy because someone from their admissions wrote to ask us to verify what he'd said in his letter.'

'What some people will do for a first-class mark,' the Chaucer man replied, biting into his duck à l'orange with evident gastronomic delight.

'Oh no!' replied the secretary, her eyes wide and bright. 'Word has it that this is quite a romance; they've been seen around town together, and apparently she's signed up to take all his classes.'

Clarissa didn't believe a word of it. Warburton had to be in his 50s; while he might have some sort of kinky sexual appeal for a dominatrix such as Monica, what 21-year-old woman would find such a paunchy, grey-haired man such a turn-on that she would alter the course of her academic career as he had risked losing his? Clarissa could, perhaps, concede that it was possible for a young woman to become infatuated with her university lecturer, but actually to transfer universities just so she could be near him was quite a serious undertaking indeed. Then again, Clarissa mused, she was hardly one to adjudicate in such matters, considering her own ill-advised extracurricular behaviour of late. Perhaps Warburton was just attending to all sides of his apparently perverse sexuality: he could play the distinguished, older father-figure type of lover to young Ms Dodwell while acting out his own infantile fantasies with the dominating Mistress Monica.

'Well, let's hope they keep it a little quieter this time, whatever their feelings,' the Chaucer expert nodded wisely, mopping up his gravy with his bread. 'True love or

186

sexual harassment: either of them's going to get you fired from *this* university.'

Clarissa sat chilled to the bone, her appetite gone, her hands beginning to shake. Certainly some tutors undoubtedly did exploit their relationships with students in dangerous and reprehensible ways, and many of these lecturers did deserve to have their positions terminated. However, Clarissa argued to herself, surely there must be some distinction between outright harassment and mutual consent? What if Graham actually did let drop that Clarissa had been seen kissing her student – and in her office, of all places? Clarissa had no doubt now that no one at the university would look kindly upon such an offence.

Then she thought to look at Monica, to see whether she had been listening to this tittle-tattle exchange. Monica appeared not to have heard, as she was merrily eating her duck, her elbow held out in that awkward, stilted manner Clarissa thought so frightfully English, her fork turned tine-side down as she delicately placed her food in her mouth. However, Clarissa thought she could detect a slight whitening of the knuckles around that fork, but she couldn't be sure that Monica had actually heard the conversation, as the head of administration was placed between her and the English secretary. One thing was certain: if Monica heard that Warburton's romance was making the rumour circuit at the university, the poor man's bottom was in for a very severe thwacking indeed.

The rest of the dinner dragged slowly on as Clarissa grew more and more tense, both with anxiety about the need to face down Graham once and for all, and with her increasing desire to turn her back on this stuffy professional duty and race over to the party where she could really have some fun. She sighed and rubbed her thighs together under the table, once again picturing Nick's tall, lean body as he'd stood in her living room earlier that day, and she could hardly suppress the grunt of relief that rose to her lips when the vice-chancellor finally took his seat after the suffocatingly dull final speech.

Without a word to anyone Clarissa dashed her chair

back against the wall and hurriedly reached for her coat, desperately trying to avoid eye contact with any colleagues on her way out. Too late – with a coy waggle of her fingers Monica flagged Clarissa down, and Clarissa had a moment of sheer panic at the thought that Monica might now want to refer, however obliquely, to what had transpired at the Glory Box. But no, she simply asked with a simpering flutter of her lashes, 'And what do you think of our Professor Anderson now, Clarissa?'

Clarissa never knew what plagiarised platitude she mumbled back in response, no doubt lifted from some comment made by someone else in her department that had lain dormant in the back of her brain. Regardless, Monica seemed satisfied, and so, finally liberated from this excrutiatingly dull dinner, Clarissa crammed herself into her car and drove away to the party at a recklessly high speed.

When Clarissa finally arrived at the location Nick had scrawled out for her, having taken several wrong turns along the way, she merely sat back in her car seat at first, staring open mouthed around her. Nick wasn't kidding when he'd said the house was set far back from the road: the gated circular drive, flanked by an impressive grey stone wall, extended at least half a mile around, enclosing a front garden so vast Clarissa imagined it must be several acres long. Yellow-flowered laburnum trees and hanging weeping willows were bordered by a profusion of riotously coloured flower beds, and there was even a sparkling fountain in the middle, with tinkling water cascading from a white stone mermaid in the centre. There were cars and people everywhere, and Clarissa had a little bit of difficulty at first finding a space large enough to accommodate her medium-sized Honda. When she'd finally managed to park, she stood nervously by the side of her car, wondering if she actually dared to go in.

The house itself was huge. It had more windows than she could count, bright lights, loud music and party revellers everywhere she looked. It was a balmy spring night, and people were obviously taking advantage of the unseasonably warm weather, for they were drinking and dancing under the stars, and Clarissa even noted a few shadowy couples embracing quietly in the gardens. She also noted that she was way under-dressed; a lot of the women were in mid-calf or full-length ballgowns, and many of the men were wearing dinner jackets complete with bow-ties and cumberbunds.

Clarissa even doubted whether Nick was actually inside; this didn't look like it was his kind of scene at all. Nevertheless, now that she was here she might as well try to find him, though how she'd be able to spot him amongst all the people, she had no idea.

Bravely she ascended the huge stone steps that led up to the double main doors complete with pillars at the top, then paused for a moment in indecision before forcing herself to pull one of them open. She was nearly knocked over by a young woman in a flouncy black dress drunkenly making her way outside with a handsome young man in tow, and as they made their way out of the door, Clarissa hurriedly slipped inside, anxious not to trip on the shiny wooden floor.

The first thing she did on entering the house was to flag down a passing waiter and grab a fluted glass of champagne. Sipping rapidly at her drink, Clarissa tried to look inconspicuous in her wool dress which she now saw as hopelessly dowdy and unfashionable compared to all the killingly elegant people she saw around her. The guests seemed to be a mix of many ages: there were stately silver-haired women escorted by devilishly handsome young men, couples in their 30s who looked frighteningly well-bred and aristocratic, and a large selection of attractive and well-dressed twenty-somethings, even, Clarissa suspected, several students from her university. She moved through the large, beautifully decorated rooms, gazing at the fabric-covered walls, brocaded furniture and important art, including masterly oil paintings of landscapes and people. Clarissa paused to stare at an impressive replica of the Eiffel Tower carved entirely out of ice which served as a bed for all manner of lobsters, prawns, oysters and caviar. She was tempted to fork out a few hearts of palm and black olives, her favourites, from one of the many tempting platters artfully arranged on the buffet table, but quickly decided against it, her stomach much too agitated to accommodate even the most delicate of foods. Instead she continued to move through the house, feeling increasingly surreal and completely out of place amongst the laughing, chatting crowd; Clarissa guessed there must be at least two hundred people at the party.

But where was Nick? Clarissa just could not imagine him feeling at home in this tastefully furnished mausoleum surrounded by monied guests in diamonds and silk, classical music softly piping from unseen speakers under the haughty gaze of forebears mounted on the walls. True, the further Clarissa moved into the party, the younger the crowd seemed to get; it appeared that most of the older guests had congregated in the outer rooms, and when Clarissa finally reached what must have been the inner library, all antique oak furniture and leather-bound books, there were only a few people gathered inside, not one of them over 21.

'Excuse me,' she cleared her throat nervously, unwilling to intrude on this obviously private gathering. A tall, pale, blond young man was seated within the recesses of one of the large leather chairs, a brandy snifter in one hand, a cigar in the other, and two giggling young women perched on the arms of the chair.

'Yes . . .?' he drawled, sucking thoughtfully on his cigar. 'Something I can help you with?'

'I'm looking for . . . for Nicholas St Clair,' Clarissa stammered, feeling uncomfortably out of place at this party. 'Is he around anywhere?'

The lad tipped back his head and blew a perfectly formed smoke ring at the ceiling. 'I expect you'll find him in one of the upstairs bedrooms,' he offered slowly, and to no one in particular. For some reason the two girls on the chair found this suggestion most amusing, for they began tittering and giggling so shrilly that Clarissa had to stop herself from marching over to smack their silly faces. Instead she merely nodded at the young man and started to make her way out of the door, but he called out after her, 'Excuse me, darling?'

She turned round, gritted her teeth and smiled demurely. 'Yes?'

'If you see one of those wandering minstrels outside, do send one in,' he said, sounding as though he'd been born to direct household staff. 'We're all frightfully dry in here.' He indicated his empty glass, then nearly disappeared from view as the two tittering girls bent their heads towards him, virtually obscuring him from sight as the three started whispering and giggling together.

Clarissa did not even bother to reply, just retraced her steps out to the main hallway and located the overwhelming mahogany spiral staircase that wound its way up to the first floor.

Once on the carpeted labyrinth of the upstairs corridor, Clarissa followed the hall along – like following the Yellow Brick Road, she thought grimly to herself – peeking curiously into sumptuously fitted rooms but seeing no one she knew. She was just about to curse roundly and give up, planning to find her car and get the hell out of there, when a tinkle of laughter from a nearby room arrested her attention, and Clarissa paused in front of an open doorway, having at last located the object of her search.

There was Nick, reclining casually on a pale pink-and-cream striped chaise longue, his head leaning on the armrest at one end, his booted feet hanging over the other side. He, at least, had quite obviously disdained to wear the black-tie dress that seemed to be ubiquitous among the guests: he was wearing his black leather jeans and a black button-down shirt, his only obvious concession to the formality of the occasion being an unexpectedly close shave.

Perched on a hassock near where Nick lay sat Lawrence Hoffman, suitably attired in a dress shirt and black trousers, his red cummerbund lying on the floor nearby and his red bow tie loosened around his neck. A cigar was clamped between his teeth and he was holding a champagne bottle in his hand from which he seemed to be freely imbibing. Between the two young men was a huge overstuffed sofa, also patterned in pale pink and cream, and sitting upright upon it was the beautiful blonde Jessica. Like Nick she was dressed far too casually for this party; she was barelegged and barefoot, wearing a short, sleeveless black clingy dress that zipped up the front and which accentuated the silvery sheen of her hair. Her dress was partially unzipped, revealing a hint of the creamy swell of her generous cleavage, and Clarissa found her eyes drawn to that temptingly shadowed divide. This was the first time she'd ever been able to get a good look at the girl, and she stared at the wide-set eyes, tipped-up nose, and full-lipped mouth painted a delicate shade of poppy. None of the three seemed to notice Clarissa at first; they seemed to be sharing some kind of intimate joke, for all were laughing away, until Nick finally raised his eyes to the door to see Clarissa silently standing there.

'Well, hello there,' he said smiling, but it wasn't an open, friendly smile; he looked as though Clarissa had interrupted something, and he wasn't going to tell her what it was. Then his face suddenly changed; he sat up and patted the cushion next to him invitingly, gesturing that she should enter the room. 'Come in, Clarissa,' he said warmly, adding, 'I was beginning to wonder where you'd been.'

Clarissa stepped hesitantly inside, quite unsure now whether she wanted to stay. Nick was smiling openly at her now, cocking his head at her in that slightly mocking way, while Lawrence merely puffed at his cigar and then took a swig out of the bottle, barely appearing to notice her. But it was at Jessica that Clarissa stared, unable to help herself: the cool beauty was regarding her with a kind of amused interest, as though she knew something about Clarissa, as though Clarissa wasn't quite a stranger to her. Something in the girl's face made Clarissa pause, but then she supposed that as she was already here, in this slightly surreal setting, she might as well advance further into it and see where the situation led.

'Come in and shut the door,' Nick called out as Clarissa continued to stand there motionless, but then she finally did just that, closing the door gently and moving into the centre of the room, hesitating over where to sit. This was obviously a private sitting room leading to a bedroom and bathroom beyond; she could see a little way into the slightly open door behind Nick, and she began to wonder exactly who Nick's mysterious cousin was.

'I believe you know Lawrence,' Nick was saying, only the slightest irony in his coolly modulated voice, 'and this,' he said, extending his hand towards the sofa, 'is Jessica.'

Clarissa nodded her head briefly in Jessica's direction, to which the young woman replied in an accent straight out of Sloane Square, 'It's nice to meet you finally, Clarissa. Nick has told me so much about you.'

Clarissa glanced at Nick, who merely smiled innocently and patted the seat again. 'Aren't you going to sit down?'

Glaring at him a little, Clarissa deliberately moved away from him and cautiously lowered herself into a wing-backed chair by the door, slightly out of the way of the cosy triangle formed by the other three, and then she leant back a little in her seat, wondering what was going to happen next.

'Drink?' Nick offered, reaching behind him and pulling out an unopened bottle of champagne from a silver ice bucket on the floor. Clarissa watched in silence as he expertly released the cork from the bottle and poured swiftly into an empty glass, not spilling a single drop. He rose and walked over to Clarissa, wordlessly handed her the glass, then sat back down on the chaise longue, his long body splayed out before him. Clarissa sipped nervously at her drink, the thick silence of the room thrumming inside her head, all sound seeming to have been absorbed by the plush nap of the carpet.

'So,' Nick began conversationally, lighting up a cigar of his own. What's with cigars in this place? Clarissa thought wildly to herself, wishing she'd brought along a pack of cigarettes. 'Are you having a good time so far?'

'It's a great party, Nick,' Clarissa replied casually,

impressed by the steady control she heard in her own voice. 'Am I going to get a chance to meet your cousin?'

'Cousin?' Nick repeated questioningly, while a loud snigger burst out from Lawrence. Nick turned to him and asked him pointedly, 'Do you know any cousin, Larry?'

By now Clarissa had decided that something really was up, and she did not feel like staying to find out what it was. She set her glass carefully down on the floor, rose to her feet and said firmly, 'OK, I've obviously interrupted something here, so I'm going to leave. Nick, I'll see you in class next week.' She was about to pick up her bag and march out of the door when Nick sprang guiltily to his feet and stopped her.

'Come on, Clarissa, I'm sorry,' he said, moving his tall body her way. 'Don't go. The thing is . . .' He paused, gazed briefly at the ceiling, then looked her in the face and said, 'There is no cousin. This is really my house.'

Blankly astonished, Clarissa could only stare at him for a moment, then murmured, 'Now I really do need that drink.' She picked up her glass, quickly drained it to the dregs, then held it out for more. 'Why didn't you tell me?' she cried out. 'What's with all the secrecy? Who are you really – and why do you live like such a poor student?' she added suspiciously, accepting her refilled glass.

Nick shrugged. 'I don't know. My mother is – ' he paused for the briefest of moments, then rapidly named one of the most famous and highest-placed women in the art world. She was a well-known philanthropist and frequently hosted benefits such as this to promote unknown talent; she was also rumoured to be one of the richest women in the county. In fact, looking around her now, Clarissa realised that she had actually seen photographs of some of the rooms in this house in the society pages of a few of the more upmarket glossy magazines.

'She's your *mother*?' Clarissa asked, still in shock, then indicated the room with a shaking hand. 'Yes, I can see why you might want to keep the truth about your ancestry a secret. This is some place.' She then asked anxiously, 'This isn't *your* room, is it?'

'Good god no!' Nick shouted out in laughter, as Jessica and Lawrence joined in. 'I don't, er, exactly have a room here. My stepfather and I . . . well, let's just say we don't get on together.' Nick grinned at her cockily and added, 'I don't hang around here very much. But my mother insisted on my coming tonight since she's hosting this reception for some bloody artist – ' Clarissa couldn't miss that sharp note of bitterness in his voice ' – and I didn't feel I could disappoint her, so here I am. And here you are as well,' he added slyly, eyeing her up and down.

'Is she here?' Clarissa asked curiously. 'I'd really like to meet her.'

Nick smiled in contempt. 'No, she and my *stepfather* – ' Clarissa winced at the sneer ' – left a little while ago for some world cruise.'

'They left the party?' Clarissa asked incredulously. 'What about all these people?'

Nick shrugged. 'They'll stay until the morning, then leave after breakfast. The staff will close the house and it'll be shut until my mother returns.' He suddenly stretched and yawned, then said dismissively, 'Let's not talk about them any more. Let's talk about something else.'

At the look on Nick's face Clarissa was instantly back on her guard. He was up to something, of that she was sure, but she couldn't guess what it was. Deciding to pre-empt him, she asked Nick abruptly, 'And how do you and Jessica know each other?'

Nick then turned his evil grin on the woman on the couch and said companionably, 'Oh, Jessica and I are old friends, aren't we, Jess?'

When Lawrence sniggered again Clarissa thought about leaving for good, and she wondered angrily at the transformation from his shy, embarrassed stance when she'd last seen him to this arrogant, obnoxious young man. At her cold stare, however, Lawrence dropped his eyes to the floor, refusing to return her look, and lit up a fresh cigar, fumbling with the lighter.

'In fact, we're all old friends here, aren't we?' asked Nick, leaning back expansively and folding his hands behind his head. 'You and I know each other quite well, don't we, 'Rissa?' he said smilingly, staring into her eyes, then indicated Lawrence with his head. 'And I know you know young Lawrence over here as well, don't you?' The wicked glint in his eye was unmistakable now as Nick gestured towards Jessica and concluded, 'But then you don't know our Jessica quite so well as we two do, do you, Clarissa?' He faced Jessica directly and said to her, 'Although I know that Clarissa has seen you before. Did you know that, Jess? Actually . . .' he paused for maximum effect, 'Clarissa's seen quite a lot of you.' He now smiled fully in Jessica's face, and Clarissa was forcibly reminded of that night she'd seen the two of them together, Nick ploughing Jessica's wide wet sex with his cock and his tongue, Jessica's naked body spread out and constrained on the bed. Suddenly the atmosphere in the room changed. Clarissa could feel her inner juices begin to gather among her blossoming vaginal folds, and she shifted a little uncomfortably in her chair. She was now not so sure that Jessica had not been aware of her presence in the room that night after all. The way Jessica and Nick were looking at each other now suddenly seemed very intimate: he was looking at her with almost the same intensity he had often turned on Clarissa.

Clarissa closed her eyes briefly against the searing pain of jealousy that twisted throughout her body as she watched Nick and Jessica eyeing each other and smiling: so this is the woman he knows so well, she thought to herself. He knew the way Jessica tasted, he was familiar with her smell and how she felt wrapped around his body; Jessica's mouth, breasts and sex were obviously well known to him, and now Clarissa wanted to know her too. She wanted to experience Jessica's body in the same way Nick did, she wanted to share in what he knew, she wanted to get inside his body, as it were, and feel what he felt when he touched Jessica – maybe that way she could finally reduce his hold over her. Clarissa thought now that perhaps she could dissolve some of Nick's potent mystery by discovering for herself how this woman felt to him. If she, Clarissa, knew what it was like to make love to Jessica the way Nick did, then maybe she wouldn't be jealous of her any more, maybe she could finally begin to let this thing go.

But she also wanted to experience Jessica as a woman would; she wanted to kiss and touch that woman's body in a way she had never wanted to before. Maybe because Nick had, or maybe just because it was time; she was ready to try it, body to body, sex to sex, woman to woman.

Clarissa rose and came to sit on the couch beside Jessica, a little uncertain of what exactly she was going to do, but willing to go along on impulse. She gazed enviously at Jessica's long, slim legs, comparing them with her own short, pale ones, and studied the difference between Jessica's large, round breasts and her own smaller, less full ones. Hesitantly Clarissa reached out a hand to run her fingers through that blonde hair, and at her touch Jessica closed her eyes and smiled dreamily, then opened them and looked Clarissa full in the face.

'You don't mind if I've watched you, do you, Jessica?' Clarissa murmured, not even surprised that Jessica didn't seem shocked by her sudden closeness. Perhaps this was what Nick had been planning after all, perhaps this was another one of his set-ups, for Clarissa to get close to Jessica, but Clarissa was now acting according to pure desire and she wasn't about to stop now, even if this was what Nick wanted.

'Such beautiful hair,' Clarissa whispered, sliding her fingers through the silvery fall. 'You know, Jessica,' she continued, murmuring even more softly now and moving a little closer to the girl, 'I've always been a little jealous of your relationship with Nick; I always knew about the two of you, and I've always wondered what it would be like to touch you the way Nick touches you.' She paused and withdrew her hand, as though waiting for permission. 'Do you mind if I touch you now?'

Jessica sighed and shook her head, looking into Clarissa's face once more and smiling gently before closing her eyes and leaning back a little, passively awaiting Clarissa's touch. Slowly, shyly, Clarissa grasped the zip of Jessica's dress and pulled it down a little, stopping just under her bra, having opened up her dress enough to reveal the large soft globes of Jessica's bosom. Hesitantly, still a little shy, Clarissa reached out her hand and laid it gently on the swell of Jessica's breast that rose so temptingly above the black cup of her bra. At the feel of Clarissa's fingers, Jessica let out a soft moan, then leant her head back against the sofa, arching up her neck as if to expose more of herself to the woman who touched her. Emboldened now, and having nearly forgotten her audience, Clarissa curved both hands round Jessica's breasts, marvelling at their fluidity and weight, slipping her fingers along the cleavage but not yet daring to stroke at her nipples. Instead she merely concentrated on familiarising herself with the feel of Jessica's breasts, gliding her hands over their smooth softness, sliding them along the full deep curves. She then passed one finger lightly over the outside of Jessica's bra, brushing over the pointed tips, then gradually worked her finger inside to seek out the puckered nub of Jessica's nipple. Clarissa closed her eyes for a moment and pressed her fingertip against that tightly raised bud, stroking the nipple with her finger, and then she bent her head to kiss Jessica's breasts.

As she opened her mouth to slide it along that delicately fragranced flesh, Clarissa opened her eyes to see the two young men silently watching her, her body leaning over Jessica's, Jessica's breast in her mouth. As though sensing their gaze and performing to it, Jessica raised her hands to her shoulders and slid down the straps of her bra, exposing the whole of her breasts, and then she placed her hands around Clarissa's head and gently guided her nipple into Clarissa's mouth. Clarissa sucked quietly on the hard brown tip, trying to memorise the feel of Jessica's nipple against her tongue. She drew in as much of the girl's breast as she could, feeling it fill her mouth completely, its soft warmth and weight seeming to vibrate a little as she sucked. Then she slowly withdrew it and just licked at the girl's nipples, moving from one to another while Jessica whimpered and sighed and moaned. And then Clarissa wanted to taste more.

She drew back and looked down at the girl, who opened her eyes and gazed at her. Then, with slow and exaggerated movements, Jessica pulled on the zip of her dress and eased it all the way downwards, revealing more and more of her glorious golden body. Clarissa watched in silence as the zip reached the bottom of the dress, then she reached forward to help Jessica release herself from it. She bent her head and breathed deeply of the girl's flowery scent, feeling the brush of warm skin against her hands while Jessica wriggled out of her dress, and then Clarissa reached behind the girl to release the hooks on her bra, dropping that on to the floor as well.

Jessica was now completely naked except for her sheer black lace underwear. She looked up at Clarissa, proudly displaying her body, inviting her gaze, offering up her beauty to Clarissa and to her male audience. She spread her legs a little and seductively arched up her back, and so Clarissa, with a brief glance at Nick, bent over the girl's body and once again took Jessica's naked breast into her mouth.

She continued to kiss those trembling cocoa-crested breasts for many minutes before sliding slowly to her knees and moving her mouth downwards, pausing to thrust her tongue into the deep well of Jessica's navel. She tasted of perfume and sweat there, and Clarissa ran her tongue around inside before continuing to move downward until she was sitting back on her heels on the floor, her head leaning against Jessica's thigh, gazing at that lace-covered mound. Finally she bent forward and pressed her open mouth against the rough scratch of lace, then with an upward glance caught Jessica's eyes with her own. Wordlessly the girl arched up her hips and Clarissa eased down her black lace panties, then pushed Jessica's legs wide apart and gazed at the shining pink vagina now completely exposed to her view.

At first she did nothing but stare, having never seen another woman's vagina so close up to her face before.

After tracing the folds and crevices with her eyes, Clarissa then used her fingers, running them up and down the plump pink lips so wet with juice, breathing in the intoxicating scent, studying the sight of the exposed clitoral nub, the inner set of lips, and the invitingly open entrance to the heart of Jessica's sex. Clarissa then placed her trembling fingers on those swollen outer lips and gently stroked, running her fingers up and down the pouting labia before spreading them wide apart. She bent her head forwards and dipped her tongue once into that rich musky wetness and then gently, slowly, hesitantly, she began to lick Jessica's melting, open vagina.

At the taste of the girl on her tongue, Clarissa felt her own sex swelling and softening, her own vulva responding to what her mouth was doing in the same way that Jessica's was. Her mouth, her sex, Jessica's sex all seemed to be joined together, all sharing in the same musky, sensual joy. As Clarissa slid her tongue over Jessica's satiny flesh, she shivered with delight, savouring the velvety wet richness that seemed to surround her. Clarissa was only dimly aware now of Lawrence and Nick looking on; instead she concentrated on the fluid delight of Jessica's sex in her mouth, her smell, her taste, her touch. As the girl panted and sighed above her, Clarissa drew back and inquiringly inserted her finger into the dewy entrance to the hidden tunnel, watching it closing around her finger as though trying to draw it in further. Clarissa worked her finger in and out of Jessica's rosy flesh, then withdrew it and inserted her tongue, pushing it in and out, feeling it sucked by the sex that she herself was sucking. Clarissa then raised her eyes over the glossy blonde fringe that bordered the mound which engulfed her tongue to see Nick's face bending over the girl, his eyes narrow and bright, his lips slightly parted; he had moved up out of his seat and was now standing by Jessica, intently watching the two women. When Clarissa saw his hand drop lightly on to Jessica's head, stroking her hair, she drove her tongue in further, feeling a moment of triumph as Jessica cried out in ecstasy. She then slid her hands up under Jessica's buttocks and pulled her closer to her mouth, working her tongue in deeper, her fingers playing at the entrance to Jessica's clenching anal passage.

As Jessica screamed and shrieked and shook, Clarissa closed her mouth round the sensitive shaft of her clitoris, running her tongue around the little round nub as she sucked, causing Jessica nearly to pitch herself off the sofa. Her face now completely buried in the other woman's sex, Clarissa was nonetheless able to look up and see Nick, his cheeks slightly flushed, his eyes riveted on Clarissa, his hand still on Jessica's head, stroking lightly at her hair. Clarissa wondered if he was feeling any of the spiked pangs of envy which had wracked her body when she'd watched him doing exactly this same thing with Jessica so many weeks before; as if to test him, she sucked harder on Jessica's clitoris, driving the girl into a virtual frenzy of orgasm. As Jessica bucked and rocked and writhed above her, Clarissa clamped her mouth even more firmly to her sex, closing her eyes now and concentrating on bringing Jessica to the fullest height of sexual satisfaction. At last the girl seemed fully spent, her gasps and moans fading to sighs, and she gently nudged Clarissa away, still leaning breathlessly against the couch.

Clarissa looked up to see Jessica smiling down at her as she touched the now-dishevelled red head in a gesture of affection. Clarissa then rose to her feet, looked Nick full in the face and slowly drew the back of her hand across her mouth. Then she turned on her heel, picked up her bag and walked out of the door.

Chapter Eleven

Clarissa woke early the next morning having slept deeply, dreaming technicolour dreams of rapidly opening roses, their blooming red petals unfurling in the heat of the sun, and of salty blue oceans, their undulating tides rising far upwards to crash rhythmically on the shore. She opened her eyes to the springtime sun streaming in through the half-shuttered blinds at her windows, then tasted the inside of her mouth, smiling voluptuously at her image in the mirror next to her bed. She stretched her body luxuriously, then ran her hands lasciviously over her round, warm breasts and down to the sleepy sweet dampness between her thighs. She pictured to herself Jessica's ripe, lush body, imagined she was again inhaling that deep musky wetness, could still taste the intoxicating marine-flavoured richness lingering in the recesses of her mouth. Clarissa felt somehow complete, more womanly than she had ever felt before, as though she'd been initiated into something that only a few select, brave women knew.

And then she thought of Graham. Graham! His angry, sneering face even momentarily eclipsed the image of Nick with which she usually awoke: Clarissa knew she simply had to get to Graham soon, now, and try to explain away her shocking rudeness in standing him up at the races before he did exactly as he'd threatened and phoned one of his friends at the university for a cosy little chat about a certain female lecturer's sexual impropriety with a student.

Clarissa glanced at the clock. 7:30. Graham habitually rose early, that she knew, whether to go for a run, read the paper or play some infernal ballistic missile computer game, so she would have a good chance of catching him at home. She showered hurriedly, oddly reluctant to wash away all traces of Jessica's pleasure from her hands, face and mouth, and then pulled on a loose pair of jeans and a comfortable turquoise cotton jumper. She was anxious to downplay her sexuality with Graham; he'd never liked it when her clothes had been too sexy, as he preferred her to look tasteful and elegant, which was Graham's definition of the sensual woman, though not necessarily hers. Well, she didn't look particularly sexy today, Clarissa thought to herself with a rueful smile, but she hoped she didn't look either too combative or too vulnerable.

With a rapid, nervous heartbeat, Clarissa ascended the stone steps to Graham's large Victorian house and gently pressed the doorbell, trying to make the ring sound as friendly as possible. There seemed to be no reply, so Clarissa pressed the bell again, a little less gently this time, as she tried to still her accelerated pulse. Still no reply, and now screamingly anxious to face Graham in person and get this over with once and for all, Clarissa was just about to pound on the door with her raised fist when suddenly the bolt was pulled back and she nearly fell inside.

'Clarissa!' Graham said, startled, and at first the two merely stared at each other, each waiting for the other to speak.

Clarissa was surprised to see that Graham looked as though she'd awakened him out of bed, for he was obviously naked beneath a hastily belted paisley silk dressing gown. His blond hair was rumpled and his eyes looked a little glazed, which was most unusual for him, as he was usually up and crisply dressed by this time, even on a Saturday. Clarissa was just about to open her mouth and say good morning when a voice from the back of the hall arrested her sudden speech.

'Graham? Is there someone at the door?'

Clarissa knew that voice, she was sure of it! It was marked by a distinct Scottish accent, its 'Rs' long and rolled, its vowels round and elongated, its rich baritone timbre decidedly, undoubtedly male. Then she knew – of course! The voice belonged to Glen, Graham's ... departmental manager! And the voice was most certainly coming from Graham's own bedroom.

Clarissa couldn't help herself uttering forth a triumphant little laugh, a knowing, mischievous smile curving her lipstick-bare lips.

'Well, now, Graham,' she began slowly, 'I think perhaps you've got some explaining to do.'

Graham looked at her helplessly and started to stammer out, 'Please, Clarissa, just let me have a – ' but she cut him off with a laugh, calling out into the hallway in a loud, clear voice, 'It's only me, Glen, Clarissa Cornwall – why don't you come out and say hello?'

A moment later Graham's immediate senior at his company came stumbling shamefacedly down the hall, clutching at a silk dressing gown knotted round his waist in a cut and colour to match Graham's.

'Hello, Clarissa, it's nice to see you,' he mumbled a bit red-faced, retying his belt and coming to stand close to Graham. When Graham moved away a little in obvious embarrassment, Glen edged in closer to the man who was obviously his lover and whispered out angrily, 'I told you we should have been open with her from the start!'

Clarissa came forward to smile gaily at the two of them as Graham cleared his throat a bit nervously and said as courteously as possible, 'Ahem – well, now, perhaps we'd all better sit down for a cup of coffee and a chat.'

'The hell with coffee!' Clarissa snorted out contemptuously, still unable to keep the laughter out of her voice. 'I say this calls for some exceptionally fine whisky – what about a bottle of that vintage Johnny Walker Black I know you keep a large stock of?'

'At nine in the morning ... ?' Graham started to mutter in astonishment, but one look at Clarissa's face sent him

204

scurrying away in the direction of his well-appointed liquor cabinet.

Once the three of them were seated on Graham's slippery leather sofa, each clutching their antique tumbler of Scotch, Clarissa took a long swallow of her drink and said easily, 'Now then, Graham, perhaps you'd like to apologise to me for your recent unpleasantness?'

Graham glanced quickly at Glen and said haltingly, 'Ah, yes, well, Clarissa, I've been meaning to tell you about this for some time, but I wasn't sure how to put it to you, um, discreetly . . .'

'What's to tell?' Clarissa cut in with a wicked grin. 'That your lover is a man? That he's your department manager? Did you think I'm so narrow minded that I would care?'

'Well now, Clarissa, I know of course that *you* might not be taken aback by all this,' Graham said stiffly, uncomfortably, 'but imagine my position – *our* position – at the company! Imagine our disgrace if anyone found out! You know how conservative the military industry is,' he said urgently, pleadingly, leaning forward towards Clarissa. But with an affectionate hand on his arm, Glen leant forward as well and cut in.

'What Graham means to say, Clarissa,' he said smoothly, 'is that he's very sorry for trying to bully you into appearing with him for the company's sake – ' he glanced frowningly at Graham ' – and he really didn't mean to cause you any distress with his big macho act.'

'You mean his ugly little scheme of blackmail?' Clarissa asked sweetly, settling back into her seat. Merrily her eyes caught Graham's and she said, 'Oh, I think I quite understand now. No wonder you were so desperate for me to accompany you to the theatre, the opera, and to your big company do – appearances must be kept up, I assume, at all costs!'

'I was never really going to tell anyone about you and your student,' Graham said miserably, still avoiding her gaze. 'I just didn't want to look awkward in front of the company. Some rumours have been circulating the office – ' here he looked over at Glen ' – and I just didn't think it was the right time to go public with our – ahem – relationship.'

'Well, *I* was all for telling you about it ages ago,' Glen said proudly, leaning companionably against Graham's arm. '*I'm* not ashamed of our relationship; I think that the world – and the company – ' here he grinned down at Graham ' – is ready to accept our affair.'

The world might be ready, but Clarissa rather doubted that Graham, with his public-school background and essentially conservative nature, was ready to proclaim to the world his erotic preference for men. Then a thought occurred to her.

'Did you two start this affair while Graham was still with me?' she asked, thankfully not in the least bit jealous, merely curious.

'No,' Glen said firmly, with a fond glance at Graham. 'Graham is far too loyal to cheat on someone, especially you, Clarissa, whom he's always greatly respected, despite his recent aggressiveness.' He turned to scowl at his lover before resuming, 'I don't want to speak for him, but I do think that his sexual awareness was a little late in coming; only after things had ended with you was he brave enough to give *us* a try.'

'I did try to tell you, Clarissa,' Graham said somewhat pathetically, refilling her glass from the bottle at his feet. 'But I just couldn't do it: for one thing, I didn't want you to think that you were in any way – um – displeasing to me.'

'Oh, really, Graham, let's not worry about that now,' Clarissa said pleasantly, feeling wonderfully warm and relaxed from the Scotch. Indeed, she wasn't in the least bit bothered by this revelation; now it all seemed to fit into place. Perhaps this was the reason why their relationship had seemed doomed from the start; perhaps Graham had really felt this way about Glen all the time, but had simply been too repressed to acknowledge it to anyone, least of all to himself. Besides, she reflected, sipping at her drink, she was hardly in a position to comment on anyone's sexual proclivities, given her own experimental behaviour the night before – though she didn't really think she'd tell Graham about her own particular epiphany, at least, not now.

'I'm just happy you've found someone who appreciates you as you deserve, Graham,' Clarissa said generously, polishing off the rest of her Scotch. She must be getting a bit drunk, she thought to herself a little dazedly; this whole scenario was actually beginning to turn her on. She looked consideringly at Graham and Glen, now relaxed and entwined on the couch, their arms round each other's shoulders, their bare legs rubbing together. They certainly seemed to be enjoying each other's company; in fact, if Clarissa was not downright mistaken, she actually thought she could spy the beginnings of an erection poking shyly out of the parting of Graham's robe.

'I hope I wasn't interrupting anything when I rang your bell so early,' Clarissa said suddenly, still furtively eyeing Graham's crotch.

The two men smiled quietly at each other, and Glen reached up to fondle Graham's hair. 'Well, actually . . .' he began with an embarrassed laugh, then his eyes were mischievously caught by Graham's.

'Oh, I *am* sorry,' Clarissa said apologetically, then gestured towards the two of them with a wave of her hand. 'By all means, carry on where you left off – go ahead and get back to whatever it was you were doing.'

The two lovers glanced uncertainly at each other, then at her. 'Clarissa, I really don't think that you – ' began Graham, but she broke in with another dismissive flap of her hand as she reached for the bottle of Scotch.

'Oh, come on, Graham, don't be so stuffy,' she grunted, generously topping up her drink. 'It's not like I've never seen your body before – though I *have* actually fantasised about *yours*, Glen,' she added with a wink at the now blushing Scotsman.

Graham stared at Clarissa, his mouth dropping open in astonishment. 'You can't be serious, Clarissa!' he spluttered, then took a deep drink of his Scotch. 'Glen and I 'prefer to keep things private between us, you know,' he said, looking decidedly ill at ease.

'Oh, why not?' she asked scornfully, rummaging in her bag for a cigarette. 'I remember having it away with you one night in my car while a bunch of my students were walking by,' she said slyly, locating her emergency ration of Silk Cut in the inside pocket. 'That little exhibitionist opportunity didn't seem to dampen your ardour at all.' Clarissa laughed wickedly and blew smoke up at the ceiling, ignoring Graham's outraged expression, whether in response to her casual reference to sex in her car or to the fact that she was smoking in his house, she didn't know or care. 'Lighten up, Graham,' Clarissa said now, absently tapping ashes on to his priceless Indian rug. 'I think you owe me a little something for being so nasty to me recently – and besides,' she added provocatively to Glen, 'I've always wanted to watch two men making love.' She then pointed directly to Graham's fully erect penis and said meaningfully, 'Besides, part of you at least thinks it's a good idea.'

Glen reached over a hand to stroke gently at Graham's rampant cock. 'I think the lady's right,' he said softly, swiftly untying Graham's sash with the fingers of his free hand. 'You've been so cruel and nasty to her lately; let's show her how kind and loving you can be.' And with that, Glen quickly lowered his head to Graham's cock and took the straining purple tip into his mouth, his face only inches away from Clarissa's knee.

Clarissa then moved over a little on the sofa to give the men more room, staring in fascination at her ex-boyfriend's cock slowly disappearing into his new lover's mouth. Graham looked as though he were in absolute ecstasy, his head thrown back against the sofa, his bared chest rising and falling with his deep, rasping breath, his small, stubby nipples prickling and erect, and his hands gripping Glen's head tightly. As Clarissa watched Glen's mouth working up and down the rosy, flushed length of Graham's cock, she felt a wild hot flush of her own sweeping up her body, igniting her sex, tightening her nipples and lighting hot fires in her cheeks. She shifted a little restlessly where she sat, staring avidly at Glen's long wide tongue as he sensuously ran it along the whole of Graham's shaft, then swirled it around the ridge under the glistening, swollen head. She could hear the little sucking noises Glen's mouth made each time it released its hold on Graham's penis, and she could nearly smell the aromatic, oddly clean scent of Graham's semen which she knew was hotly gathered in his balls, the taste of which she could easily remember herself.

Glen then suddenly took his mouth away from the stiff member, leaving it swaying helplessly in the air as though blindly seeking the warm haven that had abandoned it, and then he ran his mouth upwards over the blond mat of hair on Graham's chest to claim his mouth in a fierce, passionate kiss. Clarissa looked on in wonder as the two men wound their arms around each other, tongues deep in each other's mouths, Glen's hands caught in Graham's blond hair at the back of his head, Graham's hands gripping Glen's buttocks. Clarissa watched them kissing for many minutes, utterly captivated yet obviously forgotten and feeling a little bereft: Graham had certainly never kissed her with such force and intensity before, which was one of the reasons why she'd left him. Staring at the two men on the sofa next to her now, though, she certainly couldn't fault Graham for his taste in men. Glen was quite a fine specimen, of about Graham's height and build, but where Graham had a kind of cool, aloof handsomeness, Glen was rougher, with a darker, more sensual appeal: Clarissa hadn't been lying when she'd said she'd found him attractive. On the few times they'd met at Graham's office or at a company party, she'd been impressed by Glen's blazing blue eyes which had locked tightly with hers when they spoke. At the time she'd thought he was flirting with her, but she realised now he was probably assessing her curiously, perhaps wondering what it was Graham saw in her. Well, he certainly didn't need to think of Clarissa as his competition any more, she thought, gazing at the entwined couple now tumbling off the sofa and rolling on to the floor; she had obviously done Graham a favour when she'd suggested that they end things between them, leaving the field wide open for Glen to plough, as it were.

Graham now lay full length on Glen's body, having stripped off the other man's robe so the two men lay naked together on the floor, hands running along each other's bodies, legs tangled up together, each cock rubbing against the other. Clarissa stared with delight at the sight of the men's twin sets of balls, the two velvety sacs collapsing into one. She studied the tight globes of Graham's tensing buttocks, catching tantalising glimpses of his clenching bottom-hole as he rocked rhythmically against Glen's body. Finally Graham sat up, straddling Glen across the waist, gazing into his eyes, each man totally absorbed by the other.

'I think it's my turn to go first,' Graham laughed softly, obviously playing a familiar and well-worn game.

'It's just over there,' Glen said teasingly, pointing to his discarded robe that lay on the floor by the couch. 'I'd put some in my pocket because I was planning to seduce you in the kitchen while you were making our morning coffee.' He then glanced over at Clarissa, having apparently remembered his audience, and called out companionably, 'He does make wonderful coffee, doesn't he?'

Clarissa could only nod mutely and light another cigarette, finding small comfort in the burning thin tube for the gnawing sexual ache that had opened up inside her, brought on by the open display of male lust on the floor before her. She watched greedily as Graham located the packet of condoms and lubricating jelly in the pocket of Glen's robe, then palmed his heavy organ leeringly at Glen as he unrolled the thin sheath down over it. Glen placed his hand on Graham's and said with a low laugh, 'Hey – no cheating. I want you to save all that for me.' Glen then turned over on to his stomach, thrusting his buttocks far backwards and lewdly spreading out the cheeks of his bottom so that his puckered anal hole was open and ready for Graham. He said nothing, merely bent his head down to the floor and closed his eyes, holding himself open and breathlessly awaiting Graham's thrust.

Sitting up tall on his knees, Graham positioned himself behind Glen, gripped his manfully erect cock in one firm hand and lightly tapped it against that hairy dark cleft so patently eager for his cock. He then aimed slow and steady, easing the tip into Glen's anus and driving it straight in, bracing himself with his hands on Glen's hips, holding the other man close to his body and filling him up with his cock. Clarissa caught her breath, bit her lip and sighed at the sight of the two naked men, Graham's thighs driving steadily between Glen's, Glen's legs enclosing Graham's, Graham's head bent low over Glen's back as he delved deeply within his body. The two men were silent in their pleasure, Graham's lips tightly compressed in a thin line in an expression of erotic determination Clarissa remembered well, but the beads of sweat on his forehead and the whiteness around his knuckles that gripped Glen's hips betrayed his inexorable rise to orgasm.

Glen, too, Clarissa could see, was well on his way to climax: his cock hung heavy and low, redly distended and jutting blindly forward as though searching for blissful friction to ease its swollen tension. As Clarissa looked on, consumed by Scotch and lust, she gazed enviously at Graham's sturdy cock as it divided the cheeks of Glen's buttocks with every deep thrust, and she wished she could feel that cock inside herself – vagina, mouth or anus, she didn't much care which, so long as it was hot and hard and ready. She was astonished by the range and depth of the desire Graham was causing to rise up within her as he drove on into the secret passage of his lover's behind. Although Graham had certainly been a skilled and competent lover, whether that skill came from a manual or not, he'd lacked the heat and intensity so clearly evident in his erotic embrace with this man. Finally Graham rose up on his knees even higher, slamming his body further against Glen's, gave one briefly gasped 'ah', and slumped over his lover's back, evidently spent. Glen, however, continued to push himself desperately back and forth against Graham's cock still embedded within him. Finally Graham withdrew his cock from Glen's anus, replacing it with his tongue, his mouth pressed up against the cheeks of his lover's bottom, his lips sucking against Glen's buttocks as he thrust his tongue in and out of that tightly clenching entrance. While Graham rhythmically worked his tongue, he reached forward with one hand to clasp Glen's hotly throbbing cock, stroking it up and down in time to the movements of his mouth. Finally he turned his lover over on to his back and bent over to take Glen's cock tenderly into his mouth. He closed his lips around the thick member and sucked, and it only took a moment before Glen pushed Graham's mouth away with a sudden cry, gripped his cock around the base and shook it as the milky white semen came shooting out, spraying Graham's chest, arms and face with the thick pearly stream, almost near enough for Clarissa to catch on her tongue herself.

At last the men lay still, Graham absently rubbing Glen's seed into the flushed pink skin of his chest and throat while Glen lovingly released Graham's now flaccid penis from its latex wrapping, kissing it lightly before glancing over at Clarissa with a satisfied smile. With a chuckle he tapped Graham lightly on the shoulder, and when Graham looked up inquiringly Glen indicated Clarissa sitting wild eyed and flushed on the couch. The two men struggled to sit up, freely unashamed in their nakedness, and for a moment the three simply shared a companionable moment of post-orgasmic silence.

Clarissa was the first one to break it. 'I suppose I should go,' she said feebly, still breathless and weak from what she'd just witnessed, her own remark sounding pathetically trite and inane in her ears.

'No, stay,' Graham suddenly urged, slipping on his dressing gown and coming to sit next to Clarissa on the sofa. He put his arm round her shoulders and held her closely to him, and for the moment that Clarissa's face was pressed against his chest, she thought she could smell the lingering traces of Glen's semen on his skin. This was the Graham she knew, Clarissa thought contentedly to herself, returning Graham's friendly hug. This was the Graham who had first attracted her – warm, kind, sensitive and polite. Reluctantly she moved away from him and straightened up, waving away his offer to refill her empty Scotch glass.

'Thanks, really, but I have to go,' she said, smiling gently at the two men. 'Easter break is over now, you know; I have to be in class on Monday, and I still have preparation to do. Besides,' she added with an attempt at a laugh as she reached for her bag, 'you two probably want to be alone.'

'No, really, Clarissa, stay,' Glen said, coming to sit beside her on the couch. 'Really, we'd love you to stay and have lunch with us, wouldn't we, Graham?'

'No, truly, I have to go,' Clarissa repeated, smiling genuinely this time, relieved that she and Graham had now set things right between them. 'But I'll ring you soon,' she added, moving off towards the door. 'We can all have dinner.'

'And bring your young man!' Glen called out after her as she pulled the door open to go. 'Let's make it a double date!'

The thought of Nick suddenly chilled Clarissa's heart. She was desperate to see how he felt about what had happened last night. As Clarissa walked slowly down Graham's front steps to her car, she tried to picture Nick's face: would he be impressed by her performance with Jessica? Aroused? Jealous? – after all, she had really done it more for her own pleasure than for his. But she was desperate to see him now, to feel his arms round her and his mouth on hers, her flesh craving the feel of his warm body against her own.

But when Clarissa arrived home, it wasn't Nick she saw but Jessica, sitting on Clarissa's front step and bending over her knee, apparently about to write her a note. Clarissa pulled up behind the long, sleek Jaguar in her drive – not, she noted, the Porsche she'd seen pick up Nick the day before – and suddenly she felt a little shy and nervous about facing this young woman she'd been so shamelessly intimate with just the night before. She emerged slowly from her car and walked hesitantly up the steps, wondering what Jessica was doing there and how she should greet her.

'Oh, hello,' Jessica said to Clarissa, clearly as nervous as she. 'I was just about to write you a note.'

At the sight of the young woman's apparent awkwardness and unease, Clarissa suddenly felt much calmer and in control, and she regarded the girl with quite a friendly smile as she ushered her up to her door. 'Won't you come in?' she offered the girl warmly. 'Perhaps you would like a cup of coffee.'

Jessica's eyes widened a little as she stepped inside Clarissa's house, gazing at the odd collection of treasures Clarissa had inherited from her aunt over the years. 'Wow,' the girl breathed, slipping her Bond Street suede jacket off her shoulders. 'Nick told me you had a lot of stuff.'

Clarissa went off into the kitchen to start up her espresso machine, returning a moment later with a plate of biscuits and fruit in her hands. 'Sit down,' she said to the girl, gesturing towards her comfortable purple sofa. She then took a breath and asked bluntly, 'What did you want to see me about?'

Clarissa felt ridiculously like a university lecturer as she watched the girl take a seat, and not at all like the woman who had explored the girl's body with her hands and mouth at the party just the night before. She watched curiously as Jessica dug through her handbag for something, and wondered if she felt the same.

'Nick told me to give you this,' Jessica said, handing over a heavy cream envelope with Clarissa's name scrawled across the back. Clarissa ignored the now-urgent bubbling of her coffee machine as she accepted the expensive, elegant envelope. Slowly she opened the unsealed envelope and drew out the single sheet from inside.

'Clarissa,' she read, 'I have to go away again for a while, and won't be back until the end of term. I'm sorry about missing class, I'll see you when I get back.' It was signed simply 'Nick'.

'Still hasn't mastered the semicolon,' Clarissa muttered to herself, then glanced up into Jessica's face. 'Thank you,' she said briefly, then went to attend to the coffee.

When she returned Jessica was sitting exactly where she'd left her, nervously picking at a bunch of purple seedless grapes. She accepted the steaming cup of dark bitter coffee Clarissa handed her, then looked into Clarissa's eyes a little uncertainly.

'I also wanted to speak to you about last night,' Jessica began hesitantly, her shyness in evident contrast to her cool blonde beauty. 'I . . . I don't quite know how to say this,' she whispered, lowering her eyes, then she glanced quickly back and said, 'but I've never done that with a woman before, and I just wanted to tell you I thought it was really . . . really lovely.'

Clarissa was deeply touched and sat staring at the girl, her coffee lying neglected on the table. 'It was the first time for me too,' she confessed softly, and then said, 'but I'll always think of it as something very special.'

There was an awkward pause in the room while the two women, brief lovers, now strangers, sipped at their coffees and nibbled on grapes. Finally Jessica broke the silence by setting her coffee cup deliberately on to its saucer and boldly stating, 'I hope you didn't feel that we were laughing at you or anything last night when you asked about Nick's cousin.' At Clarissa's sharp, inquisitive stare, Jessica hesitated and nearly dropped her cup before adding, 'It's just that Nick tells so many little stories and is so secretive about everything, especially about his mother. He's very proud of her, I think, and they get along fine when his stepfather isn't around, but he's so private and mysterious, he never likes to let anyone get close to him.'

Isn't that the truth, Clarissa thought bitterly to herself, then, unable to stop herself from probing, she asked outright, 'But he's quite close to you, Jessica, isn't he?'

The girl looked up and smiled sadly. 'Well, we've known each other for a very long time,' she hedged cautiously, then blurted out, 'but I think it's you that he really wants.'

Clarissa doubted this very much, but she would have

liked to believe the girl. She simply had to know, she just had to ask: 'Did you know that he had invited me to his flat that night – the night you and he were ... well ... together?'

Jessica immediately knew to which night Clarissa was referring, and she nodded her head slowly. 'Yes, but not until afterwards,' she said, blushing. 'Believe me, I didn't know you were standing there at the time – ' she looked away in embarrassment ' – or I would never have gone along with it.' She turned back to face Clarissa. 'But when he told me about it afterwards – ' she blushed again, fiercely ' – I told him I thought that was a really wicked thing to do. I hope it didn't upset you, having to ... see us like that.'

No, actually it turned me on, Clarissa wanted to tell her, but thought it wisest not to give too much away. Relentlessly she ploughed on. 'What exactly did he tell you about me?'

'Not much,' the girl admitted, toying nervously with her now-empty cup. At Clarissa's offer of a refill she accepted eagerly, then said, 'I knew you were watching us that day you saw us kissing outside your building. I saw you out of the corner of my eye, and when you were gone I asked Nick who you were. He just said, "That was my tutor", and laughed, you know, the way that he does – ' don't I indeed, thought Clarissa ' – and then later he told me that he found you really intriguing, and he was trying to get you to react to him.'

'And you continued to sleep with him, knowing that he wanted me?' Clarissa couldn't help herself from asking, curious about their relationship. Jessica looked away.

'Nick and I – well, like I said, we're old friends,' she said, sounding a little uncertain herself, then added, 'besides, there have always been others with Nick, and he always comes back to me.' She glanced at Clarissa and clapped a hand to her mouth in such a sweet gesture of innocence Clarissa couldn't help smiling. The girl really was a child after all. 'I didn't mean that to come out the way it sounded,' Jessica said apologetically, stumbling to find the right words. 'What I mean is that I've seen him with lots of other girls in the past, but they were always temporary, momentary flings, whereas you...' She fell silent for a moment while Clarissa merely looked at her, then with a shrug Jessica continued. 'Well, he hasn't been with me since that night you saw us together – and I suppose that's because he only wants you now.'

Clarissa couldn't believe what she was hearing. 'You don't think that Nick has been with any other woman except me since that night?'

Jessica shrugged again, ruefully, helplessly. 'I don't know,' she whispered, avoiding Clarissa's eyes. 'Maybe. He certainly doesn't tell me everything – but there are always women running after him, offering themselves to him, so who knows?'

The two women sat again in silence, Clarissa trying to absorb the implications of what Jessica was telling her. She thought the whole scenario was slightly absurd, her having to glean second-hand information about her lover from a girl who could very well be a student of hers, but she had to pursue this conversation to its conclusion. 'Are you in love with him?' she asked Jessica gently, feeling a new warmth for the girl that had nothing to do with last night.

'Aren't we all?' asked Jessica sadly, gazing over at Clarissa.

Actually, Clarissa didn't really think that she was, but she did know that Nick's body seemed uniquely capable of giving her what she needed, and so she was more determined than ever to break things off soon, while she was still able to get away from this impossible situation. She wouldn't want to end up like Jessica, feeling that kind of pain, for anything.

'Can I offer you more coffee?' Clarissa asked brightly, hoping to break the girl's despondent mood, for Jessica now seemed so young and so vulnerable, and Clarissa couldn't help but feel a little guilty looking at her now.

'No thanks,' replied Jessica with a small smile, getting up and reaching for her coat. 'I really need to get going – but it was so nice to see you again,' she added shyly. As

Clarissa helped the girl on with her coat, the two women paused for a moment, their bodies close, almost touching, and then Jessica reached over to lay a warm kiss on Clarissa's lips. Clarissa felt the gentle pressure of Jessica's mouth against hers, the tip of Jessica's tongue reaching out to brush against her lips, but before she had a chance to return the kiss, it was over.

'Thank you for last night,' the girl murmured softly, her cheeks still stained a delicate pink. 'I think I'll remember it forever.'

Clarissa said nothing in reply, only touching her fingers to the girl's cheek before running them through that silky blonde hair before Jessica turned to walk out of the door. Clarissa stood for a moment in the doorway, watching while Jessica slid behind the wheel of her car then waved briefly at Clarissa in farewell. Clarissa waved back once, then went back into her house and shut the door.

Chapter Twelve

*T*he final three weeks of the semester passed with their usual dizzying mix of frenetic classroom lectures in which Clarissa raced furiously to conclude a semester's worth of work, and the mind-bending tedium of rehashing old material in order to help her students revise. Clarissa was determined to work at her best, despite the distracting blank emptiness of Nick's chair which glared at her every time she stood in the front of the classroom. Nick's abrupt departure from class ensured his probable fail for the term, and while Clarissa mourned the loss of her lover, she also fretted about the damage done to the academic record of one of her most promising pupils. She was enough of a professional to worry about how Nick would be able to continue his degree course having earned a fail in Clarissa's class as well as presumably failing the other classes he was enrolled in that semester. Clarissa couldn't help but wonder with an internal grimace whether the deliberate truncation of his academic career was a way to strike out at his over-achieving mother and the mysterious stepfather Nick so clearly detested. Well, Clarissa had other things to worry about than her nineteen-year-old boyfriend's adolescent rebellion and perversely secretive ways. Let him keep his family feuding and abrupt comings and goings for some suitably naive young girl who would cheerfully put up with his erratic behaviour, Clarissa thought angrily to herself – she had other, more important things to worry about.

One such worry was the fate of her book on the erotic. Clarissa knew that the pushy publicity officer at her publishing house had sent out advance copies of her book to all the major literary journals in both England and America in an attempt to secure it a high rating among her peers. Her editor was hoping that the book would also make it into some of the more prominent national newspapers, trying to entice the lay reader into buying an essentially academic work by appealing to their more prurient interest in sex. Clarissa didn't much care about the money she stood to earn should her book achieve the rare success of the cross-over market, but she did very much care about how the academic community and literary reviewers would receive her work.

Her other major concern was even more immediate: Clarissa's annual review with the university board was scheduled for the end of the semester, in between students' final assessments and graduation duties, and she was a bit nervous about how she would fare under the tightly budgeted scrutiny of the powers that be in academia. Despite increasing student enrolment, financial cutbacks had now become commonplace at universities such as hers, and Clarissa was concerned that her short-term contract might not be renewed in an effort by the finance committee to cut costs. She had so far made only minimal progress in publishing and research – a critical edition, a couple of reviews, some papers given at conferences – and she knew her job depended on her ability to convince the board she was research worthy, hence the emphasis on her book. She knew she was an excellent instructor, and she had many glowing student evaluations to prove it, but she also knew that good teaching was simply not enough to guarantee her a job – and university teaching was the only profession Clarissa felt herself suited for.

And, of course, she did miss Nick, especially at night when she rolled about restlessly in her too-big bed by herself. She was hurt, yes, and angry at Nick's abrupt departure, with only the briefest of impersonal notes couriered to her by a third party, and she was getting pretty damned fed up with his casual, dismissive treatment of her. She couldn't, however, erase the traces of Nick's body against hers from her physical memories: images of his lips, his hands, his penis would fill her dreams as she slept fitfully, and she couldn't see any way for her obsession with Nick to end except in heartbreak.

But she carried on through the final debilitating weeks of term, squeezing in the odd hour for a drink with Julian, planning a dinner date with Glen and Graham to celebrate the end of the semester, and writing out course proposals for teaching next year should the board look upon her application for renewal of her contract favourably.

It was, therefore, with a jolt of surprise that Clarissa walked into her classroom several days before the end of term to find Nicholas St Clair back in his appointed seat, black leather-clad legs insolently sprawled out before him, head tipped back against the wall, fingers restlessly drumming against the copy of Angela Carter's collected short stories on his desk. Clarissa closed her eyes briefly against the tumultuous wave of pleasure that rose up in her belly at the sight of her casual lover staring at her with a glint of amused laughter in his eyes. She took a deep breath as she laid her books carefully down on the desk at the front of the room, deliberately averting her eyes from that piercing hazel stare. She fought to keep still as the sight of Nick's eyes on her body caused her legs to weaken dangerously and the liquid begin to flow among the lips of her rapidly blossoming sex.

I've got to stop this and I've got to stop this now, Clarissa gritted out to herself silently as she, outwardly calm, leafed through her book to the story under discussion today. This thing has just got to end, she told herself even as she began talking out loud, directing her students' attention to the story 'The Bloody Chamber'. She refused to meet Nick's eyes, blithely avoiding his determined gaze until he evidently took the hint and stopped trying to attract her attention, sullenly doodling on his pad and pointedly ignoring her lecture.

When class was finally over, however, Nick sauntered up to Clarissa with his usual arrogance, leant over her desk and whispered only just loud enough for her to hear, 'Did you miss me?'

Clarissa's whole body was screaming out to touch him, to wrap her arms round that irresistible male body and draw his mouth down to hers, but she gathered together all her forces and mustered out a cool reply: 'It's nice to see you back, Nick.'

'I'd like to see you, Clarissa,' he said to her earnestly, his eyes blazing into hers. 'Let me come to you tonight.'

Clarissa clenched her fists together in her palms, tightened up the muscles in her abdomen and forced herself to say, 'No, Nick, not tonight. I can't.'

He looked down into her face, puzzled, for the briefest of moments, then uttered a low laugh, smiling at her quite fondly. 'Look, if you're angry that I had to leave so suddenly I can – ' he began, but Clarissa cut him off with an anxious glance at the fresh crop of students who came streaming into the room.

'I really can't talk about that now,' she said formally, professionally, beginning to walk out of the room. 'Why don't you come to my office for a few minutes?'

Clarissa's office wasn't exactly the ideal place to conduct the discussion that was to follow, especially given what had happened the last time she was in there with Nick, but she wanted to get this over with now. Obediently Nick strode down the hall alongside her, his eyes skimming over the faces of the students they passed – especially the women, Clarissa noted angrily – until they reached Clarissa's office where he quietly stood to one side while she unlocked the door and ushered him in.

'Didn't Jessica give you my note?' he asked abruptly once Clarissa had ascertained that her office door was shut – and locked.

'Look, Nick,' she began wearily, despite the slamming sound of her heart in her ears, 'it's the last couple of days of term, I'm extremely busy and overworked, and I really don't have time to see you right now.' She was pleased by her firm, decisive voice, but she couldn't help herself from adding, 'Perhaps after the end of the semester you and I can . . . get together.'

Nick simply stared at her and nodded, then started to move for the door when Clarissa heard herself call out, 'Just out of curiosity, though, Nick . . . where have you been the last few weeks?' As Nick turned to smile at her triumphantly, having at last apparently got a reaction out of her, Clarissa added hastily, 'You have missed quite a lot of work, you know – will you be able to make it all up and pass this semester?'

'I was with my father,' Nick offered by way of explanation, then paused and said, 'I spent my birthday with him at his house in Derby.' At Clarissa's blank expression he added, 'I've just reached twenty.'

'Must have been some party,' Clarissa murmured to herself, suddenly feeling the need to sit down. He'd just turned twenty and she hadn't even known! She could think of nothing else to say except, 'Well, it's good to have you back. Final essays are due on my desk on Friday by five.'

Nick looked at her, then walked over to where she sat to trail his fingers over her cheek. 'I missed you, Rissa,' he murmured, gently twisting his fingers in a few strands of her coppery hair. 'Are you sure I can't come and see you tonight?'

Clarissa felt herself weakening but willed herself to stay strong. 'I'm sorry, Nick,' she said as firmly as she could, while inside her stomach was quivering. 'I think we'd better wait until after the semester is over.' She couldn't bring herself to end this between them for good, however; the call of her body was still too strong. And so Clarissa turned her cheek to press her lips against Nick's palm, kissing the curve of his hand as it cupped her face, and then he withdrew it and was gone.

After he left Clarissa just sat dumbly at her desk for a while, staring blindly out of the window and wondering what the hell she'd just done. She'd allowed the most sexually exciting, most passionate man she'd ever met walk out of her door, possibly out of her life, and for what? Because he'd had to go away for a little while and hadn't bothered to tell her where?

No, she said firmly to herself, shuffling the papers on her desk. Because he's an arrogant, rude, ridiculously young man who could cost me my job. I just want him too much, she said to herself brutally, and he knows it – and is willing to use it against me just to see what he can get away with. Even as she tried to pull herself together, however, the thought of Nick's tender hand on her face just now nearly caused Clarissa to leap up out of her chair and go hurtling through the hallways in a mad dash to find him when the phone suddenly rang on her desk, jarring her out of her mental agitation.

'Clarissa Cornwall,' she said briskly into the telephone, hoping it was good news.

'Clarissa? It's Heidi – you are going to be very happy when you hear what I have to tell you.'

Oh good, her editor. About bloody time too, Clarissa told herself fiercely. 'Yes?' she said as dispassionately as she could.

'The first reviews of your book are in, and they are *brilliant*,' Heidi gushed over the phone. 'Two of the journals and one of the newspapers have printed "must-read" reviews – that snooty one from the university press was a little sniffy, not at all sure about your so-called populist bent, and one of the dailies thought your book was a little too rude to be strictly an academic read, but that's bound to sell more copies anyway, isn't it? The *American Feminist Review loved* it, though, especially the bit about how the early Gothic women writers were slammed in the critical journals at the time for being too sensationalist; I suppose they're just trying to show how advanced today's critics are compared to those of the eighteenth century!'

Clarissa clasped the receiver to her chest with joy. They liked it! she sang inwardly, all thoughts of Nick now totally forgotten. They really liked my book! This could be it, this could be the key she'd been looking for which would

224

secure her a permanent position in the academic world – she might never need to worry about interviewing for another job again! Clarissa exhaled a long, deep breath of gratitude, silently vowing to renew her subscription to the feminist journal that very day, and she eagerly exchanged ideas with her editor about a possible follow-up to her book, this time concentrating on the erotic in film.

When Clarissa finally hung up the phone, dewy eyed and glowing with the first sweet flush of success, another thought occurred to her which caused her heart to pound even harder. The success of her book was partially and indirectly due to the influence of Nicholas St Clair in her life, Clarissa realised, then corrected herself: it was her *desire* for Nick, not Nick himself, which had so inspired her to write with such passion and energy about the material she analysed in her book. Not Nick himself, but the way Nick made her feel had helped to stimulate Clarissa's thinking about her own sexual identity and about the nature of eroticism in the world in general, and in certain literary works in particular. Having now crystallised this realisation in her own mind, Clarissa thought that perhaps she had been a little too hasty in dismissing Nick from her office so abruptly only an hour ago. Perhaps it wasn't too late to go and find him and at least share with him her good news; maybe this affair was better for her than she had thought, maybe it was possible to go on as they had been for just a little while longer.

Clarissa quickly checked her watch as she hurried out of her office: she had enough time before her next class to see if she could locate Nick in the quad outside where she knew he usually dawdled away the time between classes. Clarissa strode rapidly down the pavement of the inner quad, now crowded with students, anxiously searching out Nick's tall lean frame with her eyes. At this mad moment she didn't care a toss for how unseemly her eager pursuit of her student might seem to the casual observer; she was joyous, no, jubilant, that her book was going to do so well, and her pleasure at her professional success was rapidly translating itself into a thrumming insistent need in her body for a more immediate form of gratification. Where was Nick? Clarissa asked herself anxiously, scanning the clusters of students grouped around the library steps and barring the entrance to the university bookshop, all seemingly taking advantage of the warmth of the early May sunshine. Disappointed in her search, Clarissa was just about to give it up and go back inside, since she was due in class soon anyway, when an animated group of students abruptly broke up, and in the space made by their dispersing bodies the figure of Nick emerged sharply into view.

He was there, leaning against the stone pillar bust of the university's founder, and he was not alone. He was laughing down into the eyes of a slim, stunningly pretty girl: she was tall, reaching up almost to Nick's shoulder, with dead-straight jet-black hair that reached to her chin in a graduated cut, and she was dressed in a lacy black top cropped at the waist and low-slung hipster jeans, her long, model-thin body obviously the figure the jeans were designed for. In front of Clarissa's horrified stare Nick bent over to place a lingering kiss on the girl's darkly painted mouth, his hand cupping her cheek and drawing her face closer to his in a way that was so painfully familiar to Clarissa.

As Clarissa stood there, tears threatening to gather in her eyes, Nick then slung his arm round the girl and together they walked away, she leaning into him, his beautiful big hand wrapped possessively round her bare toned midriff. Clarissa stood and watched them go, feeling totally helpless and suddenly very, very old. She felt as though she had just been slapped across the face. The hot dry ache in her heart had now completely drained away the euphoric joy brought on by Heidi's phone call. This wasn't at all like the time she had seen Nick with Jessica all those months ago on that damp, dark February day: that episode, she had known at the time, had been constructed solely for her benefit. No, this was different: for one thing, Nick had been completely unaware that she had seen him, of this Clarissa was sure, which made his attraction for this girl seem all the more genuine. Jessica

226

had obviously been wrong, Clarissa thought bitterly to herself: Clarissa wasn't at all the only woman Nick wanted, and probably never would be.

Clarissa wasn't sure how long she'd been standing there, a lone, still figure amongst a moving, laughing, chattering mass of people, but when she finally blinked her eyes away from the spot where she had seen Nick kissing the unfamiliar young woman, it was to find Monica Talbot gazing at her with a concerned, puzzled expression on her face.

'Clarissa?' she asked gently, coming over to lay a comforting hand on her arm. 'Clarissa, dear, are you all right?'

Clarissa bravely blinked back her tears and turned to look steadily at her colleague. 'Oh, yes, of course, Monica,' she said brightly, too brightly, she guessed, for Monica didn't look at all convinced.

'It's that student, Clarissa, isn't it?' Monica asked, indicating the direction Nick and the girl had taken with her head. 'Clarissa, dear, you must listen to me,' she went on while Clarissa was still trying to frame a denial. 'I've been meaning to say something to you for a while. Come and sit down with me over there.'

The two women sat down on a stone bench under the trees a little distance from the clusters of university students.

'Certain rumours have begun to circulate round certain quarters,' Monica began delicately, clearly straining not to alarm Clarissa.

Clarissa was alarmed, however, deeply alarmed, and in cold, sudden fear she drew back, an icy hand of fright clutching at the twisted strands of her stomach. '. . . Rumours?' she asked in a hushed whisper, too frightened to ask any more.

Monica reached for Clarissa's chilled, damp hands and pressed them gently, smiling reassuringly at her friend. 'It's not as bad as you think, Clarissa, so pull yourself together,' she said in that forthright, no-nonsense manner Clarissa always thought of as quintessentially British. 'It's just that I happened to overhear some students talking,

227

and one was describing a pretty red-headed teacher from here he'd seen at a student's party one night, dressed in a bright red outfit and asking to speak to a certain young man at about 3:30 in the morning.'

Oh god, the night of her club date with Julian! Clarissa shut her eyes and shook her head in blind agony, outraged at her thoughtlessly reckless behaviour. How could she have presented herself so boldly at Nick's front door during a party, as propelled by lust as she'd been; what if someone had seen her and Nick outside against the wall? But no, surely Monica would have told her if that was the case – but she simply had to be sure. 'Is that it? . . . is there anything else?' she whispered to Monica, her mouth gone completely dry.

Monica patted her hand and shook her head. 'I don't think anyone else on staff has heard anything, if that's what you're worried about – but Clarissa, you know you really must be careful with what you do. This *is* a small town, and the slightest indiscretion can make the gossip rounds in absolutely no time at all. Believe me, I know what I'm talking about.' Monica nodded her head at Clarissa, then paused and smiled with just the tiniest hint of indecent suggestion flickering around the corners of her mouth. 'You don't want to end up like Warburton, my dear, now do you?' she asked her.

Meeting Monica's gaze head on, Clarissa wondered to herself with a little smile if the woman knew that Clarissa herself was familiar with certain things that Monica got up to; perhaps Monica had spotted her at the Dungeon after all, but was simply not choosing to say anything. Well, Clarissa wasn't about to broach the subject herself; instead she nodded her head firmly, gripped Monica's hand in thanks and said, 'OK, I think I'm all right now. I could use a strong cup of tea before my next class, though.'

Monica smiled at Clarissa and rose, brushing off some stray twigs from her drab olive blouse. 'I think I have an emergency bottle of whisky stashed away somewhere we could use to brighten up that tea.' She held out her hand to Clarissa to help her to rise to her feet, and the two women headed back into the building.

And so the semester finally came to its close. Nick managed to make it to class for the last session, as casually arrogant and insolent as ever, looking everywhere but at Clarissa, who managed to avoid his eyes with equal aplomb. However, Monica's words of warning continued to ring in her ears, and she was tormented by the fear that now the entire student body knew of her ill-advised affair with Nicholas St Clair. Clarissa was constantly on the alert for a strange pair of eyes coolly appraising her as she walked down the hall, and she imagined she heard students whispering together, their eyes moving over her as she walked on by. She tried to tell herself she was being foolish, that of course no one was gossiping about her, but her skin constantly prickled as though tentacled eyes were actually touching her flesh, and her dreams at night were haunted by grotesque images of jeering faces which ringed her in a mocking, threatening circle, like some nightmarish sketch by the artist Masereel.

Thus her final days in the classroom were ruined, damaged by tension and nerves as Clarissa constantly fretted about her new position as grist in the university gossip mill. To be sure, she was thankful Monica had spoken to her – who knows what other foolhardy acts she might have been drawn to, as consumed as she was with desire and pain? – but Clarissa now truly dreaded facing her assessors as she prepared for her annual review with the university board.

Her unease was only intensified when she unexpectedly encountered Malcom Anderson in the corridor the day after classes ended, when she dropped into her office to collect the essays submitted by her students the day before.

'Ah, yes, Clarissa, the board will be expecting you at ten on Monday morning,' the new department head said warningly as he accosted Clarissa in the hallway, as though she didn't know the time of her own review meeting. 'As I am new to the university I will only be sitting in on the committee, not actually participating,' he said stiffly, frowning a little as he looked at a spot on the wall directly above Clarissa's head. 'I think there are some things that the committee would like to discuss with you, though,' he added darkly. Then he abruptly closed his mouth as though deciding to say no more. He gave a single curt nod in her direction and marched away, leaving a nervous Clarissa to try to decipher exactly what it was the board wanted to address on Monday morning.

She spent the weekend concentrating on her students' essays, reading straight through from early in the morning up to the night-time news at nine, breaking only for cigarettes, coffee refills and the occasional scrap of food. It was always this way at the close of the semester: the final frantic rush to award the cumulative marks for the term, and Clarissa had over a hundred students to assess. When Monday morning finally arrived with a glaring burst of sunshine that penetrated even the tightly shuttered blinds in her bedroom windows, Clarissa was perversely relieved to know that in a very few hours she would be facing her contract renewal committee and would finally learn the fate of her tenuously held position. She would also learn, she assumed, whether any rumours of herself and Nick had circulated to the upper echelons of the academic staff.

Thus she disentangled herself from her rumpled, sweaty sheets, having spent most of the night tossing and turning, her dreams alternating between Nick having sex with the dark-haired girl in an endless succession of inventive and imaginative ways, and of finding herself standing in front of a scandalised row of robed and bewigged judges only to discovered that she was, in fact, stark naked. With a groan Clarissa dragged herself into the shower and subjected herself to the stinging needle-like jabs of a jet of scalding hot water before shutting off the heat entirely and dousing herself with an icy-cold stream. Having haphazardly towelled herself dry she was reaching for the dowdiest, most shapeless and figure-defying dress she could find when the telephone rang sharply, jolting her out of her pathetic, self-obsessed stupor.

'Hello?' she whispered cautiously into the phone, feeling far too delicate to pursue any more self-possessed speech.

'Rissa? Is that you?'

At the loud, cocky tones of Julian's warm, friendly voice, Clarissa found a new source of strength and self-resolve, and she gripped the phone gratefully, clinging to it as though to a means of life support.

'Julian! How wonderful to hear your voice!'

'It is? Why is that?' Julian asked suspiciously, and Clarissa could almost see those narrowing black eyes staring her in the face. 'You usually hate it when I ring too early!'

'It's not early – it's after nine,' Clarissa found herself babbling into the phone, so happy to hear a friendly voice.

'Yeah, well, whatever,' Julian replied dismissively. 'Anyway I'm just calling to wish you luck, love – I know that today's your big day, and I want you to know that I'm wishing you the best. If those stuck-up pretentious buggers give you any grief, just tell them to stuff their smelly old job up their arses and bolt out that door!'

'Yes, and I love you too,' Clarissa smiled into the phone, blew a kiss and hung up.

Julian's call seemed to have provided Clarissa with the self-confidence she needed to walk into the large seminar room on the first floor dead on time and with her red head held high. To her surprise, the vice chancellor was presiding as head of the meeting; he usually delegated the job to the head of faculty or someone, and was rarely seen at meetings except for those directly related to finance.

'Well, now, Dr Cornwall,' he began formally, welcoming her into the room. 'Please, take a seat and let us begin this meeting.'

Once Clarissa was seated there was a general pause for several seconds before the vice-chancellor cleared his throat and said, 'Before we begin the process of reviewing your application for renewal of your contract, I believe that Professor Anderson has a matter of some importance he would like to communicate to you.'

Clarissa had to stifle her nervous fit of giggles at the

vice-chancellor's overtly formal speech, but then Malcolm Anderson rose to speak and everyone fell silent.

'You may not be aware, Clarissa,' he said, 'but this year I have been among those privileged to serve as one of the judges who present the National Critics Award for the best literary works for this year, and it gives me great pleasure to be the first to announce to you that your book, *Visions of the Erotic*, has been chosen to be among those nominated for the category of best non-fiction.'

As Clarissa gasped with surprise and excitement and the clatter of polite applause sounded round the room, the vice-chancellor also addressed himself to Clarissa, saying, 'I have had the great pleasure to read your new book and I must say I am very impressed with your scholarship and your research, and I thought it a most enjoyable read.' As he seated himself Clarissa caught the eye of Professor Anderson who was now smiling quite openly at her, and she decided that perhaps he wasn't such a stodgy and dull man after all.

The rest of the meeting passed relatively quickly. Clarissa's teaching and academic service achievements were assessed, her records photocopied and passed around the room, and the meeting was concluded with the vice-chancellor announcing his pleasure in his ability to offer Clarissa a new contract with the university on the understanding that her probationary period would conclude with the opportunity to take up a permanent, full-time position.

Clarissa walked home as though she were floating on air, feeling as though she had achieved – for the moment – the pinnacle of her professional ambitions. She couldn't wait to race to the phone to begin to share her good news, but then she thought of Nick, and suddenly she was consumed with the desire to see him. The thought of Nick seemed to sober her up a bit. She'd left things with him so tentative, and now that the question of her academic career seemed to have been settled, she wanted to find a kind of closure to the affair that was partially responsible, in however oblique and indirect a way, for her now secure professional standing.

But she certainly couldn't go and see him looking like this. Clarissa started stripping off her sexless grey linen dress almost the minute she walked in the door, ripping off her unflattering grey tights and unhooking her dull cream cotton bra in one swift motion. Naked, she was just about to reach for a new pair of slinky red satin knickers when the telephone rang, disturbing the direction of Clarissa's thoughts.

Frowning, she stared at the phone, then uttered a brief sigh and picked up the receiver.

'Hello?' she said firmly.

When Clarissa replaced the telephone fifteen minutes later, she found she had to sit on the floor, no chair being immediately available where she stood, and her legs having suddenly refused to support her. The call had been from an old college friend of hers from America, a woman Clarissa had last spoken with over a year ago, and who was now teaching at the Ivy League university she and Clarissa had graduated from over ten years before. Apparently news of the success of Clarissa's book was making the rounds of the English department over there according to Marie, who was now serving on the recruitment and hiring committee, a most prestigious appointment. It seemed that Clarissa's old alma mater was on the lookout for a new college professor to take up the modernism and twentieth-century post, and Marie was calling to invite Clarissa to apply for the job.

'It's practically assured to you if you'll only come and apply,' her friend had urged on the phone, shamelessly informing Clarissa of the secretive behind-the-scenes discussions that the hiring committee had been conducting. 'We're looking for a new face, someone who hasn't been making the usual rounds of the interview conferences giving the same dull, over-worked papers, and your name was one of the first to come up, especially now that your book is such a success. Please say you'll at least give it some thought!'

Home. Back to America riding high on the crest of her success, away from England, away from scandal, away from Nick.

Nick. Clarissa paused, still naked, still clutching her red satin underwear, still thinking of Nick. She already knew she would present herself for the interview for this exciting new job, already knew she would take up the position in a New York minute, as they say, should the committee happen to offer it to her. What better answer was there for her than to begin anew, to let go of this thrilling but potentially damaging affair with her student, retaining only the memory, the experience, the new definition of her still-emerging sexual self?

Clarissa rubbed her eyes tiredly, smearing her mascara a little, and decided there was no time like the present to break things off once and for all with Nick. She'd been planning on going over there anyway, before she'd got the call, so she might as well pull on some clothes and make her way, one last time, over to Nick's flat. If he wasn't there, she vowed silently to herself, she'd leave him a note.

As if on cue, the doorbell rang. What is this, someone's sick idea of a new version of *This Is Your Life?* Clarissa thought crossly to herself. She glanced at her reflection in the mirror; she was still naked. Well, she'd pull on a robe and go to greet whoever it was that was standing on her front doorstep. Hopefully the sight of her hastily covered body would be enough to convince them to go away and leave her in peace.

The gods must be working overtime on her behalf that day, Clarissa thought dazedly to herself as she pulled open the door to reveal Nick himself standing there on her doorstep. He had never seemed more beautiful to her than he did then, his reddish-brown hair flipped over that high, strong forehead, his hazel-green eyes burning brightly into her own, his beautifully sculpted mouth curving into a half-ironic, yet oddly sad smile as he gazed down at her.

'Hey, Clarissa,' he began as he usually did. 'Can I come in?'

Wordlessly she stepped aside to let Nick into her house,

inwardly fighting against the desire to touch him that gripped her anew every time she saw him. They just stood there a moment at first, each gazing at the other, until Nick broke the tense silence with a warm, open smile as he reached over to touch Clarissa's arm.

'I've been reading your book,' he said. 'It's really good.' At the flush of pleasure which suffused Clarissa's cheeks Nick smiled again, a little sheepishly this time, and added, 'I'm not sure I quite understand all of it, but a lot of it is familiar from class, and I can practically hear your voice as I read it.'

'I couldn't have written it without you,' Clarissa heard herself whisper, then took a step towards him, still clutching at her robe. 'I was just getting dressed to go out and try to find you,' she murmured, unable to stop herself from unbuttoning the first two buttons of his white cotton shirt. 'I have something to tell you,' she said, then pressed her mouth against the deep smooth curve of Nick's strong, muscled chest. Her body still felt starved of his, despite her resentment of his casual treatment of her, and she knew this would be the last opportunity she would have to satisfy her urgent craving for him. 'I'm leaving,' Clarissa told Nick, holding his eyes while she continued to unbutton his shirt, then she reached up to strip it away from him, revealing the shape of Nick's bare upper body in all its male beauty.

'Where are you going?' he asked curiously, not moving at all, merely smiling a little as he watched Clarissa drop his shirt on the floor.

'To America,' she replied, pressing her cheek against his chest as she wrapped her arms round to embrace him. 'I think I'm about to be offered a new teaching position at my old university.'

Nick sighed and wrapped his arms round Clarissa, holding her close against his body. 'Don't go, 'Rissa,' he breathed into her neck, his breath warm and alive on her flesh. 'Stay.'

Clarissa then thought about making some stinging remark about the girl she'd seen him kissing, but then

235

realised she didn't matter at all, no matter what her relationship was with Nick; all that mattered was this man, this body. Clarissa knew that they shared some indefinable something, not love, but greater than lust, that neither would be able to duplicate with another for a very long time. And so it was with a feeling of pure pleasure, nothing more, that Clarissa rapidly undid the buckle of Nick's belt and eased down his jeans while Nick slid Clarissa's robe down and away from her until they were both fully naked and somehow lying on the floor. Clarissa arched her hips against Nick's body and sighed, welcoming the warm, wet imprint of his mouth upon hers as she kissed him fully, passionately, her tongue searching out and locking with his as she ran her hands over his body, so blissfully familiar to her. As Nick bent to kiss her breasts, Clarissa tangled her fingers in his wonderfully thick hair, whispering out his name and urging him back up over her body until he was positioned at the entrance to her sex, his thighs braced between hers, his eyes looking down into her face. He held himself still, not yet inside her, only the tip of his penis seeking entrance to her body, and while Clarissa looked up into his eyes, she could swear she saw some moisture there.

'I could have loved you, you know,' Nick whispered to her, his eyes now gone dry but still burning bright.

Clarissa looked up at him and thought about his calculated manipulation of her, the way he'd tried to choreograph her responses to him right from the start; she thought about Jessica, about Lawrence, about Nick's frequent absences and mysterious silences, and she decided that, like the black-haired girl, none of that mattered whenever they were together, whenever her body met his.

'I know,' was all she said, and then he was inside her, moving slowly, gently, tenderly, making love to her in silence, his hands cradling her body, his cheek pressed against hers. And Clarissa gave herself up to her desire for Nick one more time, rocking his body with hers, wrapping her legs round him to draw him in even closer, contracting herself around him so that when he climaxed, right after her, she felt him stay a part of her body for a long, bittersweet moment of desire and loss, until he gently withdrew and lay still, his body still pressed against hers.

When Nick finally spoke, his voice was quiet and hushed as he pulled away to roll on to his side and prop himself up on his arm, still looking down into Clarissa's face. 'I'm leaving too, you know,' he said.

Startled, Clarissa looked up. 'You're moving away?' she asked.

'Well, I'll be staying around for a while, but I'm giving up university,' Nick replied.

Clarissa suddenly sat up, surprised by the intensity of her disappointment in him. 'But Nick, you're doing so well!' she cried out. 'Even with missing these last few weeks of classes you've managed to pull through with a very high upper second – surely you're doing this well in all your classes?'

Nick's shrug was almost as eloquent as his written words. 'Maybe I'll come back next year or something, I don't know – but I just don't think university is for me at the moment.' He then regarded her sadly for a moment, and when he spoke Clarissa could not detect a trace of irony in his voice. 'Besides, Clarissa,' he whispered, placing his hand around the back of her neck and pulling her mouth down to his, 'this place wouldn't be the same without you here, anyway.'

And just before her lips closed in on his, Clarissa looked at Nick and said with great sorrow and regret, 'Why couldn't we have met at a different time, and in a different place?' And then his mouth was on hers, and in the silence that followed there was no answer.

Three months later Dr Clarissa Cornwall stood in front of her class in her new capacity as associate professor of English in her American Ivy League university. She had just finished introducing her new course on the erotic in literature to her students and was about to read aloud John Donne's erotic poem 'The Flea'. As her finger sought out the page she had marked out in her book the night before,

Clarissa's eyes caught those of a singularly handsome young man who sat in the far corner in the back of the room. His chestnut-brown hair was pulled back into a ponytail, his skin had a healthy tanned glow, and even from her place in the front of the room Clarissa could note the startling blue intensity of his eyes. As she opened her book and prepared to read the poem, she noticed the young man staring intently at her as his hand, hidden under his desk, seemed to be moving downwards to his lap. Clarissa looked directly at the boy, smiled, and began to read.

Visit the Black Lace website at
www.blacklace-books.co.uk

LOOK OUT FOR THE ALL-NEW BLACK LACE BOOKS – AVAILABLE NOW!

All books priced £6.99 in the UK. Please note publication dates apply to the UK only. For other territories, please contact your retailer.

HARD BLUE MIDNIGHT
Alaine Hood
ISBN 0 352 33851 2

Lori owns an antique clothes shop in a seaside town in New England, devoting all her energies to the business at the expense of her sex life. When she meets handsome Gavin MacLellan, a transformation begins. Gavin is writing a book about Lori's great-aunt, an erotic photographer who disappeared during World War II. Lori gets so wrapped up in solving the mystery that she accompanies Gavin to Paris to trace her ancestor's past. A growing fascination with bondage and discipline leads her into a world of secrecy and danger. **A tale of dark secrets and female desire.**

Coming in December 2003

ALWAYS THE BRIDEGROOM
Tesni Morgan
ISBN 0 352 33855 5

Jody Hamilton is a landscape gardener who has returned from the States to attend her best friend's wedding. All is well until Jody finds out what a sex-crazed rotter her best friend is about to marry. With too many people involved in the preparations for the big day, bickering, back-stabbing and infidelities soon ensue. But in the middle of the mayhem, Jody thinks she may have found the man of her dreams. **Erotica and chick-lit merge in this sizzling tale of wedding mayhem.**

DOCTOR'S ORDERS
Deanna Ashford
ISBN 0 352 33453 3

Helen Dawson is a dedicated doctor who has taken a short-term assignment at an exclusive private hospital that caters for the every need of its rich and famous clientele. The matron, Sandra Pope, ensures this includes their most curious sexual fantasies. When Helen risks an affair with a famous actor, she is drawn deeper into the hedonistic lifestyle of the clinic. **Naughty nurses get busy behind the screens!**

Coming in January 2004

WICKED WORDS 9
Various
ISBN 0352 33860 1

Wicked Words collections are the hottest anthologies of women's erotic writing to be found anywhere in the world. With settings and scenarios to suit all tastes, this is fun erotica at the cutting edge from the UK and USA. The diversity of themes and styles reflects the multi-faceted nature of the female sexual imagination. Combining humour, warmth and attitude with imaginative writing, these stories sizzle with horny action. **Another scorching collection of wild fantasies.**

THE AMULET
Lisette Allen
ISBN 0 352 33019 8

Roman Britain, near the end of the second century. Catarina, an orphan adopted by the pagan Celts, has grown into a beautiful young woman with the gift of second sight. When her tribe captures a Roman garrison, she falls in love with their hunky leader, Alexius. Yet he betrays her, stealing her precious amulet. Vowing revenge, Catarina follows Alexius to Rome, but the salacious pagan rituals and endless orgies prove to be a formidable distraction. **Wonderfully decadent fiction from a pioneer of female erotica.**

Black Lace Booklist

Information is correct at time of printing. To avoid disappointment check availability before ordering. Go to www.blacklace-books.co.uk. All books are priced £6.99 unless another price is given.

BLACK LACE BOOKS WITH A CONTEMPORARY SETTING

☐ IN THE FLESH Emma Holly	ISBN 0 352 33498 3	£5.99
☐ SHAMELESS Stella Black	ISBN 0 352 33485 1	£5.99
☐ INTENSE BLUE Lyn Wood	ISBN 0 352 33496 7	£5.99
☐ THE NAKED TRUTH Natasha Rostova	ISBN 0 352 33497 5	£5.99
☐ A SPORTING CHANCE Susie Raymond	ISBN 0 352 33501 7	£5.99
☐ TAKING LIBERTIES Susie Raymond	ISBN 0 352 33357 X	£5.99
☐ A SCANDALOUS AFFAIR Holly Graham	ISBN 0 352 33523 8	£5.99
☐ THE NAKED FLAME Crystalle Valentino	ISBN 0 352 33528 9	£5.99
☐ ON THE EDGE Laura Hamilton	ISBN 0 352 33534 3	£5.99
☐ LURED BY LUST Tania Picarda	ISBN 0 352 33533 5	£5.99
☐ THE HOTTEST PLACE Tabitha Flyte	ISBN 0 352 33536 X	£5.99
☐ THE NINETY DAYS OF GENEVIEVE Lucinda Carrington	ISBN 0 352 33070 8	£5.99
☐ DREAMING SPIRES Juliet Hastings	ISBN 0 352 33584 X	
☐ THE TRANSFORMATION Natasha Rostova	ISBN 0 352 33311 1	
☐ SIN.NET Helena Ravenscroft	ISBN 0 352 33598 X	
☐ TWO WEEKS IN TANGIER Annabel Lee	ISBN 0 352 33599 8	
☐ HIGHLAND FLING Jane Justine	ISBN 0 352 33616 1	
☐ PLAYING HARD Tina Troy	ISBN 0 352 33617 X	
☐ SYMPHONY X Jasmine Stone	ISBN 0 352 33629 3	
☐ SUMMER FEVER Anna Ricci	ISBN 0 352 33625 0	
☐ CONTINUUM Portia Da Costa	ISBN 0 352 33120 8	
☐ OPENING ACTS Suki Cunningham	ISBN 0 352 33630 7	
☐ FULL STEAM AHEAD Tabitha Flyte	ISBN 0 352 33637 4	
☐ A SECRET PLACE Ella Broussard	ISBN 0 352 33307 3	
☐ GAME FOR ANYTHING Lyn Wood	ISBN 0 352 33639 0	
☐ CHEAP TRICK Astrid Fox	ISBN 0 352 33640 4	
☐ ALL THE TRIMMINGS Tesni Morgan	ISBN 0 352 33641 3	

To find out the latest information about Black Lace titles, check out the website: www.blacklace-books.co.uk or send for a booklist with complete synopses by writing to:

Black Lace Booklist, Virgin Books Ltd
Thames Wharf Studios
Rainville Road
London W6 9HA

Please include an SAE of decent size. Please note only British stamps are valid.

Our privacy policy
We will not disclose information you supply us to any other parties. We will not disclose any information which identifies you personally to any person without your express consent.

From time to time we may send out information about Black Lace books and special offers. Please tick here if you do not wish to receive Black Lace information. ❏

Please send me the books I have ticked above.

Name ....

Address ....

....

....

....

Post Code ....

Send to: Cash Sales, Black Lace Books, Thames Wharf Studios, Rainville Road, London W6 9HA.

US customers: for prices and details of how to order books for delivery by mail, call 1-800-343-4499.

Please enclose a cheque or postal order, made payable to Virgin Books Ltd, to the value of the books you have ordered plus postage and packing costs as follows:

UK and BFPO – £1.00 for the first book, 50p for each subsequent book.

Overseas (including Republic of Ireland) – £2.00 for the first book, £1.00 for each subsequent book.

If you would prefer to pay by VISA, ACCESS/MASTERCARD, DINERS CLUB, AMEX or SWITCH, please write your card number and expiry date here:

....

Signature ....

Please allow up to 28 days for delivery.